DOCTORING
DUST

MEL A ROWE

Also by Mel A ROWE

Receive exclusive insights, and news on upcoming releases by joining: https://melarowe.com/newsletter/

COPYRIGHT

**Caveat: As a courtesy, since there may be some sparse language choices in this story that may represent an obstacle for the reader, I am offering this warning. Please note this language and cultural references are purely for fictional purposes only and not designed to offend any individual persons, culture, or religions implied.

The following is written in Australian English

I consider the ELSIE CREEK SERIES a love letter to the unique individuals that continue to shape the Northern Territory into a truly amazing part of Australia.

My dad would've loved it.

One

*H*e traced one thick finger down her forearm, sending her nerves into hyper-drive as a pleasurable shiver licked its way up to her shoulders. It pushed a warmth of pleasure so deep into her bones she forgot the world, the universe, even how to breathe.

Except through his kiss.

A kiss that was so soft, so warm, so deliciously clever, it only stirred her cravings deeper with desire. She gripped his shoulders to steady herself under the sweep of emotions, undone by the way his tongue caressed her lips. Leaving her to forget everything but how to touch. Taste. Hear. See. The love of him. That was everything. With this man. Who—

The joey poked her head out of the pouch, dragging Alice Meadows from the story, with the book precariously held open in her lap.

'Melody, I was really getting into that.' Alice inhaled deeply to calm the heat inside, shifting the baby carrier resting across her chest, ready to read more. *This book is getting good.*

But the pleading eyes of the baby wallaby sucked her in.

'Fine, last feed for the night.'

Flinging out of her rocking chair, Alice placed the novel on the shelf of her nearby wall-to-ceiling bookcases. The wooden floorboards in the living room creaked under her workboots. Tonight, it somehow seemed louder than normal.

As the microwave whirred in the background, heating the formula, she stood in her darkened kitchen and glanced out the window. From her elevated house, Alice saw everything on this side of town. It was an industrial area that rarely got any traffic, even during normal business hours, and nothing after dark. In the daytime her kitchen window's view stretched over the fire station to the nearby airfield, and the stockyards beyond, where road trains filled with cattle would glide like a brown snake shifting across the outback sands to meet the freight trains.

But the only thing worth watching at this time of night was the town doctor, Doctor Stewart Mannen. The Hot Doc.

Leaning her hip against the kitchen sink, Alice plucked a fresh strawberry from a bowl. The berry was so sweet and perfectly ripe against her tongue—her dessert, perfectly timed to enjoy as she admired Stewart's sturdy stride.

At the same time, every night, he'd walk the road from the hospital like a ghost. A blond-haired, mouth-wateringly hot and honeyed ghost, with a look that made her toes curl, making her suck harder on the tart-yet-sweet juice from her plump, homegrown strawberry.

As the town's most eligible bachelor, Stewart was a prize catch for someone special. Pity he didn't know she existed.

Come on, the guy was a big-city surgeon. While she was nothing more than a woman wearing a uniform of khaki grunge, who everyone called the *new* ranger.

Ding.

She opened the microwave and gave the baby bottle a good shake.

Melody excitedly shifted in her baby pouch with one of her long wallaby toes jabbing Alice in the ribs.

'Oi! Watch those paws, kiddo.' Alice winced at the sharp pain, readjusting the baby carrier that had seen better days. It was so well used, she'd forgotten how many she'd carried over the years. *See, not a new ranger.*

Alice dabbed a few drops of the milky formula against her wrist. The perfect temperature. 'Here you go, Melody.'

At least the wallaby could hold the bottle these days.

'Shall we get back to the story? I have a TBR pile I want to get control of.' The pile of books waiting to be read was as big as the side table that stood next to her rocking chair.

Scooping up her romance novel, she headed to her chair, keen to read all about her latest book boyfriend—who somehow, always, ended up looking like the Hot Doc in her imagination.

As Melody snuggled deeper into her makeshift pouch, Alice noticed the dry dirt on her uniform. Maybe she should run a bath and read another chapter while soaking—

The floor creaked. Loudly. As if a microphone was pressed to the floor, with the stereo sound echoing down the corridor to the bedrooms.

The little joey stopped suckling, creating a resounding *plop* as she dragged her mouth free from the baby bottle's teat. Wide-eyed and alert, her big ears twitched, scanning the room like a radar at an air force base.

Alice always trusted the instincts of an animal, no matter how young.

Especially when she felt it too.

Her eyes widened as the wooden floorboards shifted beneath the soles of her boots.

With her heart hammering, she gently shifted her weight, but that was met with a series of groans. She stopped breathing.

Seconds seemed like hours as she waited.

But then there was a large snap, and the floorboard panel splintered into cracks that followed the wood grains. She went to jump—and that was when the floor collapsed.

'Augh!' Alice fell through the hole in the living room floor.

Only to jerk quickly to a stop as she became wedged in the hole, with floating dust irritating her eyes. The stench of old dry wood and sawdust made her want to sneeze, as her ribs were squeezed tight by the broken floorboards scratching at her stomach, where she was stuck in the middle of the floor with a baby wallaby in her face.

'Gimme a break!' Alice tried to wriggle free, but the straps of the baby carrier were snagged on the jagged edges of the floorboards.

Determined, she tried to swing her legs to catch on something to push herself up.

Then there was another loud creak.

This time, she felt it through her bones as the sharp boards pressed against her ribcage.

But what stopped all movement as pure ice rushed through her veins was her wall-to-ceiling bookcases.

All four of them were now leaning towards her. On the top shelves, her most prized hardcover book trophies slowly slid off the edge, one by one, as if pushed by some invisible fairy. They spilled around her head, crushing pages, snapping spines. She cringed, holding the baby carrier closer to her hammering chest, where the baby wallaby's instinct was to burrow deeper inside. With one arm protecting her head, the books rained down around her.

She swallowed hard, forcing down the acidic taste of fear, while ignoring the pounding whoosh of blood in her ears that competed with the spine-tingling creaking of the wood pushing against her ribs.

A line of sweat trickled down her brow as she tried to find her courage or a solution.

Death by bestsellers? Hmm, how would that read in the morning news?

'HELP!'

But who would hear her out here, when she lived alone?

Two

Six weeks to go and Stewart would be free from this outback hellhole of red dust, cattle, and extreme weather conditions.

He kicked at a stone. It rolled down the dark road that ran from the small bush hospital to the outback highway.

Highway? Ha. There was no such thing as traffic jams in this place where time slowed down to a freakish crawl, dragging boredom along with it.

Sent here against his free will, by his old bosses, but in six weeks he'd be back amongst the gritty city's chaos, working back in his old hospital that was bigger than this town's main street. Back in a workplace where you'd walk in the door on a Friday morning, blink, and it'd be Monday night when you left.

Here, in Elsie Creek, as a surgeon stuck in the outback—pfft!

Sure, it had its challenges, from farmers to cowboys playing with trucks, tractors and livestock. Most of the time it was dehydrated, sunburnt tourists, a few elderly patients on hospice, and children doing childish things.

It was nothing compared to the cut and dice world of limbs, aches, and ailments you got from working in a big city hospital. A place built to serve over a million city-dwelling souls who didn't get along with their neighbours.

Here, in this tiny town, they'd bake cakes for their neighbours.

Most of all, they were in his face. All the time. Period.

The locals in Elsie Creek knew who he was, that he was stuck here on a limited-time only contract, as well as who and what he was working on. All while trying to set him up with Daisy May's milkmaid cousin, daughter, granddaughter, niece and second-whatever. It's where he'd tell them all the same answer: *I'm not getting involved with anyone because I'm only here to finish my contract. Period.*

Six weeks to go.

'Heeeeeeeelp!'

Head down, Stewart focused on the red dirt and listened harder.

'Hello? Is somebody out there? I need help!' It was a female voice.

Stewart searched the thick cloak of darkness. Before him was the road to town, then the railway line and empty stockyards. Beyond that was nothing but scrublands. On his left stood the silent airfield, perched on the edge of the outback. The council buildings and some other businesses were on the right, but they were all closed. Behind him was the hospital at the end of the road shared by the police and fire departments.

'HELP!'

Was a woman locked up in the police station?

'Please help or *I'm gonna die!*' The level of distress was clear in her voice.

'Where are you?' His footsteps echoed down the tarred road, passing the silent fire station. As he passed the police station, his shadow lengthened from the bright spotlights positioned on the roof.

'I'm at the ranger station.'

Pausing to get his bearings in the dark, his eyes landed on the beefy four-wheel drive parked under the elevated house that stood a little off the road. He ran down the driveway where the low light shone from the house upstairs. 'I'm here.'

'Oh, joy. Me too.'

He skidded in the soft dirt, coming face to face with a pair of boots at the end of khaki cargo pants that hung low enough on the hips of a woman to show the pink lace panties she was wearing. Her flat stomach was exposed, showing the edge of her lacy pink bra. *Matching underwear! For real? In this town.*

'That's not the doctor, is it?'

He grinned. 'Are you the new ranger?'

'Hey, I've been in this town longer than you.'

His grin grew wider. He'd seen the woman around town. Did she have a temper to match her fire-red hair? 'Well, I'm right beneath you.' He gently gripped her ankles, putting her sturdy workboots on his shoulders. 'Can you come down using my weight?'

'I'm caught on something, otherwise I would have lowered myself.'

Based on the tight muscles of her stomach, she was fit enough to do a dozen chin lifts for fun.

'The front door is open. Or do you need a formal invitation, Doctor?'

He raced up the front steps as the entire house creaked and shifted like a boat at sea.

'SLOWLY.' Her voice was laced with fear as the house moaned and twisted as if it was about to fall like a house of cards.

He pulled out his phone. 'Sit tight, Ranger—'

'My name is Alice, Doctor Mannen.'

'Stewart. I'm calling for help.' He pressed dial as he pushed open the front door and his jaw dropped at the scene.

Poor Alice was stuck in the floor with a group of bookcases leaning precariously over her head. If they fell, she was …

'Elsie Creek Police,' came the gravelly voice over the phone's speaker.

'Porter, where are you?' From the house landing, he looked over his shoulder at the police station.

'Home. Why? Is that you, Doc?'

'I'm at the ranger's house. The building is about to collapse, with the ranger stuck in the floor. Who do we get to help?'

'Jax. He's got the equipment in the fire station across the road. But he's got the keys and lives twenty minutes out.'

'I don't think the floor will hold that long.' The house shifted like he was standing on a wooden sway bridge shifting over an abyss, the creaking noise making the hairs on his neck stand up.

'I could call the new ranger. She's got more tools than —'

'Didn't I just say I'm at the ranger's house looking at the new ranger?'

'The name is ALICE.' She wriggled with pure frustration only for the house to groan louder as her bookcases leaned closer to the woman trapped in the hole in the floor. Heavy books, the size of bricks, fell around her head.

'Alice. STOP.' Stewart held up his hand like a traffic cop. 'Porter, we need help. *Now*.' Tucking his phone into his pocket, he crouched lower to face a woman with pure fire in her eyes. But her fear he felt. 'Alice?'

She narrowed her green eyes at him like he'd gone and upset her. 'Give it to me straight. How bad is it?'

'Those bookcases are ...' He pointed, as the entire house shuddered. Ceiling panels cracked, paint chips fell, and the house lights flickered.

'We don't have long.'

Alice was right.

'Got any suggestions?'

'Grab some rope from the back of my ute and a knife.'

'You want a kitchen knife? It's not safe.' The fridge was leaning towards the bulging kitchen floor. The monstrous noise of wood grinding against wood irritated his ear drums.

'I've got some knives strapped inside the driver's door. The ute keys are sitting next to my phone, on the table by the door. You'll find the switch for the outdoor lights on the doorjamb above your head.'

'Got it.' He snatched the keys and gingerly trotted down the stairs that shifted beneath him as if in an earthquake, while the house angrily groaned above him.

In the back tray of the beefy ute, with Park Ranger emblems covering its doors, he found a load of ropes lying beside shovels, assorted wire cages, fuel drums, and a chainsaw. He grabbed a neatly bundled coil of rope, its coarse fibres prickly against his palm.

He opened the driver's door to be met by an unexpected fragrance of tangerine and lime. There was an assortment of lethal-looking knives strapped to the inner door panel, complete with an axe resting across the cab's rear window. Talk about rugged.

He tugged free a chunky pocketknife that had a ring on the handle.

'Are we there yet, Doctor?' Alice was very calm, considering her immediate danger.

'Coming.' With her feet dangling over his head, and with the lights on, he frowned at the angry scratches along Alice's sides, and the jagged wood digging into her ribs. It made him run faster up the stairs.

'We'll be okay, Melody. You wait, the Hot Doc is going to rescue us.'

Who is she talking to?

He crouched down by the open front door as an empty baby bottle rolled off the kitchen cupboards. That's when he realised that what he'd mistaken for an apron was in fact a baby carrier strapped across her chest. His heart dropped. *She has a baby!* 'What do you want me to do?'

'Tie the knife to the rope and throw it to me. I'll tie the baby carrier to the end of the rope. Then I'll cut the straps so you can pull it to you and get the hell out of this house. Got it?'

He threw the rope tied to the knife. It landed with a heavy thud on the floor.

They both froze as more hardcover books dropped like

bombs around her head.

'Alice ...' He held his breath as she reached for the rope, dragging the knife towards her.

'Baby carrier first.' She tied the rope around the wriggling baby carrier, then flicked open the knife's blade, which looked as sharp as his surgical tools.

'Ready, Stewart?'

He pulled the end of the rope connected to the baby carrier until it was tight. 'On three?'

'One ... Two ... Three.' Alice cut the straps.

Hand over hand, he dragged the wriggling baby carrier across the floor as the house screamed with the pressure of a bubble about to burst.

Then there was a thunderous crash. It was deafening.

Holding the baby pouch to his chest, he jumped down the twisted stairs to come face to face with a blinding dust storm.

'ALICE!'

He waved at the dust, as it settled with the rubble, spitting out some grit. The dining room and parts of the kitchen floor had collapsed leaving only a house with a roof and walls, that still had its lights on.

The baby carrier in his arms wriggled, and a head popped out.

'What the hell?' He held it out at arm's length. It was an enormous rat, or a deformed dormouse.

The mountain of books shifted.

'Alice?' Tucking the animal into the back of the nearby ute, he rushed under the house and pulled away a bookcase, as books with glossy book covers shifted beneath his shoes. 'Alice?'

'Here.' Her voice was muffled, as more books slid down the sides of the pulsing pile of rubble.

He shoved the broken floorboards aside, digging under the pages to grab her hand. It was a firm grip.

A police siren wailed in the distance as he kept digging, getting paper cuts from the pages. Until she was finally free.

'Thank you.' Covered in red dirt, her red hair was everywhere. Her flushed feminine face looked like a miner being dragged free from a cave-in.

'Are you okay?' He grabbed her wrist, checking her pulse. It was as erratic as his own. He gently brushed her hair free from her face, discovering some cuts and a lump growing on her forehead.

'I'm fine.' Alice brushed his hand aside. 'Where's Melody?'

'Who?'

'The joey.' She limped over the pile of books.

'You had me rescue a kangaroo?' He pointed at the ute, where the animal with enormous eyes, was busily sucking on a baby bottle like a toddler watching cartoons on TV. 'I thought it was a baby. A human baby.'

'Melody *is* a baby, she's an agile wallaby baby.'

He frowned with disgust, he didn't do animals. Then something bit his lower leg, sending a searing sting across his skin. 'Ow.' He brushed at his jeans.

Alice was beside him. Concern was clear in her green eyes. 'Are you okay?'

'Something bit me.' He raised the leg of his jeans. 'Ants?'

'White ants.' She brushed it away from his leg. Pulling out a heavy torch from her ute, she directed its beam of bright light at the gaps in the floor. 'Friggin' feral!'

'What?'

'I'm trying not to swear.' Her slender neck craned back as she inspected the remnants of her fallen floor. 'It looks like a white ants house party.' The cavity was crawling with large termites burrowing into the floorboards.

'Now we know what happened to your house.'

'My books! They'll have a fat picnic with this.' She scooped up some books, dusting them.

'Probably why they attacked this house.' But he wasn't worried about the house, only the patient. 'Let me take a look at you.' He pulled Alice away from the books and made her face him. He'd never realised how pretty she was. 'Hi, remember me, the doctor?'

'I'm fine.'

'Your ribs are bleeding.' He pointed to the blood patch growing on her khaki work shirt. 'And that's a nasty bump on your head.'

'No way?' She lifted her shirt to expose an angry gash running along the side of her rib cage.

'You need stitches.'

'What I need is to save these books.'

A siren alerted them to the arrival of a police van, its blue flashing lights bouncing off the ute and pile of books. Porter climbed out of the cab, adjusting his police cap. 'What happened?'

'White ants,' Alice said.

Porter unclipped a torch from his police belt. Its light beam was nowhere near as bright as Alice's. 'Doesn't this place get regular termite inspections? We had ours a few months back.'

'I have no idea.' Holding her bleeding side with one hand, Alice frowned as she followed the torchlight highlighting the thick group of white ants falling from the house floor, directly onto her pile of books. She winced, reaching down to scoop up her books, shaking some free from the termites.

'Porter, can you take us to the hospital, please?' Stewart gently gripped her arm. 'Don't fight me on this, Alice.'

'Jax is on his way. He can have a proper look at the place,' said Porter. 'I'm sure his volunteer firemen will save your books.' He picked up a copy. 'Did you know Marcus's new missus is a famous author? Do you have any of her books?'

'No. Been meaning to ...' In defeat, Alice's posture softened to lean against the ute, her hand gently patting the baby wallaby, as she looked over her books as if they were friends.

Stewart gently tugged on her slender wrist. 'Come on, let's get you looked at first, then you can come back and rescue your books.'

Her plump bottom lip quivered as she lifted her gaze, her glassy green eyes met his. The level of sadness was suffocating.

He slid an arm across her shoulders, giving her a gentle squeeze. 'Now that we've met, let me fix you. You know, me, the hero …' He gave her one of the charming smiles that had been known to win over many of his female patients.

Except Alice only scowled at him as if he'd gone and done the wrong thing!

Three

The doctor examined her like she was nothing but a lump of meat. The Hot Doc now up close and clinical, with Alice lying on her side on the cold examination bed. The scents of warm musk and cool mint beneath the layers of sterilising solution, and Stewart's sexy-as-hell blue eyes, had Alice curling her fingers into fists to stop herself from reaching out and running her fingers through his thick, blond hair.

'Ouch.' Alice winced at the sting of a needle. 'Are you meant to fix me or add to my pain?'

'That was just a needle to numb the area, so you won't feel the stitches,' said Stewart.

'I suppose I can't get them wet for the next few days?'

'Not for at least a week.'

'But you can annoy us every day to change your dressings, Alice,' said Jenny, the head nurse assisting. 'Can't she, Doctor?'

'Hm-hmm.' Stewart wasn't even listening, looking at her body of flesh and blood as if there wasn't a person attached to it.

'How many stitches am I getting?' Alice asked him.

'About twelve.'

'How big is the cut?' Alice tried to sit up, but he pushed her back down.

'Do you want me to tie you to the bed?'

'Hmph. I heard your bedside manner sucks...' Apparently it's what got his sweet butt kicked out from his old hospital to end up here. 'So I must be getting the royal treatment.'

'Is that any way to treat your hero?'

'Hero?' Jenny grinned, looking between Stewart and Alice.

'That's right, Jenny. I'm the hero, and it didn't involve surgery.'

Even his arrogant smart-arse smirk was sexy. She needed to leave this room.

'Yeah, okay, I'll give you that. Thank you, Stewart, for being our hero. Who knows how long I would've been hanging there.' Or what condition she would've been in once the house collapsed.

'At least Melody is okay.' She lay back, sharing a soft smile at the joey sniffing out the emergency room. Even though the Hot Doc baulked at her for bringing a baby wallaby into his ER, there was no way Alice was leaving Melody alone. She could be very stubborn when it came to the animals in her care.

Jenny secured the IV to Alice's wrist with tape, checking the drip from the clear bag of saline hanging off the tall stand.

'Is that bag necessary? I'm not dehydrated.'

'It is. Unless you want fifteen different needle marks in your arm.' Stewart's warm breath brushed against her skin. But the wet, sweeping wipes of cold solution on her skin made her cringe.

She'd planned to end this night with a warm bath, her new book boyfriend, and a yummy glass of red wine. Now here she was, wincing at the pain, in between sharp shocks of cool solution stinging her many scratches. 'A mild painkiller would be good.'

'Already on it.' Jenny flicked at the syringe, then injected it into the IV. 'How long have you got Melody for?'

'A few more weeks and she'll be good to go.'

'Go where?' Stewart slipped on a face mask, leaving his blue eyes exposed.

'Um, I—' She cleared her throat, choosing to focus on the

wallaby roaming the room.

'Alice rescues the wildlife and then returns them to the national park,' explained Jenny.

'Why?' He gave a shrug.

Oh, come on, did she have to spell it out to the surgeon? She tapped the ranger's patch on the sleeve of her khaki work uniform. 'It's my job. Park. Ranger.' *I'm not a bad guy.*

'It you move again, I'll strap you down and knock you out with anaesthetic. Period. Now let me do my job.'

'Pushy, much.' Alice lay back on her side. She didn't even have her phone on her to keep her occupied. And no book. *My books!*

'I'd like to do an X-ray—'

'No need. Nothing feels broken.' What she wanted was to get out of this place and go rescue her lifelong belongings.

'You didn't even notice you'd cut your ribs until I told you.'

'I feel it now.' Along with the thrumming, thumping headache.

His hand was gentle on her shoulder as he lowered his mask to speak with her. 'I just want to be sure, Alice. And I want an X-ray of your head to check for concussion. Do you have a headache?'

She didn't know where the tears came from or why. Was it the combination of his tender tone and the open concern he had for her? Alice could only swallow the lump in her tight throat.

'Hey, I'll take care of you. And we'll try to find someone to monitor that—' Stewart nodded at the wallaby like it was some feral rat.

'Night shift would love to take care of Melody,' volunteered Jenny. 'Do you have any formula?'

'There's a fresh box in the front seat of the ute.' Which was lucky, because Alice wasn't sure how anyone could get to her kitchen cupboards when she had no kitchen floor anymore.

Stewart slipped his surgical mask back on, his eyes becoming cold and focused. 'You can't go back to that house. It's not safe.' Even his voice had a cold clinical tone to it.

'I guessed that.' Alice sighed in defeat, her cheek pressing against the cold pillow. 'Let's hope my boss doesn't see it as an excuse to ship me out.'

Working on her side, both Jenny and Stewart looked up with a frown.

'What do you mean by that?' asked Stewart. 'You manage the local park, don't you? What's it called?'

'You haven't been there yet?' She arched an eyebrow at the doctor.

'I'm not a tourist.'

'Good. I do my best to avoid tourists.'

His blue eyes narrowed at her. With the mask hiding his mouth, she didn't know if he was smiling or scowling at her. 'Aren't rangers meant to help tourists?'

'Hmph. We're there for the land and its inhabitants. The Elsie Creek National Park, all two hundred square kilometres, is my patch of paradise.' A tiny park so far off the beaten track, most people passed it on their way to Kakadu National Park. Which was fine by Alice, who did her best to avoid people—especially tourists who wanted to talk, take photos, and annoy her for tips on where to go. That's where she'd point them to Kakadu, so they'd leave her little park alone.

If she could, she'd cordon off the entire area with signs that said *Park Closed*. But she had to be careful, or it would be closed permanently, and that would ruin her plans.

Oh no … With nowhere to live what did that mean for her plans for the park?

Her heart fluttered as her stomach churned, and she sank deeper into the hard pillow, feeling woozy. 'Sadly, my new boss is all about budget cuts. That's why I'm always getting shipped off to Kakadu, Mary River, and all the other NPs.' Her boss, the honourable horrible Harold, was nothing more than a prickly patch of cactus crowns. One spike and that prick was under her skin, irritating her to no end.

'What's an MP?' Stewart's mask shifted as if he was screwing up his nose.

Again, she tapped on the embroidered patch of her khaki uniform that clearly spelled out *National Park*. 'N. P. You don't do social media, then?'

He sharply sniffed, then went back to work.

'Is that why we never see you around?' Jenny spoke to Alice while passing shiny metal tools to Stewart.'

'I'm around. But if I have no house, Elsie Creek may lose their ranger.' Not that anyone would miss her.

But Alice needed to stay in town. She had to. She was so close to achieving her dream. If she couldn't stay here her dream would be nothing more than a pile of dirt, like her precious books under her broken house.

She fought the urge to move, to wriggle, to leave this room, as the cold wave of helplessness rushed through her system. Or was that from the IV's clear liquid drip-feeding into her bloodstream?

She clenched her teeth, desperate to think of somewhere to stay. Or did she kiss everything goodbye?

'So, what'll happen to the park if you're not there?' asked Jenny. 'I love the local park.'

Alice couldn't answer, as the fear prickled over her scalp. She tried to shrug, only copping a scary scowl from Stewart as he held some thread and a sharp tool thingy in his hand.

'Sorry.'

'Good girl. Now don't move.' His eyes focused on her ribs.

It wasn't the sexiest part of her body, now made uglier with a side-serving of stitches.

'I wish we had a spare room in the nurses' quarters. I'd let you stay there,' said Jenny.

'That's okay. Thank you for the offer.'

'Why not stay at the pub?' Stewart asked.

'My boss would love that.' Her words dripped with sarcasm, picturing the honourable horrible Harold's reaction.

Her boss was the most miserable miser she'd ever met, a man who'd re-use the same tea bag for a week. Starting his workdays by counting out the paperclips on his desk, while wearing the same striped nylon shirts he'd bought back in the eighties. Telling her boss about the house was going to crinkle his comb-over!

'Do you know of anyone renting out a spare room? Even a couch would be fine by me.' If she got desperate, she could always pitch a tent in the park.

'Stewart, don't you have two spare rooms in your house?' asked Jenny.

'Hm-hmm …' Stewart worked on Alice's stitches, his concentration was impressive as he held a fancy curved needle with some nylon thread. Complete with blood.

Alice's stomach started doing slow churns, as she struggled to swallow a wave of nausea. Which was surprising because blood had never bothered her before.

'You could let Alice stay with you,' suggested Jenny.

Ha! Like that would happen, not when the sexy doctor only looked at Alice like a stitching bag. 'Very funny, Jenny. You know, we only met tonight. And I hear Stewart's leaving soon. Is that right?'

'I am. Six weeks to go.'

'Which means when Stewart goes, the house will be empty, until we find another doctor.' Jenny's eyebrows knitted together as her lips tightened while watching Stewart at work.

'So, it's council housing?' Again, Alice tried to sit up, as the hope rose in her chest.

'Hey! Last warning.' Stewart's fingers were strong, his frown was ferocious, leaving her with no choice but to lie down. 'Forceps.'

Jenny passed him a set of long tweezers. 'Alice could take a spare room. Then she could talk to the council about switching over the lease after you leave.'

'That's a brilliant idea, Jenny.' Alice nodded, full of hope.

'Don't I get a say in this?' With scissors in hand, Stewart snipped at something.

It made Alice cringe, trying to ignore the tug on her skin.

'We're talking about my house. Where I live.' He stripped off his gloves, then his mask, throwing them into the trash, before turning to wash his hands at the sink.

'Can I move now?' She was ready to move in today.

'Not until Jenny bandages you up.'

Alice peered down at her side, screwing up her nose. The skin was all puffy and red, marred by black stitching knots, covered in an icky brown solution. 'Will it scar?'

'My finest work ever, so I doubt it. I should have been a plastic surgeon.'

'With your bedside manner?' *Oops.* So much for playing nice.

'But it'll be perfect!' Jenny interrupted them, as she placed a bandage over Alice's side.

'What? My bedside manner?' The doctor arched an eyebrow at the nurse as he dried his hands on a towel.

Jenny gave a short laugh. 'I'm talking about letting Alice stay with you.'

'I'll be quiet. I'm gone before daybreak and usually back at sunset. And you hardly leave the hospital.' Alice should know, watching him stroll the streets every night.

'How do you know?'

Err—awkward.

'Alice is right.' Jenny rolled her trolley of tools to the bench. 'You live here at the hospital more than at that house. Your cleaner says she doesn't have to clean anything.'

'You have a cleaner?' *Oh hello, heaven.* Alice would rather read another chapter than do housework.

Stewart flicked back the sides of his white doctor's coat like a superhero's cape to put his hands on his hips, slowly shaking his head.

Alice put on her sweetest smile, dousing her desires for the guy, because this was all about saving her dream and she'd do anything to keep it, even if it meant living with a stranger. 'What do you say, Stewart? Please? Be my hero for the next six weeks? You won't even know I'm there.'

Four

Somehow both women had backed him into a corner. Even as Alice was wriggling off the examination table like a rabbit ready to bounce for the door, she had enthusiastically grasped onto Jenny's suggestion about moving in with him. It was a ridiculous idea. Stewart didn't live with anyone. Period.

The emergency doors opened, and a set of sturdy footsteps entered the ward. 'I heard our park ranger is in need of assistance.'

'Hello, Doctor Mannen.' Alice's smile made Stewart's heart falter.

'My dear sweet Alice, how many times have I told you to call me Thomas.' Thomas gently sandwiched her hand between his palms.

'Yeah, hi, Dad.' Stewart rolled his eyes. In this town they called his father Doctor Mannen *Senior* while Stewart copped the *Junior* tag like he was some toddler.

'What happened to your house, Alice?' Thomas asked.

'White ants. But your son saved me?'

'Oh really? Are you saying Stewart got his hands dirty for a change?'

Stewart frowned at his father, and at the smile that was both sweet and sinful from the ranger, whose red hair spilled free around her head and shoulders. He had to look away, only for his eyes to land on the long-tailed, oversized rat at his feet. 'I also rescued a baby *something*?'

'That's not little Melody? She's grown so much.' Thomas

leaned down to greet the wallaby.

Stewart wanted to barf at his father gushing over the feral creature. 'You two know each other, obviously.'

'I see Alice on the road all the time. She's pulled me out of many bogholes during the wet season. And I've helped Alice rescue a few of these little fellas on the road myself.' Thomas hugged the baby wallaby affectionately.

His father was never like this with Stewart. Ever. In his entire life. If his father had only bothered to give his family half the attention he gave to his patients, then their family wouldn't have been torn apart.

'Porter was telling me your house is uninhabitable,' Thomas said to Alice. 'Where are you going to stay?'

'Alice is staying here for the night.' Stewart butted in, matching Alice's frown.

But then she winced, rubbing at her forehead, just above her eyebrow. Alice was in a lot more pain than she let on.

'You've just received twelve stitches, and you have a suspected concussion. I want you X-rayed. Jenny, can you arrange that, please? We'll also talk about some shots you may need, like tetanus to start with.' He wasn't letting her walk out of here, even if she was rolling those pretty eyes at him. Alice was smart enough to accept the inevitable.

Sure, he was stern when it came to patients, because most of them ignored doctor's advice. But this was the first time he actually felt bad for it. 'Come on, don't make me hate my job for being right.' He gave her hand a squeeze, and what do you know, it was forgiveness with a sweet smile.

Clearing his throat, he stepped away from the redhead and her hopping rat. *Not happening.*

'We were trying to talk Stewart into letting Alice stay in one of his spare rooms,' Jenny said to Thomas.

Stewart eyed the double doors to his freedom. If he avoided both Jenny and Alice, they wouldn't be able to talk him into anything. He didn't live with people or do houseplants. And he certainly didn't do animals. Especially lanky-legged, big-nosed, awkwardly loping baby critters. And he wasn't going to live with some random female who looked like Alice with her silky soft skin, shiny satin hair, with her aroma a sweet and potent aphrodisiac.

In his entire career no patient had affected him like this. Not when he'd come from a world where patients barrelled in and out of his old hospital's front doors like a supermarket selling half-price caffeinated sports drinks right next door to a sold-out rock concert.

'Great idea.' Thomas nodded at Alice. 'Stewart will do it. Won't you, son?'

'Dad?' Stewart rubbed his eyes, surprised at the feel of gritty dirt.

'Of course, he will.' Thomas patted his son on the shoulder. 'You're leaving. Why should you care who lives in the house after you're gone? I'll come check on you later, Alice. Glad to see you and Melody are okay.'

'Thank you, Thomas.' Alice was positively beaming at him. 'And thank you, Stewart. You don't know how much this means to me. Unless you don't want to …'

He had to say no, now.

Yet he struggled to speak with Alice looking at him like that.

He tugged at his collar, clearing his throat, about to share the bad news like he'd done with many patients over the years. *She's just a patient.* Period.

'Of course, he wants to. You can move in tomorrow. Stewart, I need your assistance on a consult.' And just like that Thomas exited the room.

'Hey—' The emergency doors swung shut behind him as he followed his father's long gait eating up the corridor. With hunched shoulders and head down, Thomas was deep in thought for a man who could be utterly thoughtless.

'You can't do that.'

'Do what?'

'Tell Alice it's okay to move into my house. I only just met her a few hours ago.'

'Alice is a lovely girl. You'll like her.'

'She's a rugged, outdoorsy, female who owns a chainsaw.' Everything he'd always found unattractive in a woman, that he did not want under his roof. Period.

His father stopped and faced Stewart. 'I have a lot of respect for Alice.'

Yeah, and what about your respect for your family, Dad? He so wanted to say it. But he never did.

'Alice is an amazing young lady with a big job. Her new boss has cut back all of her funding, leaving that poor girl to run that park on nothing but a prayer.'

'I doubt being a park ranger is as important as being a surgeon.'

Thomas frowned. 'You sound like your mother, a proper city snob.'

Stewart's voice deepened, as did his scowl. 'Why are you here, Doctor?'

'I brought in a patient. Young Eskie. He's a stockman.' Thomas led the way down the corridor. 'He got his hand crushed in one of the gates in the drafting yard. He'll need surgery.'

'Are you doing an evac?'

'The Flying Doctors are on another job, and it'll be a six-hour wait. I was at a nearby community and heard them on the radio trying to get help. I made them meet me on the highway. The kid's lost a lot of blood. He's having X-rays now.'

Side by side, they walked down the hall to the X-ray room, discussing the case. They never had a problem when it came to work, patients, or the hospital. They just avoided anything personal. Besides the job, the looks, and the surname, they had nothing else in common to show any form of father-son bond. They were just work colleagues. Which was why Stewart was surprised that his father had gotten involved in his private life over Alice moving into his house.

His. House.

Inside the X-ray room's office area, the two doctors checked over the results.

'This patient—'

'Eskie.' Thomas shrugged. 'It's how he introduced himself. They live by nicknames out here.'

Names didn't matter, not when surgery was on the table, with his fingers itching to get to work. 'The patient will need extensive digital nerve repair, or he'll lose the use of his hand.' Stewart pointed at the patient's X-ray film.

'Agreed.' Thomas traced a finger over the outline of broken bones that made up the cowboy's hand. 'Have you done many microsurgical procedures?'

'A few. I trained with some of the best. You?'

'Less than I can count on two hands.'

Stewart groaned at the lame joke. 'I know an orthopaedic hand surgeon who may offer some advice.' He looked at his watch. It was almost ten. 'If you're willing to hold off for half an hour?'

'It'll take that long to get the patient cleaned and prepped for surgery.' Thomas nodded at the pale cowboy in severe pain, being moved to the wheelchair. His jeans and long-sleeved shirt were ingrained with sweat and dirt.

'Don't start without me.' Down the corridor, Stewart turned left, then right, and into his office that was as plain as the day he'd arrived. Dropping into the chair behind his desk, Stewart pulled out his mobile phone and dialled a number he hadn't rung in almost a year.

'Hey, babe.' Her voice was soothing. He could hear Dr Oliva Sinclair's smile. 'Are you still stuck in the outback?'

'Six weeks and I'm outta here.' Making it the perfect time to start making professional connections again, especially with Liv. 'Have you got time to talk, because I have this patient ...' He discussed the prognosis just like old times, coming up with a surgical plan because hands were her specialty. 'Thanks for the help, Liv.'

'Anytime, babe. So, are you coming back to Melbourne?'

'I am. My apartment is there.' He scribbled a note to contact the real estate agent about the rental lease agreement ending in a few weeks. *I'm coming home, baby!*

'The hospital board was stupid to let you go.'

'I'm still under their ironclad contract.' He'd kill it as soon as he could, and work elsewhere. But in the meantime, it meant fronting up to the place for a dressing down by the overlord—the CEO.

Specialised hospitals were all about profit for the privilege. A place where he'd had a surgical team bigger than the entire staff running this bush hospital. Back home doctors drove luxury cars, not utes. They wore suits and ties, or medical scrubs, and could walk anywhere with no one knowing who they were in the big city.

Not like Elsie Creek. Where everyone butted into his business. He'd thought he could chill on the dress code, wearing baseball caps and T-shirts. Until another red-headed female told him to be more professional and dress for the job. Her name was Kat, a regular visitor to a terminal patient.

Stewart had kissed her once, but then Kat looked at him like her uncle's illness was his fault and ended up marrying her childhood sweetheart just before her uncle passed.

Women in this town meant nothing to him—not with six weeks to go. And certainly not with his ex-fiancée on the phone.

'The hospital's heart's surgical team has just announced a job vacancy that might be perfect for you,' said Liv.

He arched an eyebrow. 'Who's the head of surgery?'

Liv gave a light laugh. 'Babe, I think you should go straight to the chief surgeon and skip the whole job interview process.'

'Why is that?'

'Dr Benjamin Harrington is in charge.'

He groaned, dropping his head. His stepfather.

'When did you speak to your mother last?'

'It's been a while.' With his mother in Melbourne, he'd been able to avoid her.

'Want me to email you the details?'

He hesitated.

'Do you still want to be the best cardiothoracic surgeon in the country?'

'Send it.' His teeth clenched as he nodded to the empty room.

'Already on its way, babe.'

His shifted the mouse, waking his PC screen, waiting for her email to land. 'Got it.'

His eyes opened wide at the job ad: *specialised cardiothoracic surgeon to join Australia's leading cardiothoracic surgical team.*

It was his dream job!

The excitement was like fire pumping through his blood stream. *This was good.* It was better than good. He now had an exit plan out of this place.

Suddenly it didn't matter who lived in his house that sat behind this tiny hospital. After being forced to live in this town, that house was nothing more than a fancy prison to him.

Jenny, dressed in surgical scrubs, pushed opened his office door.

'I've got to go, Liv,' he said over the phone, shutting down his PC. 'We'll talk soon.' Maybe he could pick up with his ex-fiancée, considering they'd parted as friends.

'I'd like that. Good luck with your surgery.'

'Nothing to do with luck, it's all skill, sweetheart. Skills I have.' With six weeks to go, his plan of being a specialised surgeon was back on the table, making Elsie Creek nothing more than a quickly forgotten nightmare.

Five

Alice gingerly grabbed some empty boxes from the back of her work ute. She slowly dragged them to the edge of the rubble pile and started packing the books she could save from under her house. Dusting their covers, straightening out their pages, she placed them tenderly in the box, while wincing with pain every time she moved. It was going to take forever to move her gear, especially when the stupid stitches were a literal thousand stabbing thorns in her side.

She hated moving house. The whole process of packing and unpacking was such a chore, and the time wasted trying to settle into somewhere new was even worse. It's why she'd taken this permanent placement that came with a house, so she wouldn't have to move until she was ready.

Well, didn't that plan joyously end up facedown in the red dirt.

With the nurses volunteering to babysit Melody for the day, Alice was hoping to knock this over and meet with Stewart for the keys. But, not even halfway through packing her first box, she was reaching for the painkillers and guzzling back on the water.

Then her phone rang.

She cringed at the phone's screen, so tempted to ignore it, but she couldn't. It was her boss, the honourable horrible Harold.

'Hello, Harold.' Gripping the phone tighter she prepared herself for the lecture.

'What's this rubbish about you being off sick for a week?' His hoarse voice always made her cringe.

'I emailed you the sickness cert—'

'What did you do to the house?'

'I didn't do anything, it's the white ants fault.' Even now, in the harsh light of a new day, those pesky termites were having a party eating though the exposed floorboards. Their termite trails were everywhere. She was lucky the house had lasted this long.

'Listen here, little lady, are you sure it wasn't your books that broke the floor by overloading it? All I see in the photos from the council are books. Smutty books.'

She reached down, wincing at the pull of her stitches, to grab one of her favourite hardcovers with its pretty painted edges that used to sit on her top shelf with pride. 'They're fiction books.' Amazing worlds that allowed her to escape the dramas of her day—and her boss.

So what if they were romances, with some stories so spicy they came with heat-level warnings. They were great reads.

Should she pack them by genre?

'Hey, how would you know what genre my books are?'

Harold cleared his throat. She pictured him tugging on that oversized collar of his retro nylon shirts, while his comb-over sat like concrete on his head. 'Where are you staying?'

'A local doctor has offered me his spare room.' Not that poor Stewart had much of a choice. But thanks to Thomas, she was in. 'It won't be any change to the budget.' She was quite willing to pay her own way to stay in town.

'This department can't afford any more bills, little lady, or we'll have to shut down the park.'

'You can't.' Not when she was so close to achieving her dream.

'I'm the boss. I'm the one with the budget I'm busily balancing to keep those wretched parks open. Just know, your little park isn't the only one on the chopping block. Be sure to send me an email when you're back on the job. I'll send you out to Judbarra to do some spraying for a week.'

A week of playing with liquid death. *Oh, the joy!*

She slid her phone into her cargo pants' deep pocket, gingerly crouching to pick up another book.

She used to love going on holidays, dragging out her suitcase or dusting off her backpack. But not since the horrible Harold made her live out of her suitcase at other ranger stations for a week at a time. Even if they were much nicer places than the run-down hovel she'd called home these past three years, she preferred staying close to her park. It was unsettling for a socially awkward person not having a routine and a home to come back to.

The crunch and pop of car tyres on the gravel alerted her to the white ute parking in her driveway. It belonged to Ron, better known as *the Station Hand*. The man was a living legend in this town, who worked part time on the council. Sliding on his large, sweat-stained Akubra, he walked towards her.

Ron, like many of the local cattlemen, despised rangers for interfering with their pesky laws on wildlife and land conservation. As this was cattle country, sadly she'd been given the thankless power of controlling the stock routes that she'd annually closed due to poor weather conditions. It made her the bad guy in the eyes of the locals.

Could this day get any better?

'Morning.' She lifted her chin, ready for whatever the Station Hand dished out.

'Morning, Alice. I'm here to do a report for the council.' Ron held up a clipboard, which didn't suit the semi-retired cattleman. 'I see the white ants had a party.' In his wide-brimmed hat, Ron craned his neck up at the hole that used to be her kitchen floor.

'If this is a council house, who handles the maintenance issues?'

'The rangers' office. We bill 'em for any work we do.'

'Isn't this sort of termite damage completely preventable?'

'It is.' Ron gave a sharp nod. 'Council's got this pest guy who treats their properties annually. Now, according to the records them girls keep in that air-conditioned council office, no one has done a termite inspection on this place for a few years.'

'Why not?'

'The rangers said they'd take care of it themselves.' Ron arched an accusing eyebrow at her. 'And you've lived here for how long?'

Humph! She crossed her arms over her chest—only to wince at her stupid stabbing stitches. 'When I got the job as senior park ranger, it came with a house that makes up the ranger station.' She looked at her office desk facedown in the dirt, with her television smashed alongside her filing cabinets. 'I was told this house came with a gardener and to call you guys for any maintenance issues. I'm never here, except to sleep. Otherwise I'm out at the park.'

Ron pointed to her large backyard with its basic security fence. 'Young Rigsy reported the ant mound along the fence line, and the ant mud trails along the concrete paths around the house when he did some yard work. I filled out the paperwork and gave it to the girlie in the council office who emailed it to your supervisor a few times. Look, Alice ...' Ron paused, pushing up the brim of his hat. 'This isn't council's fault, and it's certainly not yours. This is management's issue.'

That's a first. 'So, who gets my insurance claim?' Her bookcases, part of the personal library she was proud of, were ruined.

'Just put in the paperwork, like we're doing. Then let 'em do what they do, while we keep on doin' what we do.' Ron dropped a heavy hand on her shoulder as his voice softened. 'I heard you'd spent the night in hospital and got some stitches.'

'Stitches suck. Otherwise, I'd be rigging up my rock-climbing gear to find my clothes.' Exhausted after a restless night at the hospital, she needed clean clothes and her toothbrush.

'I could ask Rigsy if he has any volunteer firemen mates who'd want to come around and practise their rigging skills. It'd be safer if they played Tarzan to swing into the house while you rest up.'

'Thank you.' Glancing at her watch, she noted she was running out of time. She'd agreed to meet with Stewart in an hour and was hoping to sneak in a load of gear now.

Then she narrowed her eyes at the big man. 'Are you being nice to me, so I'll keep signing off on Karma's permit?' There were specific housing guidelines needed to keep protected wildlife, especially a man-eating crocodile. And she'd gone toe-to-toe with Ron for over-feeding that beast for bets.

'Well …' Ron gave a cheesy grin. 'We know you're doing that for Karma's welfare. But this'll keep us both out of the office.'

Even though she no longer had an office, she did have a pile of insurance paperwork to complete.

'Is it true that you're staying at Doctor Mannen Junior's house?'

'I'm hoping to take over Stewart's lease to make it the new ranger station.'

'I was going to suggest that. We can help you move.'

'Really? What's the catch?'

He gave a sly shrug as his eyes practically sparkled with mischief. 'Of course, we'll bill your boss for it. That way, we can use the truck and do it in one load.'

She laughed. 'Done!' The day suddenly got better. 'Do you have a tow ball on that truck? I've got a few trailers that need moving.' She pointed to her large yard that stretched beyond her patch of lush lawn, to where her quad and fuel drums rested on one trailer. It stood next to three other trailers holding her river boat, her airboat, and an empty crocodile cage. And those were only some of the tools she needed for her job. Did Stewart's house have a big enough yard to become the new ranger station? Should she have warned him?

Six

Alice parked her work ute in front of the doctor's house, situated at the rear of the hospital. It looked deserted. The front was devoid of lawn, pot plants, or anything to give it that lived-in look of a home.

Her boots crunched on the gravel path that led to the house, as she hauled her large money tree to the front door. Again, the stupid stitches twinged. But she had so much to do before the painkillers wore off, especially before the Station Hand and his groupies brought over her ranger's gear this afternoon.

She turned the pot plant around, checking for the right angle with its lush foliage. 'There … welcome home, Penny. That spot was made for you.' It was a miracle it had survived the fall from her collapsing front stairs.

The front door opened, and the aroma of rich roasted coffee floated outside, along with that of the good doctor, which made her mouth water. 'Is Penny another pet?'

'No, a money tree.' She tickled the leaves of the healthy tree. 'I don't do pets.'

'Are you superstitious?'

'When I want to be.'

'So why the tree?'

'They say if you keep a money tree by the main entrance it brings luck and abundance.' Which is what she needed. Was there a special pot plant for making a man fall in love with a woman without seeing her flaws?

She returned to the chunky work ute that held all her

personal worldly belongings, those that had survived.

'Here, let me take that. You've still got stitches.' He took her suitcase.

'It's annoying.'

'What is? Me, your potential landlord? Or the stitches?'

She tried to stop her grin, honestly, she did. But she had to mirror his smile.

'What's in the boxes?' He pointed to the back of her ute.

'My books.' It hurt seeing them boxed up like that. 'I have no bookshelves anymore.'

'You can put them in the spare room, or the garage I never use.'

'Do you have a vehicle?' She'd never been around the back of the squat one-level country hospital where the doctor's house sat. But behind the house they had a magnificent view of the open countryside. And no neighbours.

'If I need a car, I'll take one from the hospital. Not that I go anywhere.' With her large suitcase, Stewart led the way inside the house.

Carrying her old backpack, she tried to ignore his easy stride and cute butt in his loose-fit chinos, and the muscular outline under his crisp linen shirt. He carried a city-chic to him, while she trudged along in her khaki cargo pants, boots, and old T-shirt. *You're way outta my league, Doctor.*

'I'm happy to chip in with the bills.'

'Don't worry about it. It's all part of my contract, which you'll have to renegotiate in six weeks.'

'My boss can do that. Once he's stopped yelling at me for destroying the ranger's house.'

'You didn't destroy that place, the white ants did. If I hadn't heard your call last night …'

She would've been in a whole rubble of trouble. Suddenly her throbbing stitches didn't feel so bad.

'Come on, I'll give you a quick tour of the place before I do my rounds. You can then rest up.'

She tugged at her sticky T-shirt, following the guy who was her walking daydream. People said *never meet your heroes*, and here she was about to live with hers. *Yikes.*

'The cleaner shows up on Thursdays.'

'I've always wanted a cleaner. I'd rather read than do housework.'

He tossed a dynamic grin at her over his shoulder while dragging her suitcase down the skinny corridor's sturdy floor. 'This is your room. It's at the end.' Stewart gently leaned her case near the queen-size bed, where the linen and blankets were folded back like a hospital bed.

Alice dumped her bag on the floor, opening the large built-in cupboards. She didn't have enough clothes to fill a tenth of that space.

'There's more cupboards in the hallway I never use.'

Did he use any space in this house?

'How many rooms does this place have?' It was so quiet. Her footsteps didn't creak under her feet, no fans whirled in the air, and there were no sounds of birds or a breeze filtering through the windows. It was as quiet as a hospital ward after visiting hours.

'It has three bedrooms. I'd kept one room open for my father, but he never stays here. He prefers his van, or the couch in his office.' Stewart frowned before heading back down the corridor. 'The bathroom is there.'

'Where do you stay? At the hospital?' Because there were no personal items anywhere. Hotels had more personal touches than this place.

'I'm in the main bedroom.' Stewart tapped at the closed door closest to the front door.

Alice poked her head inside the living room that led to the dining and kitchen area. 'I mean, do you even live here. You've got no pictures on the wall, no knick-knacks.'

'I hate knick-knacks and dust-collecting clutter. Period. So, I'd better warn you now, if you have any lace doilies it'll kill any form of friendship.'

'Do I look like a girl who does lace? Except for my lace underwear, you're safe.'

He choked out a cough.

'So why the fear of lace doilies?' Back at the ute, she grabbed a shopping bag and a small box labelled *kitchen*.

'My mother.' Stewart scooped up a larger box, also destined for the kitchen. 'Can I be blunt here?'

'Go for it.'

'My mother has a house full of clutter, she's a sucker for art pieces. While I like a house free from coasters, tablecloths, or any dust collectors. I've always wanted a place that'll take care of me for a change. Somewhere I can put my feet up and not worry about some priceless art piece, or what the neighbours think, where I'm free to be me.'

'That's what makes it a home.' It was Alice's idea of home, too. 'Being a doctor, you'd need that break from the stress.' Even if he worked right across the road. 'Don't worry, I hate clutter too. So, anything else you don't like about housemates? Or any pet hates that'll ruin this deal?' Because she needed this to work.

'I don't do birthdays. Period. So don't expect me to blow out any candles on a birthday cake.'

Who doesn't like their birthdays? And what did the guy have against birthday cake?

'Also, I don't like dishes in the sink. It's a pet hate. As a surgeon I always have a clean sink to wash my hands. We have a decent dishwasher, but I never use it.'

'Fine, I'll watch that in the future. But I need space for my work gear. It's a desk and some filing cabinets.' This place did have a big kitchen with plenty of cooking space.

'You can use the dining area. I don't eat here, and the hospital does my laundry … I think the laundry area is out the back somewhere in the garage?' He nodded at the closed back door with its venetian blinds covering the window.

Did the guy hate the outdoors, hiding from the sun behind closed windows and curtains?

'I'll find it.' She opened the blind and peered out to the backyard. *Eureka!* It was huge, with a cool patio area, too. 'Any problems with me using the yard?' She held her breath for the right answer.

'Go for it, I never use it.'

Well, she was about to use every inch he had. Poor guy. 'This place is a hundred times nicer, and so much bigger than my house.'

The corner of his mouth tugged into a slight smile. 'Do you need anything else?'

'I usually have a space set up to watch the park's CCTV cameras.' She headed for the open lounge area.

'You spy on people in the park?'

'I *watch over* the park. If people, or any of the animals are in trouble, I can help. It's great for watching road conditions, fire spotting, that sort of thing.'

'When do you get the time to watch when you're out all day?'

'I used to cast it to my TV and let it play on fast forward like some screensaver in the background. But my television set scored itself a one-way ticket to the dump.' Like most of her gear did, but the doctor had a flat screen that took up an entire wall.

'Feel free to use mine. I never bothered connecting it.'

Understandable when he had nothing to sit on besides the round table and chairs that made up the dining area.

'You don't watch movies? Or do you binge medical romance series?'

He shared a mournful groan that contradicted the shine in his eyes. 'I watch the football when Marcus is working at the police station.'

'So, what space can I or can't I use?' Not that she had many personal belongings to begin with, but she had more than Stewart.

'Don't touch my coffee machine. Period. But fill the cupboards and fridge as much as you want.' He opened the fridge to reveal one bag of coffee beans. And nothing else. She'd never seen a refrigerator that empty.

'Your coffee machine is quite safe.' It had to be the gold-class standard for shiny coffee machines. 'I prefer tea, and I don't mind sharing.' She placed her brightly coloured ceramic teapot on the barren counter that was as sterile as the hospital ward.

Except for his fancy coffee machine, the rest of the place was bare. There were no mats, no family pictures, no half-read books or magazines, no pot plants. Nothing. It made her simple teapot and tea tins of many flavours instantly brighten the room.

'How many types of tea do you have?' Stewart lifted the lid of the large tea box.

'I used to belong to this online tea club who'd send me stuff monthly. I'm still making my way through it. Being a doctor, you'd know all about the benefits of drinking tea.'

'Don't you drink coffee?'

'Oh, I used to. Big time.' She laughed, shaking her head at the memory, heading back to her ute to collect more gear. 'I got addicted to the stuff. When I ran out while camped miles away from anywhere, I suffered severe withdrawals—of the crippling kind.' Last night's headaches didn't even come close to the caffeine headaches she'd endured.

'I swear half the time my blood is nothing but pure caffeine, that when I do stop, I'll suffer those crippling withdrawals, too.'

'Well, peppermint tea and a ton of water and whatever the good doctor prescribes may help.' She giggled at him as she pulled on her rocking chair sitting on the ute's rear tray. Only to wince. 'Ouch.'

'Let me help. Stitches remember.'

'I'm so used to being on my own, I'm not …'

'Used to having people help.'

She exhaled heavily, trying to ignore those pesky stitches. 'Yeah. You?' Should she explain she was socially awkward, too?

'With my home life …' Stewart faced the house. 'I've always lived alone, so this is new for me.'

'Me too. Are you sure you're okay with this? I know your dad pushed you into this, so I promise to not bother you. I have noise-cancelling headphones, so if you want to play your music and stuff, it won't bother me. Like I said, I'm gone at dawn—when I'm not wounded.'

She waited for his response, standing under a cloudless winter sky, free from humidity. Yet her T-shirt was sticking to her clammy skin. 'You can say no, Stewart.' Giving him the chance to pull out now before she truly moved in.

Stewart gave her a wink, then picked up the heavy end of her rocking chair and helped her carry it into the house. 'So, I won't need to worry about you making noise if I need to sleep.'

The smile wouldn't leave her face. She was in! 'The loudest you'll hear from me is boiling the kettle or turning the page in a book.'

'And does this rocking chair creak?' He placed it in the middle of the lounge area.

'Absolutely not.' She gasped at him, while tenderly stroking the chair. 'My father and I made this rocking chair when my parents were stationed at Iguazu National Park.'

'Where's that?'

'Argentina. The locals showed Dad how to do it and he fell in love with woodworking. Dad had us making our own chairs with him. It's part of home …' It was her favourite reading chair that now sat in the middle of the lounge room. But it desperately needed a mat, some cushions, and books to make it feel like home. So back to the ute she went to collect more gear. She hated moving house.

Stewart followed. 'What were your parents doing in Argentina?'

'Work. I blame my parents for my chosen career path. Like you with your dad, huh?'

Again, he frowned. 'Doubt it. My father and I only talk about patients and procedures. Period.'

'I meant that you're both in the field of medicine. My parents are passionate nature enthusiasts. We were forever taking family trips to national parks, it was like this lifelong apprenticeship for me. You?' She dumped a load of soft furnishings in the lounge, ready to get more before her fancy painkillers wore off. Which wouldn't be long now.

The boxes filled with her books would have to wait until she found a trolley or something.

'I didn't spend much time with my father as a child. He was too busy dealing with his patients or hospital politics. I only saw my father out here again after ...' Stewart sighed heavily, narrowing his eyes at the ugly hospital standing a few hundred metres away. 'Twenty-two years.'

'Wow!' What else could she say.

Stewart carried a box into the kitchen and this time she followed him. How could she not, when chinos never looked so good on a man?

But she had to ask. 'Aren't you here to reconnect with your father? Because there are plenty of outback hospitals that would've gladly taken you on, no matter how bad your bedside manner is.'

'I thought I was getting better.' He dropped the box marked *kitchen* on the dining table and followed her back out the door.

She shrugged, giving him a shy smile as they headed for the rugged ranger's ute swamping the suburban-like driveway. 'I know your father loves that you're here. Thomas has said so, many times.'

The scowl on Stewart's face was a warning to stop speaking.

But Alice was well skilled in never backing away from an angry face. 'You guys don't talk much do you?'

He barely shook his head.

'Well, I must confess, this is the most conversation I've

had that doesn't involve the park or my job. I'm so weird.' She rolled her eyes, grabbing another smaller box labelled *bathroom*. She couldn't wait to dig out her toothbrush and wash her hair. Oh, wait, stitches. *Damn!*

Stewart gave a hearty laugh, with the sun shining on his hair like a halo. 'I get it. I only talk medicine. But do you live under the reputation of a saint, like my father is in this town?'

'It's probably the same as when my parents were the professors teaching the classes I needed for my double degree. We do weekly video chats to talk shop, which is cool as they keep me up to date with the latest technology and news.' She paused to tenderly touch the bruising on her forehead. 'Although, I may have to buy some make-up to hide the war wounds for their weekly call.' The lump on her forehead wasn't pretty.

'Are you okay?'

She wasn't used to sharing her worries with anyone. 'Sure. You? And stop looking at me like a doctor, your work is over there.' She pointed to the ugly building across the dry field.

He shared a different smile, one that softened the hard lines around his mouth and the crinkles around his eyes. It was a delicious look. 'I didn't realise we had that much in common.'

Did they? Dumping her garbage bag of linen on the bedroom floor, she swivelled in her boots that were so quiet in this house and went back down the corridor to the open front door, streaming sunshine and fresh air into this clinical environment.

'Can you cook?' Stewart asked, meeting her at the ute for more gear. 'With all of these boxes labelled *kitchen* I assume you can.'

'I'm a vegetarian. I even grow my own greens.' Already planning the layout of the back patio area as the perfect space for her vegetable garden. 'I don't mind cooking, I just hate cooking for one. It makes little sense to mess up the kitchen, so I don't mind cooking for the both of us considering you eat hospital food.'

He shrugged as if not wanting to commit to her meals. Mealtimes. Or her.

As if she was going to wear some white frilly apron, ringing a brass school bell at the front door to holler across the paddock 'Dinner is ready.' She bit her lip to stop herself giggling at the image.

'How about I leave the meals for you in the fridge and put your name on it? You can help yourself at any time, no commitment.' He wasn't charging her rent, but she wanted to contribute to the house somehow, especially when she was about to take over his backyard. The poor guy. 'As a recent guest, I can promise you my meals will be an improvement in freshness compared to hospital food.'

'Deal.' His smile was so bright and dynamic she wobbled with weak knees. She had to walk away.

She lifted two garbage bags that clanged of metal pots, tossing them over her shoulders like sacks. Again, she winced at the stitches, as the sweat trickled down her forehead. Moving house was such an ugly chore.

'Don't worry about cakes, I get one delivered to my office daily.' Stewart followed her inside carting another box into the kitchen.

'From patients? Or the single ladies?' She dumped the bags on the dining room floor with a thud and headed back outside with Stewart following. 'Hey, will it be an issue for me living here? I don't want to interfere with your love-life. Should we work out some signal when you're busy?' She picked up the box of kitchen plastics.

'I never bring them home.' He gave her a sly grin. It was wicked. And sinful. And —

She pinched herself to not fall into some lustful drool, shoving all her emotions down deep as she carried another box into the house. They were just housemates, that's all. Besides Stewart only looked at her like a doctor to a patient.

But she had to ask, 'Why don't you bring them home?' Did she need to install soundproofing for her bedroom walls?

'Because they'd never leave.' A devilish grin spread across his soft lips. 'But now, with you moving in, it should keep them off my back for the next six weeks.'

'It'll be sending the gossips into overdrive.'

'Tell me about it.' He sighed heavily, his smile gone. It was as if he'd lowered his doctor's mask, with the burden showing across his slumped shoulders.

'Is the pressure from the matchmakers that bad?' Come on, the guy was a gorgeous doctor, making him an everyday hero. In a town full of cowboys, Stewart was top-shelf, A-grade, el-primo choice of male rarely found on the single-men menu in this outback town. Certainly not in her world. This guy should be on some international endangered list of worthy, eligible bachelors.

'Emelia and her father, the mayor, are the worst. I don't know if they're trying to set me up to stay in town, or Emelia wants to be a doctor's wife. But with you here—'

'I don't want to be a doctor's wife. It's bad enough being the daughter of two professors keen on saving the universe.'

'Good.' He nodded firmly.

Hmph—she'd just been friend-zoned!

'Hey, do you want to come and steal lunch with me? I'll sneak you in through the nurses' entrance, then I'll check on your dressings.' He tugged on her sleeve, heading for the door. 'Let's find someone else to unpack the rest of your stuff.'

'Normally I wouldn't bother to ask anyone.'

'I don't want you pulling any stitches.'

Aww, he cared. Like a doctor to a patient and nothing else.

'Let's go.'

She followed him like a puppy. A pathetic, lovesick puppy.

Stewart pulled the front door shut behind her, then held

up a set of keys. 'This is the front door keys, and the back door keys I never use.'

'So, you don't use the backyard?' Their fingers barely touched, and yet a rush of warmth raced through her skin to her scalp.

He cleared his throat, his impeccably clean hands tugging on his collared shirt, its crisp collar a thousand times sharper than her work shirts. 'No.'

'How come you don't cook? Or do you just leave it up to the town's single ladies?'

Again, he groaned as he led them down the well-beaten path to the hospital. 'My mother never cooked, our housekeeper did. I never had the time to learn.'

How rich was this guy? Was that why his house looked so sterile?

But with a week off, she could try to turn this empty shell of a house into a home.

She quickened her step to catch up, only to be jabbed in the side. 'These stitches suck.' She had to stop and breathe slowly until the pain subsided.

'Easy does it. I don't want you pulling them.' He tenderly patted her shoulder. 'Please tell me you'll rest this week. Don't make me put you on my rounds list.'

Oh, that's tempting.

'I'm okay.' She started walking again, hoping to walk off the pain. 'I intend to put my feet up shortly and tackle my TBR.'

'Is that another acronym for the park or some new swear word?'

'TBR is the *to-be-read* pile of books.'

He arched an eyebrow at her. 'You read that much. Wait—I forgot all those books nearly crushed you.'

'Near-death by bestsellers.' She rolled her eyes at him as they walked side by side. 'I read for fun. Like you, I don't watch TV, except the CCTV.' And she needed to change the subject away from her weird self. 'Hey, where do you call home?'

'Melbourne. I have an apartment there.'

'That's why your house isn't lived in?' She pointed back to the house that looked so much better with Penny, the money tree, guarding the front door and her ranger's ute filling the driveway.

'That house is more lived in than my apartment. My mother is always threatening to send in a decorator.'

'Really?'

'I arrived here with a suitcase, one bag and my work satchel. I bought the TV and coffee machine when I couldn't get out of my contract. Back in my apartment, all I have is my bed and TV. But you collect books and tea varieties.'

'Don't you collect anything, or have an after-hours hobby?'

He shrugged. 'Besides making coffee—'

'Coffee?' She arched her eyebrow at him.

'I worked as a barista just to learn how to make a decent coffee while in medical school. So, yes, I like my coffee. And I'm always working. You?'

'I live for my job. I love it so much, it doesn't feel like I'm working.'

He stopped to stare at her. Again, that soft smile crossed his lips, softening his features into a whole new heavenly level of handsome. 'I thought only doctors felt that way.'

She really liked that look of his, it wasn't his doctor's look. 'Your career is everything to you?'

'Yeah. You?'

'I have a plan. A dream.' She just couldn't share it, not when she was afraid of word getting out to the wrong people, who'd shut her down before she'd begun. 'What's your big picture goal with your career?'

'I want to be the best cardiothoracic surgeon in the country.'

'So, you're all about *hearts*!' Her own heart started pitter-pattering in a schoolgirl swoon. Did she dare call him Doctor

Love?

Seven

'How's my favourite patient today?' Stewart strolled into the hospital room. The eye-catching colours of the orchids by the window brightened the room, as the beams of sunshine highlighted the bed where the frail, ninety-four-year-young Iris lay.

'I bet you say that to all your patients, Doctor.' Her many wrinkles crinkled as her smile widened, emphasising her hollow cheeks. Wearing a soft scarf over her hair, Iris put her book flat across her bony frame as she struggled to sit up. 'I'm fine. You can go bother someone else.'

'Why? When I can spend time with you.' He peeked at his watch. 'For a whole three minutes.' He scrolled through the reports on his tablet, then checked her vitals. 'Another book?'

'From your new housemate. I'm about to get to the hot stuff, so you'd better leave.'

'Hot, huh?'

'It comes with all these naughty content warnings.' Her sprightly giggle made him smile.

'Do I need to know?'

'Not unless you want to blush, Doctor. I know I did. But they're so much fun. It's a series that Alice is lending me.'

'Are you and Alice—'

'Friends. Yes.' Among the crinkles, Iris's light blue eyes sparkled with intelligence. It was just her body that wasn't keeping up. 'She's a lovely girl, Alice.'

'Hm-hmm …' He instantly recognised the tone of

someone trying to set him up. He wasn't having any of that. 'Alice is my housemate, who I never see. Can you sit up for me, please?'

He lifted her bed to help her, then placed the stethoscope on her back to listen to her chest. 'All clear.'

Iris leaned back into her pile of pillows. 'Alice made these marvellous truffles out of cottage cheese the other day. No sugar. I just loved them.'

'Hm-hmm …' He checked her blood pressure, scribbling the results onto her chart. 'Alice makes me lunch and dinner, so that's a bonus. Even though I told her she doesn't have to.'

After years of eating hospital food, he wasn't picky. But it had become a daily surprise to open his once-empty fridge to find it brimming with fresh fruit and vegetables. Alice had even arranged a shelf for him holding assorted tubs labelled: *Eat me for lunch. Eat me for dinner. Drink this juice to dance the day away. Take this snack to share if you dare.* Complete with smiley faces and other simple cartoon scribblings on the post-it notes. It was fun.

Ravenous, he'd stand at the fridge, savouring each mouthful that had his tastebuds dancing. The crisp crunch of lettuce, the sweetness of snow peas, the juicy plump strawberries. It was becoming a regular thing to sneak out of the hospital to eat at home. He'd never done that before.

'Alice doesn't like cooking for one,' said Iris, tucking in fine grey wisps of hair under her scarf.

'Alice told me that the day she moved in.'

'Do you like her food being vegetarian?'

'I'm not complaining.' *It beats hospital food.* He just didn't want to get used to it, or Alice.

'Do you see your housemate at all?' Iris straightened out the brightly coloured crocheted blanket that lay over her hospital sheets.

'Alice starts work early …' Leaving a heavenly aroma trail behind her. Combined with the scent of her herbal teas, her nightly bath bombs, and scented candles, Alice was growing on him when she shouldn't.

After being stuck all day inside a highly sanitised environment, filled with sterile solutions, walking through his front door was like being bathed in a layer of relaxation. These days he'd inhale deeply when he crossed the threshold, dropping all that day's stress as he dropped his keys on Alice's handy side bench where she recharged her walkie-talkies, mobile phone, satellite phone, and fancy camera.

In the kitchen, they'd squeezed her desk and filing cabinets against the corner wall, where her laptop lived. Along with a powerful and sleek-looking telescope, and an antique world globe that he'd spin like a basketball.

Alice's large work board sat above her desk, displaying her to-do lists, and lots of photos of Alice standing on large mountain peaks, on sand dunes, in forests and jungles. There were photos of Alice being hugged by an orangutan, snuggling up to a sloth, wrapped in an elephant's trunk, or with a giraffe tenderly wrapping its long neck around her in an embrace. Images of Alice as a young girl, wearing that same smile, with her long red hair in the same braid. Various caps or wide-brimmed hats shaded her shiny green eyes through the years, where she became progressively more beautiful the older she got.

There was nothing glamorous about her. Alice didn't wear make-up or dress in fancy clothes, yet her photos captured her natural beauty along with her smile that shone from her soul.

Iris put her bookmark between the pages and carefully closed her book. 'Alice says you don't like her leaving stuff out.'

'I don't like clutter and Alice has a lot of gear.'

'In the house?'

Well, Alice had her cooking gear, and he liked her cooking, so he wasn't going to complain about that. In the bathroom she had the most luxuriously thick bath sheets, he was thinking of buying some for himself.

In the living room, she had a large mat, a coffee table sitting beside the rocking chair, and a towering stack of books Alice called her TBR pile. His television set now resembled a secret home base where the large screen was filled with smaller screens set to spy on the national park.

'I'm talking about my yard,' he said to Iris. 'Alice has taken over my entire backyard.'

'I thought you didn't use your backyard.'

'Well …' Normally he didn't.

Not until he wandered out into the kitchen to his coffee machine, as part of his morning routine, to find the back door wide open. Fresh air and sunshine flooded the kitchen through the screen door. Hanging from the open window, dainty crystals cast rainbows around the room in ways he'd never seen. It was fun and frightening all at the same time.

But it's what Alice had done outside that shocked him more.

His back patio was full of white industrial pipe used for growing vegetables. He'd assumed vegetables grew in pots and tubs with some sort of dirt for a growing medium. Not Alice and her towers that were free of dirt, producing food crops in air and water. It fascinated him. Walking around the plastic totem poles, filled with pockets of spinach, tomatoes, strawberries, and even broccoli and kale. No digging, bending, just plucking, and eating.

But it was the noise that was killing him.

'Alice has turned my house into a zoo. I have a menagerie of cages filled with birds that squawk at sunrise,' he complained to Iris. 'A joey that thumps up and down my hallway playing with baby toys. There's this lizard that scurries around in the shower, while this evil-eyed turtle does laps of the bathtub.' The turtle lived in a large fish tank by the kitchen bench, set at the perfect height to give Stewart the evil eye whenever he went near his coffee machine—it was so much worse whenever he went to eat his lunch.

'They're injured animals, waiting to heal before Alice

releases them back into the wild. It's just like letting some of your patients free.' Iris frowned at him.

'She could have warned me about the birds.'

'Alice normally doesn't keep them, it's just that one of her wildlife carers is on holidays. That's why you have them.'

Well, didn't that make him feel like a nitpicker.

Speaking of the khaki-dressed devil, Alice strolled through the door. Wearing her workboots and cargo pants, her ranger's cap shadowed her eyes, with her hair in one thick braid that hung like a pretty python over her shoulder.

'Hey, roomie.' Her grin was a punch of sunshine, right in the guts.

'Hey.' Did he speak, or did he just imagine he'd said that?

'Hi, Iris, I've got your dinner.' She held up a set of plastic containers he recognised from his fridge.

'Do you cook for Iris, too?' They hadn't spoken much since the day Alice had moved in. Their last conversation was when he took out her stitches, a few days ago.

'Alice doesn't like cooking for one,' said Iris again.

'That's true.' Alice removed the new baby carrier where the wallaby, Melody, eagerly poked her head out.

Iris's reaction was beautiful to watch, with her eyes sparkling as brightly as her smile. She held out frail hands, eager to pat the joey.

He should have said no animals in the hospital, but he didn't want to upset Alice. The way the sun highlighted the fire in Alice's hair, combined with her shiny eyes and smile, she was dazzling him.

Alice wasn't polished, she didn't wear make-up and he doubted she owned a hair dryer. All he ever saw her wear were her boots, cargos, and vintage T-shirts.

The real beauty of Alice was she never annoyed him, leaving him to do his thing, only leaving notes to eat her rabbit food in the fridge. Except for the animals, Alice was easy to live with, just as she'd said she would be. He was also making it easier for her, too, because he was avoiding her.

Hold on—in his pre-Alice days, Stewart rarely spent any time at the house, so technically, he wasn't avoiding her. He was just doing his job.

Only five weeks to go.

Alice put the joey on the floor to explore the room. It had grown in a week. But it also made his heart do weird things, especially when he'd opened the front door of his house to hear the thump-thump-thump of Melody rushing up to greet him at the end of his workday. He'd never had that before.

But that turtle giving him the evil eye ruined the house party. Hey, it was still his house.

'I was telling Alice how much I'd love to see the sunset again,' said Iris.

'Sure.' He pointed at the closed window. His house used to be the same, all closed up too. But not since Captain Kale had crash landed, opening the house curtains at dawn with the windows permanently open.

'With my furry, four-legged friend, Cecil,' said Iris.

Stewart frowned. 'I'm not having a water buffalo walk through these halls. It's bad enough I've got Melody in the house thumping down the hallways.'

'Sorry.' Alice scooped up the wallaby. 'I forgot you don't like animals.'

Foot. In. Mouth. He inhaled deeply. 'This is a hospital for humans and not the place for animals.'

Iris raised her chin with her shoulders back. 'And I'm the patient who wants to watch a sunset with my old friend Cecil. I haven't seen him since I've been forced to stay here. How many months is that now, Alice?'

'Six.'

No way! For six months Alice had been visiting Iris in this small hospital and he'd never seen her until today. How was that possible?

'We can arrange something, can't we, Stewart?' Alice gave him a pleading yet determined look, while offering him a chance to play the hero again. Giving him the illusion that he was the one in control. And he liked being in control. Even though he wasn't in control when it came to Alice. How did she do that?

'I know nothing about Cecil.' Stewart did his best to avoid animals, including that beefy water buffalo known for wandering the main street of town. But since Alice had turned his house into a zoo, it was getting harder to avoid them.

'I've known Cecil since he was a baby,' said Iris. 'Every morning Cecil would show up to my verandah to give me a nod, as if to say good morning. Then he'd do the same at sunset. For a lonely old woman, Cecil was a wonderful companion.'

'Didn't his owner come after him?' Stewart asked.

'Esther would whistle, and he'd gallop off like a floppy dog,' Iris giggled. 'It was Cecil who found me when I broke my hip. Cecil dragged Esther's grandson, Luke, by his shirttails, bleating at them to come. And they did.' She straightened out her bedsheets that hid her frail legs she couldn't use anymore. 'I'd like to thank Cecil, to see him just one more time. If I could.'

'Um … Sure?' He looked at Alice for help. He didn't know how to wrangle a water buffalo.

Alice gave him such a sweet smile and a firm nod. 'We'll work on something for sure.'

It made him feel like they could do anything together — yet they weren't a team. They were two separate people who shared a roof. That's all.

'I've got rounds …' He needed to be somewhere else, far from Alice.

Stewart dropped off his paperwork to the nurse's station near the front entrance where the glass doors slid open letting in the local brewer, Alex, with his heavily pregnant partner, Verily.

'Hey, Doc.' Alex waved, wearing a smile that was positively beaming. 'She's about to pop, right?'

Verily scowled at her partner. 'I'm pregnant, not a water balloon. And you do realise this is the scariest thing in my life?' Her American accent echoed down the corridor.

Alex put a tender hand on her belly. 'Babe, you'll breeze through it. You're a world champion who can handle anything. You've got this.'

'You sound just like a softball coach,' said Stewart.

'We've only got a few more days left and our coaching clinic is done for the season. Then we can return to normal softball practice with the Dusty Dingoes.' Alex helped Verily into one of the waiting chairs. 'I told you we should have cancelled the coaching clinic.'

'I'm not running or swinging.'

'But your ankles are swelling.'

'It's our first clinic, Alex. Besides, it was you who suggested we run the softball clinics.'

'That was before Nugget crashed our party.' With his large hand on her baby bump, he leaned down and spoke to her stomach. 'Don't worry, Nugget, we'll have you playing soon enough. I'll be sure you have a spot at the next coaching clinic.'

Stewart did everything to control his grimace over the tender family moment he normally avoided. 'Are you here to see Jenny?'

'Jenny has got us doing weekly mummy checks.'

Verily sighed heavily, her small hand on her large stomach. 'I feel fine.'

'Babe, you wanted this.' Alex's voice dropped, as did his smile. 'It'll put all our minds at ease.'

'As I've said before, Verily, you are a healthy mum-to-be, and Jenny is the best midwife I know.'

'Thanks, Stewart,' Jenny said, approaching them. 'Coming from you, that's a rare compliment. I'm ready for you both. This way.'

Alex and Stewart helped Verily to her feet to walk alongside Jenny.

'Doc, got a sec?' It was barely a whisper from Alex, obviously to not alarm Verily.

'Sure. When is Verily due?'

'Four weeks,' said Alex. 'Aren't you leaving then?'

'Verily will be fine.' Judging by the size and shape of Verily's abdominal area, it wouldn't be too long before the town had a new addition to its small population.

Alex brushed fingers through his hair. 'Mate, I know you said Jenny's great, and I adore Jenny, I do. But I want you there, too.'

'I'm not a midwife. I'm just the backup.'

'Hey, I'm a team player, and I'm Verily's backup. But it'd put my mind at ease knowing you were around.'

'If I'm not, I'll make sure my father is.'

Alex screwed his nose up at the place. 'No offense—I like your old man, he's been my doctor since I was a kid when I was doing my best to avoid the guy and this place—but I want a genius to be nearby helping the love of my life. And I know you're a genius. Jenny said so. And so did your old man.'

'Why don't we just wait and see—'

'I'll name a beer after you. Or I'll supply you with a lifetime of beer, if you just promise to be here when Verily goes into labour.'

'I rarely leave the hospital grounds now, so I don't see it being an issue. Even though my contract expires soon, Alex, I'll make sure both Verily and the baby—'

'Nugget.'

'Are well taken care of.'

Alex clutched his head as if desperate to capture the overwhelming responsibility that came with newborns.

'Are you okay?'

'The stress is killing me, Doc. Verily lost her mother and brother during childbirth. Her father is in the States freaking out, and her Aunt Molly is the same. We all want to wrap Verily up in cotton wool.'

'Verily is fine.'

Alex stopped pacing to grin. 'She's perfect, mate. And she's perfect for me. That's why you've got to be here when we get to meet Nugget. Even if it terrifies me, I can't wait.'

'Your baby is lucky to have you as their father.'

Alex was going to be one of those doting dads who showed up at sporting events, and doctor visits, and anything else that a child could ever want.

'Go be with Verily.'

'Thanks, Stewart. Just be here when Nugget arrives. And for the after party, too.' Alex gave a wave, before entering the door to the consultation room.

Stewart avoided delivery rooms and maternity wards. It was never his thing in Melbourne. Yet in this hospital, he'd watched Verily's baby bump grow. With it, the level of excitement grew amongst the staff, patients, and their visitors, all looking forward to baby Nugget's arrival.

This level of sentimentality never happened in the hospitals he'd worked at. He never got attached to any of the patients that endlessly rolled in and out of the hospital's main doors like a wave shifting across the sands on an incoming tide.

It was time to focus on the world of normality.

Stewart opened his tablet to the job application for the position at the cardiothoracic surgical team, Olivia had mentioned. He'd painstakingly filled it out, edited it, and re-edited it countless times this past week. He was ready to send it, which meant making a phone call he'd been avoiding for months.

Eight

For days Stewart had stared at a particular name and number on his phone. With a deep breath, tonight, he finally hit the dial button.

The hospital's automatic doors slid open, allowing a burst of fresh air to greet him, a stark contrast to the temperature-controlled corridors. With the sunset long gone, it left only the stars shining over the deserted visitors' car park.

'Priscilla Harrington speaking.'

'Hello, Mother.'

'Oh, my darling boy. It's been far too long.'

'I've been busy.' He winced at his lame excuse, adjusting the grip on his phone.

'Listen, my darling, as much as I'd love to, I can't talk long. I'm meeting Benjamin at the ballet. He's sent a car for me.'

Priscilla was always at some luncheon or fundraising event. She never left the house without her hair perfectly coiffured, and her outfit carefully coordinated, right down to the colour of her nail polish from her weekly manicures. 'Olivia told me you'd called.'

'I did. I needed advice for a patient.' The stockman they called Eskie was healing nicely, with a full recovery expected. It had been a very successful six-hour surgery.

'Olivia also told me she sent you the application to join Benjamin's team. Please, darling, tell me you've filled it out.'

'I have.' And he'd been editing and re-editing it for days.

'Have you sent it yet?'

With another childlike wince, he dropped his head to rub the back of his neck. 'Would my stepfather want me on his team? It's a bit nepotistic, don't you think?' Going back to a world that kicked him out, and having his stepfather hold his hand, wasn't a good look.

His mother's tittering laughter floated over the phone. He recognised it from the many times it drifted above the crowd of her fancy fundraising functions she regularly hosted, that he did his best to avoid.

It was such a different world compared to the outback that spread out before him like a gothic painter's canvas with its many shades of rich violets and deep mauves to the blackest of blacks, punctuated by a supercity of stars.

'Darling, be a good boy and send me the application. I'll be sure that Benjamin gets it.'

'I want the job on my merits, not because my mother is married to the chief of surgery.'

'What's the good of having family connections if you can't use them now and again, hmm? Besides, Benjamin knows how good you are, darling. Benjamin told the board how silly they were for sending you away. How long before you're free from your penance?'

'Three-and-a-half weeks to go.' The ticking clock was getting louder. 'My tenants have just moved out.'

'Wonderful. Want me to send in a decorator?'

'Just a cleaner, Mother. And one that cleans the windows. Period.'

'I have always admired your apartment's view of the city.'

He liked that view too. When he wasn't sleeping in a deep comatose state, he'd watch the constant flow of traffic adding another layer to the city of lights so bright you never saw the sky.

Yet here there wasn't a car on a road that had no streetlights.

Craning his neck to the galaxies that were so clearly defined, he playfully reached out to touch them. To then size up the brightest five-star constellation shaped like a kite. It was the Southern Cross, held between his thumb and forefinger. Pointing in the direction of home.

'Fine. I'll find you a cleaner, and a regular housekeeper who cooks too. Are you still eating hospital food?'

'Not lately.' His grin spread, tapping his well-satisfied tummy.

'Please tell me you're not walking the corridors scoffing down vending machine food.'

'I've actually been walking home, taking a lunch break.' Where he'd slowly rock in Alice's chair with Melody the wallaby, watching CCTV footage of the national park on his big screen. Then he'd have a scowling contest with the evil-eyed turtle as he ate his greens, while the water monitor hid under a fake log in its cage in the kitchen.

Thankfully, the large bird cages were gone from the backyard, making it a quiet place to hang out. He'd kick back in Alice's outdoor seating near her totem-pole garden, where a few wind chimes shifted with their soft tunes, as he enjoyed the uninterrupted view of the outback.

The way Alice had set it up, he couldn't see her industrial work equipment that was part of her job. And the lady had lots of boys toys, including two boats, motorbikes, and large cages hidden around the corner.

'Good, you need that downtime, darling. Take advantage of it now because it won't be long and you'll be busy all over again, then I'll have to visit the hospital to see you. So, I'm booking you in now for a welcome home dinner. Lucella makes the most divine lamb dish, you'll love it.'

'Thanks, Mother.'

'It'll be so good to have you home. Now, email me that job application, pronto, young man. I'll start buttering up Benjamin tonight at the ballet. Oh, I'd better get a wriggle on out the door. I hate being late for date night.'

'Have a good night, Mother. Thank you for your help.'

'Anything for my darling boy.'

He stared at the silent phone. The guilt for not calling sooner made his stomach squirm and his shoulders tighten. It didn't feel right using her about the job, either.

An incoming text message flashed across his phone's screen: *Stop procrastinating, and email me that application, darling. Love Mum. Xx*

With a smile creeping across his lips, he emailed it to her.

There. It was done.

Now all he could do now was wait for an answer.

In the meantime, he needed a distraction to take his mind off the application for his dream job, and the pressure of returning to a place he'd been shunned from.

His eyes narrowed on the silhouette of someone walking along the deserted country road past the police station. *Hello, roomie.*

Nine

Under the sky filled with a glistening sea of stars, Alice followed Melody thumping along the road's verge, to nibble at the grass.

At her old house she grew grass just for this purpose, but it was currently nothing more than a construction site of rubble as the Council was in the process of demolishing her old house. She made a mental note to pick up some grass seed and a sprinkler for the doctor's house the next time she drove through town.

Playing the part of a drover, she herded Melody to eat the grass along the road. The nocturnal agile wallaby's white stripes were becoming more noticeable on the sides of her slender face, common for her breed. And her skills at hopping had improved immensely. Suddenly Melody swung her head around and bounced off into the dark.

'Where are you going, Melody?' She flicked on her flashlight.

'It's only me.' It was Stewart, crouching down to pat Melody.

She turned off the light, preferring the stars. 'I think Melody has a crush on you.' Not the only one. Because once you got past his arrogant smart-arsery, Stewart was a really nice guy.

Too bad he only saw her as a housemate. *Welcome to the friend zone.*

'Are you doing your nightly walk?' She noted the time. Stewart didn't normally start his walk for another hour, when she would be home, hiding in her room to not bump into the guy.

But it was getting harder to avoid him, not only sharing the same living space, but now she was bumping into him regularly at the hospital whenever she visited Iris. Although, it was getting easier to talk to him and not get all tongue-tied with her words, and she'd stopped walking into doors or strange rooms to escape him.

'I am. You?'

'It's feeding time at the zoo.' She shrugged at Melody bouncing a few feet ahead to nibble on some grass getting slick with the dew. 'Sorry about the birds in the backyard last week. There's a volunteer who looks after them as part of the local Wildlife Rescue Organisation, but she's been on holiday.'

'Are there many people in town who do that?'

'A few, with room for plenty more. I'm always looking for potential helpers considering I'm the only ranger in this area.'

'Anyone I know as carers?'

'There's the lovely Flo Wayfaren-Barnett with her backyard billabong. She wears the most amazing wardrobe.' Alice tugged on her drab khaki uniform. Nothing sexy or colourful about being dressed to blend with the scrub.

'She's got the duck head on her walking cane?'

'That's her. Flo's a water diviner, who has created an amazing refuge for any injured ducks and geese I come across.'

'So, they're babysitters for wildlife?'

'Some are, others just keep watch, like Verily and Alex are monitoring a large family of quolls on their mango farm.' These past six months visiting Iris, she'd seen Verily regularly attend the hospital, always with her partner Alex at her side. 'Verily is due soon, isn't she?

'It won't be long now.'

They walked side by side as the wallaby continued to nibble on slender grass shoots, then hopped towards something better.

'The water monitor is going back tomorrow. A course of antibiotics, and a daily salt bath, his eyes have healed. Poor little guy. I found him on the side of a creek, suffering with conjunctivitis.' She was looking forward to returning him to his home.

'What about the evil-eyed turtle? What's up with his nose? It looks like a pig snout gone wrong.'

Her laugh echoed down the dark road. 'Piggy-paddle is a pig-nosed turtle. His breed has been around since the dinosaurs.'

'Let me guess, piggy for a pig snout, and the paddle?'

'They're a rare breed of a freshwater turtle that has flippers like a sea turtle. It makes them quite clumsy on land.'

'It keeps giving me the evil eye, especially when I'm eating my lunch. Or it's because he hates the name Piggy-paddle.'

She matched his smile. 'You might be right. His breed is known to be quite moody. Or he's doing some Jedi mind trick to get you to feed him. He loves lettuce, strawberries, and celery leaves. You can feed him anytime.'

'I don't know how to feed animals. Especially turtles. Do they bite?'

'No. PP doesn't have the strength to chomp. When I found him, trapped in an illegal crabbing net in the river, he was starving. His jaw had been badly torn. He won't survive if he goes back to the wild.' She struggled to swallow down her pain for the poor creature.

'What are you going to do with him?'

She shrugged. 'Find him a home. Sadly, they're a high-maintenance animal that can live for thirty years, so I'm not sure who'll take him.' Yet PP seemed happy at the house, free from the daily fight for survival, being hand-fed fresh greens twice a day. Did she dare tell Stewart she'd been letting PP cruise around the house while he was at work?

'And this one?' He pointed to the joey.

'Now that she's grass feeding, Melody is ready to go back. I hope you're not too attached, Doctor.'

'Should I be asking you that question?' There was a level of gentleness in his tone.

'Melody will be going back to where she belongs, she'll be happy there.'

'Do you normally look after wallabies?'

'No. There are a few carers who do. Iris, at the hospital, used to be a wildlife carer for wallabies. But Melody was a special case.'

'How so?'

'We weren't sure if her spine would be an issue after the accident.'

'Accident?'

She rubbed her arms, suddenly feeling a chill in the cool outback air at the sheer luck that had saved the joey. 'Melody's mother was crushed on one of the stock routes and I found Melody in her pouch.' Alice had fought with large carrion birds to drag Melody's mother off the outback road, minutes before a large cattle truck barrelled through, bringing along a rain of red dust.

'She's hopping around now.' Stewart nodded at the wallaby as it wobbled to hop awkwardly sideways. It paused for a moment, only to hop in the direction she'd first intended.

'I know of a good wallaby troupe she'll be safe with.'

'In the park?'

'Yes.'

'I imagine your job is like a holiday?' He sighed, shoving his hands into his pockets.

'How so? Because I imagine your job is elbow deep in blood and guts.'

'Some days it is. You? Dirt and dust?'

'That's normal for the dry season. Then it's nothing but mud and mozzies in the wet. But I do get to cruise around in the ute, the quad, and the boats.'

'Sounds like you've got all the hunters' toys.'

'I'm no hunter. I refuse to get involved with any form of animal culling.'

Again, they walked in silence. They'd reached the police station, the spotlights eye-wateringly bright.

Stewart broke the silence first. 'Marcus sent me a postcard from Bali today, bragging about being on some beach, drinking beer, while learning to surf with Wren. He did that to make me jealous.'

'Like some boy's game?' She arched an eyebrow at him.

'It's what we do—did.' He shrugged. 'We're both from Melbourne, living for our careers.' Stewart playfully kicked at a stone, sending it tumbling along the road.

It made Melody look up from her roadside feast, before nibbling on something else.

Stewart looked back at the police station as if missing his friend. Then turned away, rolled his shoulders, sniffed the air, and resumed walking. Each step was a distinct disconnect, as if putting it all behind him.

He seemed as lonely as she was. Except for Stewart it was by choice, because he had lots of single women vying for his attention. While Alice had found that some men struggled with independent women, especially when she was considered the bad guy in this town.

'Have you been to Bali?' she asked.

'No. You?'

'Most years my parents and I usually meet there for Christmas to surf or snorkel around the West Bali National Park that's free from crocodiles. For presents, Dad gets a few new T-shirts, Mum gets us to hold her hand while she gets another tattoo, and I get a voucher to spend on books. I imagine that's not your idea of Christmas.' Stewart probably spent it with his mother, standing before an enormous tree that touched the ceiling. Wearing a suit and tie, sipping fancy wines, nibbling canapes, talking about medicine and the opera while the staff prepared their ten-course meal.

'I can't remember having a holiday. Whenever my ex-fiancée and I got two days rostered off together, we'd book into some hotel to just sleep for a few days with no interruptions.'

'You were engaged?'

'We were interns together.' He gave a dreamy smile to the stars.

'Another surgeon?'

'Olivia is an orthopaedic surgeon who specialises in hands.'

'Wow. Talk about a power couple.' And so out of her league in khaki grunge and tacky retro T-shirts covered in wallaby hair.

'Back at the hospital, we lived in Liv's office.'

'You didn't have your own office?'

'Liv had her own bathroom. She's like you with her special chair and her special coffee cup. Must be a girl thing.'

'I have certain teas that require the whole pomp and ceremony. I'm weird, right?'

He chuckled. 'I like your totem-pole vegetable garden. Those cherry tomatoes look great. Where did you get the idea?'

'From social media. Then I sold the idea to my dad. We're in a competition to see who can grow the best veggies. Dad is always sending me videos of his latest trophy heritage butternuts, he's even started naming them.' She scrolled her phone and opened a message. 'Here, he calls that one Nutmeg and that one's Spice.'

His chuckle suited the sexy smile. 'Like how you named your money tree Penny?'

'That's actually her short name. Her full name is Moneypenny. Weird, right?'

'It's playful.'

'The latest scientific studies show that plants may not have a brain, but they react to their environments, especially to sound and touch. Even though they haven't conclusively proven it, that if talking to plants brings a person joy and a sense of connection with nature, there's no harm in doing it. Is there?' Now she was rambling utter nonsense in the dark. She dropped her head hoping the night's shadows hid the heat radiating from her cheeks.

'You read science manuals?'

'Nowhere near to the extent you would.' His world of medicine was so clinical and sterile, nothing like hers.

'So why do you read romance novels?' He screwed his nose up.

'They're fun. With a guaranteed feel-good ending that has nothing to do with my work. My Mum loves her Spanish tele-novellas, reading the subtitles as her way of kicking back on the couch. Dad does comics. I'm sure you're aware of the health benefits to recreational reading. It's an excellent form of relaxation and stress relief, Doctor.' She playfully nudged his side. 'You do know what that is, don't you?'

He shrugged.

'When was the last time you had a day off?'

'Not since I arrived here. But I don't mind.'

'Why not?'

'There's nothing to do.'

She stopped, her eyes widening at him. 'You're kidding me! Don't you realise you live on the edge of one of the world's most amazing natural wonderlands?'

'Are you talking about the national park?'

'Your backyard, alone, is an amazing place for a sunset. Tonight's sunset was spectacular. I enjoyed it with a yummy red wine that Bottle-shop Luke recommended to me.'

'Luke?' He scratched the back of his head. 'Why do I know that name?'

'Esther's grandson. She's Cecil's owner … the water buffalo.'

He narrowed his eyes at her. 'Did you speak to him about Iris's request?'

'I did.' She sighed, feeling that pressure across her

shoulders. Even though she hated the idea of being delegated to perform Iris's last wish, she'd do anything for the lady. 'Luke is talking to Esther tonight, and they're going to visit Iris tomorrow. I'd thought about wheeling Iris out the back door of the hospital and over to your backyard to spend time with Cecil. But the gravel may be a challenge with her wheelchair, and if Cecil knew I had all those greens growing at water buffalo height—'

'He'd eat us out of house and home.'

Again, they shared a grin, resuming their stroll down the road following a baby wallaby under the stars.

'So go on, tell me more about the park.'

Did she have to?

'Um …' She cleared her throat, tugging at the neckline of her T-shirt. 'We're home to some of the most unique waterbirds in the country. Every year scientists from across the globe will visit to study our lightning storms and our impressive waterbirds.'

'Birdwatching is not my thing.'

'Or you've never tried it. Not if you're working all the time.'

He shrugged. 'That's true.'

'Birdwatching isn't about some middle-aged dude dressed in tweed, tooting on some bird whistle, you know. Most of my bird counts and observations go towards scientific research as the park is home to thousands of waterbirds during breeding time. It's impressive to see them all gathering in the one location, because it's so rare these days.'

'What do you mean by that?'

'They're an important gauge of our ecosystem's health. The cleaner the air and water, the bigger the bird population. Down south they're losing their habitats. Yet we can boast that we have one of the largest, condensed waterbird populations in the country. Just down that road. And you've never seen it.'

He shrugged as they stopped at the end of the road. Across from them lay the railway line with the deserted stockyards behind it. On the left, was the central Australian outback that swallowed the highway in a heavy layer of empty darkness.

'You need to see Elsie Creek National Park before you leave, Stewart. You can't come out all this way and not visit Mother Nature's wonderland that people put on their bucket lists.' She gently poked his chest. 'When is your next day off?'

Again, he shrugged.

'Pick a day. Go on. Any day.'

'Why?'

'I'll take you with me. We'll take the tents and stay overnight.'

He frowned. 'I've never been camping.'

It was her turn to wrinkle her nose at him. 'Then allow me to show you. All you'll need is a bag with a change of clothes, something to swim in, and your coffee. I'll bring the rest. Do you have anything else to wear besides white?' She playfully flicked at his white doctor's coat that made him stand out like a ghost.

'It's the uniform.'

'So is this.' She tugged at her khaki shirt. 'I want to introduce Melody to that wallaby troupe. There's a mother who's recently lost her baby, and she's pining. I think she'll be the perfect stepmother for Melody.' She also wanted to show him there was more to life than work, especially the amazing world that was only down the road from the hospital. 'It's my way of repaying you for your generosity for letting me take over your backyard.'

'I've told you before, Alice, it's okay.'

'Listen, I never give anyone a tour of the park as I do my best to avoid all tourists.'

'So I'll get—'

'A once-in-a-lifetime, behind-the-scenes, VIP access to Elsie Creek National Park. What do you say, Doctor?'

Ten

Stewart didn't want to go, and certainly not at four in the morning. But he'd been talked into having two days off, with Jenny refusing to let him wriggle his way out of it.

Alice seemed so excited about their adventure, meeting nightly to walk along the road to feed Melody, planning for this event. He'd honestly tried to find the same drive and energy Alice had whenever she spoke of the park, but he had nothing to compare it to. He just didn't want to go.

'Why so early?' Stewart rubbed the sleep from his eyes, flicking on his coffee machine, avoiding the pig-nosed turtle's grumpy glare. He stared at his phone, willing it to ring. He'd take on a case of sniffles to stay.

'I want you to see the sunrise for breakfast. It'll be worth it, trust me.' By the front door, Alice slid her feet into her boots. She brushed back her hair, to tie up the laces. 'I'm thinking of making you cook. I'll supervise.'

She was like a rabbit bouncing around the place as she packed her ute and got them ready for their overnight camping trip. All Stewart had to do was fill his overnight bag and his coffee thermos.

Putting the coffee beans back into the now-full fridge, he plucked a few leaves from the lettuce head and dropped them into the nearby turtle's cage. It had become a habit to avoid the turtle's glare. 'I don't cook, I only do coffee, little rabbit.' *Woah-up. Where did that come from?*

Alice snorted out a giggle, checking on the turtle's fish

tank pump, food pellets, and lights. 'Stop looking for an excuse to wriggle out of this.'

'Who me? Or the turtle?' He narrowed his eyes at the smug pig-nosed turtle, who only smiled for Alice, while Stewart scored the scowl. 'You're such a suck-up, Piggy.'

Again, Alice giggled—her good mood was annoying. But she did look cute in her khaki ranger's uniform, sliding her leather belt through the loops of her cargo pants, to clip on her walkie-talkie and mobile phone.

'Oh, hey, I got you this gadget that might come in handy.' She dumped a brown box on the bench beside him.

'What's this?' He opened the box to remove a small coffee pot. 'Does this plug into something?'

'The ute. You can even plug it into your laptop, for your office at work.'

Her habit of sharing things with him was truly endearing. Alice was always thinking of others, including her meals, that he was now sharing his morning tea with Iris at the hospital. His life was changing without him even realising it.

'Are you going to have any coffee?' He'd never made her one.

'Sure. Thanks. Here's my travel mug.' Her smile was dynamite with her green eyes sparkling, plonking down her scratched and dented coffee mug on the bench. 'But just the one. I'd hate to suffer those caffeine withdrawals again.'

'Which is why you bought me the travel pot?'

Again, she tossed that grin over her shoulder, as her hair fell like fiery waves of silk down her back. Her hand hovered over her assorted hats hanging from the stand made from an old tree branch that even his museum-loving mother would admire.

'Do you have a hat? I've got plenty of A-grade sunscreen.'

'You'd need it with your skin. Hey, with your red hair and freckles, have you ever had your skin tested for melanomas?'

'Every year as part of the job. I'm not your patient, Doctor.' She effortlessly braided her hair, shoved on her well-worn work hat, before snatching another hat from the rack 'This is yours, and this long-sleeved shirt to get dirty in.' Both bearing the National Park Ranger emblem. 'That way you won't look like a tourist.'

'Because you do your best to avoid all tourists.' He chuckled at her cheeky smile.

'Here, Dad sent you this in the mail.' She giggled, passing him another package.

'I don't like that giggle.' He was also unsure of the lightweight package. 'Why is your father sending me things?'

'You should see what he sent me.' Again, that giggle was full of mischief. It was infectious. 'Go on, take a peek.'

'I'm scared to.'

Her laugh grew louder as she slipped her laptop into her chunky workbag.

Under the scowl of PP, munching on his lettuce leaf, Stewart turned over the parcel bearing his name: *Doctor Stewart Mannen from Professor Robert Meadows*.

Was it a science manual? He knew her father was a highly respected professor in the field of wildlife biology, while Alice's mother was a professor in geoscience, both working at a Sydney university. Was it any wonder Alice had such impressive qualifications that she could work anywhere. Instead, she was out here, in the middle of Woop Woop. Was she stuck in Elsie Creek, like he was?

Stewart tore back the tissue paper, unrolled the material inside and then tilted his head at his gift.

'What did Dad send you?' Alice's minty breath blended well with her floral scents, which had become his personal flavour of pheromones, making him inhale deeply.

He pointed at the T-shirt that had a Bugs Bunny image saying: *What's up Doc?* 'Was this your idea?'

'No. Nothing to do with me. Dad does T-shirts, it's his thing.'

'My father does poor-taste medical puns. But I thought woodworking and comic books were your father's thing. As well as making up names for butternut pumpkins.' Alice was right, her family was weird. But they made him laugh, just thinking of their antics.

'It's a good fit for you.' Alice held the T-shirt up to his chest. 'Mum won't let Dad buy any more T-shirts, she's run out of room. She's told Dad that for every new T-shirt he acquires, he has to get rid of an old one.'

'Does he?'

'My dad?' Her laugh pealed around the room, even the turtle lifted its head from his lettuce feast to listen. 'Dad found a seamstress to make office curtains out of his T-shirts, with plans for a couch-cover in the near future.'

'Crafty.'

'That's Dad. Some days he's just a big kid. Do you think you'll wear it?' She covered her mouth to hide her laugh, going red in the face it highlighted her freckles.

'I, um …' He didn't want to upset her.

'We'll take it with us. Get a selfie wearing it and send it to Dad, he'll be happy with that. Then you can do whatever you want with it after that.' She deftly rolled it up like a backpacker, putting it on top of her bag that sat on the kitchen chair.

It wasn't what he normally wore at all. 'That's why you have all those seventies shirts?'

'You should see the latest one Dad sent me.'

Dressed by her father! He'd never met a woman like her. Sure, he'd met plenty of women who shopped, or had personal shoppers to select their wardrobes, but never had he met a woman who wore clothes picked by their father. 'What shirt did your father send you?'

His eyes keenly zoomed in on her nimble fingers, unbuttoning her work shirt. Was he about to see her lace underwear, which waved at him from the clothesline he never used?

Instead, she revealed a dark T-shirt that she pulled down over her flat stomach that read: *an apple a day keeps the doctor away*.

Her laugh filled the corners of their kitchen. Before he knew it, he was laughing, wiping at the happy tears threatening to spill from the corners of his eyes.

He couldn't remember the last time he'd laughed like that.

'Well, I'd better get into my uniform then.' He snatched back his new T-shirt, sliding off his polo shirt, and swapping it for a T-shirt that was so much thinner in material. But her wide smile, with her slightly upturned nose that had her freckles shifting, was so worth it as his reward.

He paused, struck anew by her astounding natural beauty. There was pretty and then there was Alice pretty. And that was pretty special. Period.

'Ready to go?' She plonked a ranger cap on his head.

He slid his arms through the sleeves of the khaki shirt. 'I'm ready.' He just had to remember they were friends, even though he struggled with the temptation to brush the fine fiery strands outlining her face.

But then the shine in her eyes dulled, and her smile fell, as she picked up the baby carrier.

He gave the hand that held the baby carrier a squeeze and gently tugged it free from her fingers. 'Come on, Melody. It's time to take you to your new home.'

The *thump thump thump* of the joey coming down the hallway had been his daily greeting since the day Alice and her entourage had moved in. He was going to miss it. Which surprised him, when he rarely connected with anyone, not when he knew that all of this was temporary.

With the joey bundled into his arms, Alice hoisted her pack over her shoulder and scooped up their coffee mugs and together they left through the back door he never used.

Eleven

'*There wasn't a place on her body he hadn't discovered. No part he hadn't conquered. And yet, he had never wanted her more. With his palm cupping her jaw, he turned her face to accept his mouth as he greedily—*'

'Stop!' Alice wanted to die. Absolutely, completely die. Her face was on fire as she ripped out the USB cord from her ute's dashboard, the male narrator's voice still ringing in her ears.

'What was that?' Stewart asked from the passenger seat.

'An audiobook,' she mumbled.

'So, you not only read romance, but you also listen to it.' He laughed harder.

She dropped her head, feeling the heat pulsing through to her ears. 'We don't get radio …'

'We can listen to—'

'Music.' She whipped her head up. 'Got any playlists?'

'Do you? Or is it all romantic music?'

'No. I mean, yes, no—I have a few playlists, but it's an eclectic mix. Melody likes it. She likes all music.' Her shirt stuck to her clammy skin as she fumbled with her phone to connect to her playlists.

'Now I get why you call her Melody. Let me guess, your parents influenced your music tastes?'

'Excuse me?' She narrowed her eyes at him. He may snub his nose at her for her love of romance novels, but no one talked badly about her parents. 'I like my parents.'

'Me too. They seem like nice people.'

Embarrassingly, they'd met Stewart one day when he'd come home for lunch, while she was on her weekly Zoom call with them. Hence the T-shirt he was being made to wear.

As the beefy diesel engine hummed in the background, the warm air of the exhaust turned to a misty smoke blending with the cool air. She strapped Melody's baby carrier into the middle of the front seat. Turned on the two-way radio hanging above her head. She slipped her chunky satellite phone into its pocket, her tablet in its cradle, then flicked on the GPS. It was her normal routine for starting the long drive to work. Always prepared for the adventure, she ensured everything had its secure spot due to some of the extreme road conditions that were just a part of her day job.

Normally, she'd listen to an audiobook, but today she had a passenger with the divine scent of warm musk and cool mint weaving its way around the cab that blended perfectly with the rich roasted coffee aroma.

He was just too big for this cab.

She swallowed nervously. 'A musician I met once told me that the best era for original music was the seventies through to the nineties. It's why there seems to be so many cover songs these days.'

Stewart clipped on his seatbelt, then checked his mobile. Again. 'Was he a boyfriend?'

'No. We were passengers stuck in this crummy airport lounge, waiting for our delayed flights, sharing his duty-free bottle of tequila.' She opened the cup holder for him. 'We had twelve hours to kill, and he was determined to educate me on the wrongs and rights of modern music. But I'm no music groupie.'

'You never mention an ex or a past boyfriend?' He slid his coffee mug into the holder.

'Nothing serious.' She shrugged, as her self-esteem over her non-existent love-life dissolved like a drop of water baking under an outback sun.

Didn't he think she was good enough to be with anyone?

'My job had me moving around a lot. Until I scored this permanent placement.'

'So, this is it for you? This ...' He sniffed at the windscreen, as if looking down his nose at her life choices. 'Isn't there somewhere else you'd rather work than here?'

'There is ...' But that was a conversation for another day.

Alice flicked on the headlights, put the ute into gear. 'Ready?' Was it too late to tell him he could stay home? Or did she continue with her plan of showing him the wonders of the outback?

'Just don't make me spill my coffee or drive the way Marcus does.' He shared one of those grins that always made her warm inside.

She wished he'd stop that, while also wishing she could stop reacting to the guy.

'I don't do high speeds, not in this workhorse. But she'll get you anywhere you want to go.' With music playing in the background, she tapped the dashboard of the beefy diesel and headed down the deserted outback highway to greet the dawn.

Seated behind the steering wheel, and through the side mirrors, Alice watched Stewart lock the sturdy steel gate behind them. He looked good dressed like a ranger instead of a doctor. The drive alone was already having a positive impact on him. His posture was straightening, his shoulders no longer stooped as if he were carrying an unseen burden, and those permanent worry lines had softened across his forehead.

'Did you lock it?' The gate had a *Do Not Enter—Restricted Access Only* sign in the middle of it.

'Yeah. Where do I hook this up, again?' He held up the key with a long tag.

'There.' She pointed to the correct clip on the dashboard where numerous sets of keys to various areas of the park lived. They all bore the *Ranger—Parks and Wildlife Commission, Northern Territory* tag, just like the patch she wore on her uniform's sleeves. It was the same emblem on the sides of the ute that was her mobile office.

'Why do I have to open and close the gate?' He complained as he climbed into the cab. 'I'm the guest, remember? Or is that why you have me wearing the uniform?'

She grimaced, trying to hold back the foolish giggle. 'It's the shotgun rule. Whoever gets the privilege of sitting in the front passenger seat has to open and close the gates.'

'You made that up.' Stewart was so serious.

Her laugh bounced off the car windows. 'I did not. Apparently, it's a thing from back in the stagecoach days, where their coach drivers needed a shotgun-carrying guard to save them from the highwaymen.'

'You're full of facts, aren't you?'

'Well, hold on to your wild brumbies for this, cowboy.'

He scoffed at her, crossing his arms over his chest. 'I'm a doctor, little rabbit.'

Her smile faltered. The nickname was new, but there was nothing fun in his tone.

She drove up the rocky road, then over the ridge to her favourite place in the park. Cutting the vehicle's lights, she killed the engine to let the ute quietly roll down the hill.

Stewart shifted in his seat, his eyes narrowing at the view, only for the frown to start. 'What is this place?'

'It's a billabong.' She parked by a group of trees. 'I'll make breakfast here. Just don't make too much noise, you don't want to scare off the wildlife.' She gently pushed the door shut. No slamming here.

Climbing out of the ute, Stewart sniffed the air as if he was at some smelly city garbage dump. But the air was invigoratingly fresh.

'Here's your chair. You sit right there, drink your coffee, and watch the sunrise.' She opened the camping chair for him.

Back at the ute, she checked on Melody.

'Is she still sleeping?'

'Yeah …' Her little paws cuddled the bottle like a baby who was growing too fast. Alice lifted the baby carrier and hooked it on the ute's rear tray to keep an eye on her. The wallaby didn't move. Neither had Stewart from his spot beside the ute, except to peek at his stupid mobile phone as if willing it to ring or something.

'Here, take these.' She passed him her binoculars and camera, gently pushing him towards the chair. 'Take some happy snaps, if you want.'

Stewart didn't look happy, wearing the expression of some city snob discovering rodents rummaging through the rubbish pile at the back of their favourite restaurant.

What was she thinking? She was here for Melody's sake and shouldn't be wasting time trying to impress Stewart. For what? To be friend-zoned again?

It was like dumping a bucket of water over a pile of burning papers, dousing her stupid schoolgirl crush on the guy who was crushing her self-esteem by turning his nose down at this place that was her job, and her way of life. He had no right to do that. No one did.

She rolled her shoulders as if shrugging off the dead weight. It shouldn't matter what Stewart thought of this place, or her job, or what she wore. She'd never cared what people thought of her, not out here where she'd worked damn hard to become the head ranger of her own park. She loved her job, and she loved this place.

It no longer mattered what he thought. After all, Stewart was just a tourist. And, like all tourists, they'd eventually leave—especially Stewart who had a daily countdown: *three weeks and three days to go*.

Twelve

Stewart brushed his fingers down his jeans. Folded back the cuffs on the borrowed ranger's shirt. Adjusted the clasp on his ranger's cap. Cleaned his sunglasses. Fidgeted with his coffee cup. Tapped his heel on the dirt. Removed the cap again to brush fingers through his hair. Looking for something—anything—to do, he got up from his seat.

'Don't you dare.' Alice aimed her egg flip at him like a weapon, from where she was cooking breakfast at the back of the ute.

'I was just—'

'Sit.'

'But—'

'Sit.'

He frowned, dropping back into his seat to stare at a large land mass of nothing. How the heck did he get talked into this?

Normally he had paperwork to annoy him, medical staff, patients, or other people to talk to. But he wasn't at work. Here all he had to occupy him was his coffee, his silent phone, a set of some serious binoculars, and her camera.

Oh, come on! He was a man who always had something to do. Constantly on the move throughout the hospital, shifting from patient to patient, with his mind going over their medical prognosis. The only time he did nothing was when he slept.

But here he was, being made to sit and do nothing for

whatever the heck this was?

It was just another sunrise. So what? He'd seen plenty over the years from the roof of the city hospital, even from his city apartment.

Stuck in the large valley, or gully, or whatever field of something, lay a billabong that was so big it should have been called a lake. There were no houses, no powerlines, nothing to show any form of human touch. He was lost. 'What am I meant to do?'

'Sit. Wait for breakfast and watch the show.'

'Alice—'

'Shh.'

Pfft.

He tried, but there wasn't much of anything to see. 'How long for breakfast?' So they could eat and run.

'You're rather impatient for a man who handles patients.' She added a pinch of salt to her dish.

Annoyance filled him as he narrowed his eyes at her. He huffed, sitting back, defeated. Crossed one leg over a knee and sipped on his coffee. *This sucks.*

As the sun rose higher, the shadows shifted into shapes to reveal an area crowded with lots of strange birds. Hundreds of birds. Some sang, whistled, cawed, and some sounded like the group of elderly women who played bridge in the hospice ward.

'What is this place?'

Alice's smile was so soft and tender. The colours of the warming sunrise reflected in her glassy eyes, while giving her hair of fire a soft glow. She was both beautiful, powerful, and tender all at the same time. 'Look at this like a maternity ward, Doctor.'

'That big bird bath?' *As if.*

'You walk quieter when you enter those places, you talk softer, and maybe you hold your breath when you peek at a newborn in their crib. This,' she said, pointing at the scenery, 'is Mother Nature's birthing suite. It's the waterbirds' breeding grounds, containing some very rare and precious creatures. And you've got the best seat in the house.'

Did he really? When all he could smell was dirt and a tang of water, mixing with the aroma of frying onions.

He lifted the heavy binoculars that were blurry. 'I don't see much.'

'Here.' She adjusted the binoculars, giving him a quick lesson.

'They're like my surgical loupes that have these small magnifiers on the lenses.' He raised them to his eyes. 'But these are a thousand times clearer. I see everything—'

'Shush.' She gave him a sly wink and went back to cooking.

Through the powerful binoculars he could follow the bend of each grass blade to the iridescent wings of a resting blue dragonfly. He followed the curve of the vibrant pink petals of a wild lotus flower bud, to the emerald-green and brown speckled frog sitting on a nearby lily pad.

Adjusting the lenses as she'd shown him, to refocus from micro-imagery to the colours and textures of various feathers that belonged to assorted birds, big and small, becoming clearer under the new dawning light.

It reminded him of some children's book filled with fantastical creatures that were tugging at the corner of his mind. A mishmash of characters that blended to form a chaotic scene spread below him. A place where tall pink-and-grey cranes blended with the pastel sky, only to be outdone by glossy black flamingo-like storks with their thin red legs.

A few fruit bats screeched overhead to crash through the treetops where a group of clumsy black-winged geese were nesting. An astonishing gathering of colourful birds bounced over the water in clever aerodynamic displays. A few crows cawed, and lots of ducks quacked, and geese clucked. Other birds whistled, hissed, clicked, with many flapping their wings. It reminded him of a doctors' convention, with the attendees wanting to know where the decent coffee was, and what time did the bar open.

Beneath the cacophony of feathers were various species of lizards. Some lay across fallen logs that ran from the grasses to rest among the water, right beside a few long-neck turtles. He zeroed in to see if there were any like PP with his pig snout.

Then something made him sit back, look up from the lenses, then peek through the binoculars again. It reminded him of a dodo bird from a childhood story he'd read. Only to shrug off the memory because he didn't read books—unless it was to do with his work. 'Am I imagining it or does that bird have a spoon for a beak?'

'It's a spoonbill.' Alice deftly flipped the ingredients in the pan. The spicy fragrant aromas blended with the fresh air, heavy with dew.

Again, he lifted the binoculars to spy on white, black, brown, tall, short, fat birds. There had to be thousands of them. Some waded along the edges, others floated in groups. Others gathered on fallen trees with their wings spread wide, as if drying their feathers under a rising sun.

It was such a busy place he didn't know where to look with everything happening at once.

'Look at you, birdwatching.'

He grinned. 'It seems I am. Not that you gave me much of a choice.'

She winced at him like she'd done the wrong thing. But he couldn't deny this place was fascinating, and Alice had gone to so much effort, so he gave her an encouraging slight smile. 'Food smells good.'

'Here.' She passed him a tin plate. 'Smoky *huevos rancheros*. I hope you're hungry.'

Two tortillas held a serving of beans, on a bed of assorted greens and red capsicum. A splash of smashed avocado topped a fried egg, garnished with freshly torn coriander. 'You made all of this out here, on that?' He nodded to the ute filled with assorted equipment.

She shrugged, going shy. Which was a rare thing.

Alice would get quiet and studious, playful and intelligent. Even after her embarrassing moment earlier when she started the car—which he would tease her about for the rest of his life—her smile never ceased to amaze him. Especially the way she looked at the scenery with that soft smile and a shimmer to her eyes. It showed how deeply she cared for this place.

A world that had never interested him before.

Alice dropped into the chair beside him. She rolled up her tortilla and began eating, very much at home in this place. She washed down her mouthful with a sip of her fragrant tea, as the steam curled in wisps from her sturdy travel mug. 'Did I do the right thing?'

He wiped his mouth on a paper towel after devouring his first tortilla. The coriander and kale combination with the smoky beans were heaven on his taste buds. 'The breakfast is amazing.' He'd never had a female cook him breakfast like this, in a place like this.

'Thank you. But I meant this …' She pointed to the massive billabong filled with assorted birds. They flew in waves like the way the housekeeper would shake out a set of sheets before making the bed.

'I don't know what I'm looking at. What is that log thing?' He pointed as the birds flew away from it. 'It's moving.'

She picked up the camera and expertly zoomed in. 'It's a crocodile. I call him the Awesome Jawsome.' She showed him the screen on the back of her digital camera giving him a crystal-clear movie image of a man-eating crocodile.

'How many are here?' He frowned at the black, angry-looking beast.

'Jawsome has two females, Splash and Dash. They're nesting over by those tall grasses the locals call croc grass. They'll have a clutch of about thirty eggs in each. Normally, I'd drive around that side, but not while they're nesting.'

'Are they protected?'

'They are. But this is more for our safety, as they're aggressively protective of their nests.'

'So, what do you do with those crocodiles and those babies?'

'Nothing. This area is protected. It's not open to the public, and one of the perks of this job.' She inhaled the crisp morning air, with her eyes on the scenery.

'So, what have you got planned for us today?'

'As part of my patrol, I want to check the water tanks, the emergency phone boxes, and the hiking trail to the falls. We'll also be participating in a biodiversity survey by doing a feral buffalo count near the waterhole. Don't worry, you won't need to wrestle any crocodiles today in the wetlands.'

'But you said it's a billabong?'

'It is. In the wet season this connects to the swamplands and flood plains to become part of the river system as one massive gateway for barramundi. It's the perfect breeding place for Awesome Jawsome's family.'

'Will Melody be okay out here?' He shouldn't be worried about something that didn't even belong to him. It was ridiculous.

'That's why I want her to get acclimated as quickly as possible. But I'll need your fine needlework skills to insert a teeny tiny GPS tracker.'

'Seriously?' The relief was enormous to know someone was watching over the floppy footed thing.

'Dad's university is providing the tech tools as part of a wallaby study he's running this semester. Having family connections helps with the job.'

'I bet.' Considering he was doing the same with his mother for his dream job.

'But you're okay with this?' Again, she pointed to the view.

The shift from night to day had been dramatic. The sun now shone its golden spotlight over the billabong's tranquil waters, which shimmered a rainbow of vibrant colours. The air was flavoured with a sweet, earthy fragrance that carried whispers of the outback's ancient stories. It was a place set apart from the modern world, where time seemed to stretch, allowing him to capture this single moment all in the space between two breaths.

He'd never seen such beauty in the simplicity of a sunrise. It truly was a powerful event. 'It's impressive.'

But her smile was even more glorious.

'Well, if you like this, wait and see what else is in store.'

Thirteen

Their shoulders swayed in sync as Alice steered the ranger's ute, with its beefy tyres rolling over large rocks, she tried to avoid the deep trenches in the cracked soil.

'Where is the road?' Stewart's voice was tight, with his wide eyes scouring the scrublands surrounding them.

'It got washed away by the floods.'

'Is this safe?' Stewart gripped the handle above the passenger door, with his other hand pressing on the roof. When the ute leaned precariously sideways, he was staring at the dirt. *'Alice!'*

She bit her inner cheek to suppress a giggle. 'It's fine. Not my first rodeo. This is just another day on the job, as part of my patrol as a ranger. Did you know this little park has a class 1A biodiversity rating, due to its extensive geological and geomorphic landscape? It's backed by a few international conservation societies giving parts of the park, like the bird billabong where we had breakfast, an IUCN category six rating to protect it while still allowing for Indigenous cultural purposes.'

'I don't know what that means?'

'It's like having top class compliances for hospitals, or a five-star review on a book. This little park has some pretty impressive street cred compared to other parks. It took me a while, but I've managed to get her recognised on a world-class standard ratings system.'

'And that's important because?' He nodded at the tall

grass that hemmed them in on both sides.

'To protect and conserve it. This park has some highly valued and unique habitat. It's filled with different varieties of animals, plants, fungi, and even microorganisms like bacteria that make this natural world a home to some endangered species, which includes the extensive wetlands and waterbirds.' Now she felt like a tour guide.

The ute straightened up with a solid thump, forcing Stewart to jump in his seat, grabbing the dashboard's handle for support. But nothing else inside the cab moved, all locked down like a boat at sea.

'Alice?' Again, the pitch of his voice was low and loaded with warning.

'Don't you like women driving?' She steered the ute, using the hefty bull bar to push over the long grass.

'Usually, I'm driving in places that have roads.'

'This is a road … of sorts.' They barrelled through the grasses and bounced onto a dirt track, barely big enough for the ute to squeeze through. She shifted easily through the gears as a plume of red dust rose behind them and the thick grasslands gave way to open plains. Finally, Stewart started relaxing in his seat, in between the times he checked his phone.

Around them were wide-open fields of low, soft cream grasses, where towering ghost gums punched through the red soil. The engine roared as the tyres churned through a thick pocket of red sand. 'This powdery sand they call bulldust. Horrible, isn't it.'

'What if you get bogged? Or sink? You can't call a tow truck out here.' He looked at his phone, again. He had a habit of checking it every few minutes. 'You can't call anyone out here. I have no bars.'

She wanted to toss his stupid phone out the window and off a cliff, to force him to enjoy the adventure of this glorious day.

'Relax, I've got winches, shovels, and stuff.' It'd be a test for the guy who gave out business cards with four phone numbers on them.

'You don't walk further than mobile phone range, do you?' Their nightly walks were getting longer, with Melody getting gamer, but Stewart was forever checking his phone.

'What do you mean by that?'

'When you walk around the hospital you'll only go as far as the mobile phone coverage.' Stewart also kept the hospital in sight, as if wearing some invisible chord chaining him to that place.

But his face fell with a mix of anguish, shifting into anger. 'I do that for the hospital, because I'm always on call.'

She backpedalled fast. 'I get it.' *I'm an idiot.* 'I don't drive in the city.'

'You what?'

'I can't handle the traffic. I suffer with road rage. After four-wheel driving on remote roads so much, I'd rather drive over the curb and steer down the sidewalk than get stuck in peak-hour traffic.'

He chuckled. 'So, who drives when you're in the city?'

'Mum. I've always been that way. Mum will slap a book in my hands to read until I can't keep my eyes open.'

'And miss the view?' He sniffed with annoyance, tossing his thumb at the low-lying scrublands that passed his side window. Admittedly, it wasn't the prettiest place in the park.

'It comes in handy waiting at airports. I'll watch the bags, reading, while Mum tries to rescue Dad from the bar before he accidentally upsets someone with his latest T-shirt.' She giggled, glad to get a smile out of him. The poor guy was well out of his depth and probably bored by now.

'You don't go to the bar with your father?'

'Sometimes.'

'Have you been to the pub here?'

'Only to check on Karma, the crocodile. You?'

'A few times …' He rubbed his jaw thoughtfully. 'The last time I went was for a patient's wake. Rowan Peddler. Did you know the guy?'

'Yeah, I knew Rowan through the Sandfly. Didn't mind the guy. I went to the funeral at the church.' Where the commercial fishermen scowled at her—she could feel their daggered stares in her back—and she'd seen Stewart standing with his mate Marcus in full police uniform.

'What's the Sandfly?'

She narrowed her eyes at Stewart, while taking them deeper into the national park. 'I don't know if I should tell you.'

'Why not?'

'Your friend is a cop.'

'Believe me, there are things I don't tell Marcus. I'm bound by patient confidentiality. Go on, share.'

'Sandfly is this little bar that sits on Goat Island. You can only get there by boat.'

'Sounds cool.'

'It is. Although not that much fun for me.' She frowned, driving alongside the dry creek bed. To the right was a towering wall of tall grasses, reminding her of North Queensland's sugarcane fields.

'Why?'

'I have to play the bad guy.' She pointed to the glistening creek that ran along their left side, where a few kingfishers were swooping down to gorge on the bugs. 'I'm responsible for the waterways and that means checking on the fishermen's hauls. There is a bag and size limit for certain fish and crabs. We don't want the waterways over-fished.'

'How often do you do that?'

She shrugged. 'I have a monthly quota to do random checks.'

'Is that why you don't get involved in this town?'

She arched an eyebrow at him. 'Excuse me?'

'Besides Melody and me, who else do you hang out with after hours?'

'I'm like you—I work. And I visit Iris.' *And I have a*

thousand book boyfriends to amuse me.

'You're like Marcus, as the town's top cop he has to play the bad guy, too. Being a doctor, like me, everyone loves the doctor.'

'Hey, I'm the good guy here. Looking after the bigger picture.' She tapped the embroidered ranger's patch on her shirt's sleeve. 'I watch over millions of birds, animals and insects and …'

She cut off as she noticed a large group of carrion birds circling above a group of trees. They were a death omen or a warning sign for bushfires.

Her eyes narrowed to the area of trees where their shadows ominously circled.

She slammed her foot on the brakes. '*Friggin' ferals!*' She unclipped her seatbelt, grabbed her machete from where it was strapped to the door panel, and climbed out of the ute, slamming the door behind her.

'What's wrong?'

'Mongrels.' She jumped a fallen log, using the machete to make the wallaby trail wider through the underbrush and into the clearing.

'What is it?' Stewart came up beside her.

The noise was horrific as birds screeched, desperate to flee, caught in odd angles, as they fought against the nylon strings of a large heavy bird net.

'Why is there a net here?' Stewart asked.

'Poachers.' Her heart squeezed at the ghastly scene. Their panicked cries for help were deafening. 'I hate this.'

'I'm sorry I ever complained about the birds at the back of our place.' Stewart had to shout over the noise, while rolling up the sleeves of his shirt. 'How can I help?'

'You?' *Hmph!*

'Hey, I am wearing the uniform. Let me help.'

'Thank you.' It meant the world to her. 'I'll cut this net here. If you can take that corner, I'll take the other one, and we'll peel the top layer back.'

'To open it up?'

'For those that can fly. Some may not. I've got gloves in the ute if we need them, and some cages should any need treatment. But I'm hoping this net hasn't been here long.'

With a sharp whack of her machete, she cut the rope on all four corners of the net, and with Stewart's help, they opened the net, setting the birds free.

'What are those black birds called?'

'The red-tailed black cockatoo.' The heaviness in her heart lightened as she watched them fly, thankfully leaving only a few feathers and birdseed behind.

'How much do those birds go for?'

She snapped a few photos of the scene with her phone's camera before rolling up the net, removing the ropes from the nearby trees. 'On the black market, the black cockatoos will sell for over thirty thousand dollars each.'

'No way.'

She pointed to the clear skies, where only a few raptors remained, gliding on the thermals, overshadowed by the expansive wings of a white-bellied sea eagle. 'Those birds can fetch up to two hundred thousand dollars each. Their eggs are a big prize for poachers, because they're easier to smuggle.'

'Are poachers a common problem in the national park?' He looked at her, bewildered. 'Are they here?'

'Probably.'

'How can you be so calm about this?'

'Do you panic when you see a patient bleeding on your operating table, Doctor?'

He frowned at her. 'It's not the same.'

'It's still life and death, Stewart.' She started dragging the net back to the ute. 'This is the part I hate the most about my job. Think of it like this, you've just saved all those birds. All of them.'

'You helped.'

She tapped his chest to make a point. 'With. *You.*'

'Hmm ...' He arched his neck at the birds high in the trees, fluffing up their feathers, to rub and nestle against each other for support. A serene calmness seemed to come over his stern stance.

She recognised that feeling. 'It's rewarding, isn't it?' It was also a humbling experience for a man who played God for a living.

'How can we stop it?'

Fourteen

Trudging through the dry weeds where grass seeds speared into the sides of his jeans, Stewart helped Alice carry the cumbersome bird net back to the ute, still remembering the harrowing cry of those trapped birds. Normally he never got involved, because normally he lived safely indoors, having nothing to do with animals or the great outdoors. Yet here he was. 'I mean it, Alice, I want to help. Period.'

'First, let's get you kitted out, then we'll work out a plan.' On the back tray of her ute, she opened a long metal toolbox and rummaged around inside.

It was like she'd shed her shyness to reveal her true nature, and he was in awe of her. He'd been getting glimpses of her true self for weeks now, and finally it was all on show. She was strong, smart, fearless, filled with wonder and curiosity about the world around her, but she was also protective. It was a potent combination for a woman who was forcing him to struggle with his attraction towards her, while making him see the world in a completely different way.

'These should fit you.' She held out a pair of workman's gloves.

'Gloves? Whose are they?'

'They're new. I bought them for you.'

'Why?'

'I'd hate for you to get splinters or hurt your hands.'

'I'm not useless.' It was bad enough Alice drove better than he ever could, she also had two chainsaws and a toolbox that you'd expect most men in the outback to have. His masculinity was seriously copping a bashing by the shorter, slender, stunning redhead.

'I didn't mean it like that.' Her hand on his arm, her dainty chin tilted towards him, and he was swimming in those pretty green eyes. 'I know how incredible a tool your hands are for surgery.'

'Oh.' Now he felt like a different kind of tool for saying such a thing.

'You can slip these on, too.' She held up what looked like two small khaki skirts.

'What are those?'

'Gators. For over your boots. It'll stop those grass seeds filling your socks.'

'What else is in that magic toolbox?'

'May as well wear the neck gator to prevent your neck from getting sunburnt, they also double up as a good mask in dust storms. Oh, talking about being sun-smart, be sure to put this sunscreen on, roll down your sleeves, and here are some safety glasses too.' She dropped them into his front pocket. 'You can leave your fancy sunnies and your mobile phone in the ute. I'd hate for them to get lost or scratched out here. They'll be safe in the glove box.' Opening the passenger door, she opened the compartment.

It was like putting on surgical scrubs, just of a different kind, with the khaki shirt, hat, gloves. He hesitated before putting his phone away, but once he did Alice slammed the compartment shut and his phone was gone. He swallowed hard. 'So, what's the plan?'

Her eyes shone with a whole new level of seriousness. She was a highly intelligent female with a passion for her job, and he always had a healthy respect for smart women.

'We need to scout this whole area for more traps.' Sliding her sturdy pocketknife into her belt, she passed him the machete and a couple of heavy-duty sacks. From the underside of the roof of her ute's back tray, Alice removed a garden rake and a shovel that had been well concealed.

'What's the rake for?'

'For the birdseed. Sometimes poachers lace their bait with a drug to knock the birds out. Their traps are designed to trip when they reach a certain weight. We'll need to remove the junk, with you taking plenty of photos before we pull them apart.'

'What are the photos for?'

'The case files.' She passed him the digital camera, that he added to the pile of tools she was gathering. 'It's now a criminal case.'

'I thought you guys were only about animals.'

'And the land. Where it's hard to stop poaching on a land that is open to the public.'

'That's why you have the CCTV set up at home.'

'How's your skill at using a drill?'

'Surgical drills, sure.'

'Good. You'll have no problems managing this industrial drill then.' She pulled the trigger and the drill whirled. 'I want to set up a camera to monitor this region.'

'Good idea.' He was lumbered with the heavy tool as she headed for the other side of the ute. His head tilted as he noticed how cute her butt looked in those khakis.

From behind the driver's seat, Alice pulled out a large case, a black bag, and a map. She then dropped the ute's rear tray to create a table, where she unwrapped the black bag to reveal a camera attached to a black solar panel and an aerial. 'I'm thinking of putting this camera up in that tree.' She pointed to the massive ghost gum. 'I'll park the ute next to the trunk and use the roof for higher leverage. The higher we get it, the more area it'll cover, and the less chance the poachers will notice it.'

'I didn't know you were such a security specialist. You're a real gadget and gizmo girl, aren't you?'

'I like tech tools that make it easier for me to do my job. And if you're nice, I might let you play with this gadget.' Her grin was the same one she had this morning when she gave him his t-shirt, full of mischief as she hoisted the heavy case onto the flat tray and opened the clips. 'Have you ever flown a drone?'

'I stand corrected—you're a gadgets queen.'

'Don't see me wearing no crown.'

'I was thinking you were Captain Kale with your totem-pole garden of rabbit food, but now you're a digital diva.' At least he had her laughing. 'Hey, aren't drones illegal in the national park?' He'd seen the sign at the park's main entrance.

'See this ...' She tapped on her ranger's patch with that beautiful smile a marvel. 'That's our licence to play.'

In a matter of moments, she'd assembled the drone, activating its camera. With a buzz of its engines, the blades stirred up the red dirt, then it was in the air.

'Here, you play with it.' She handed him the controls. 'I want to check on Melody.' She rummaged around in the ute to get the wallaby comfortable in her baby pouch. She then dug around in the esky, returning with two bottles of cold water. 'Got the hang of it yet?'

'I do. This is great.' His thumbs shifted the joysticks on the bulky controller. Its large video screen displayed the world, as the drone buzzed like a loud bee in the air. 'They're like the surgical robot tools I've used. This is seriously cool.'

'I agree. Can you increase your altitude to follow these tracks.' She showed him the areas on her rolled out map.

'What are we looking for?'

'We need to find where those poachers got in.'

'To arrest them? Can you do that, being a ranger?'

'Rangers have 'Special Constable' powers for certain sections of the criminal, animal welfare and environmental acts.'

'Like a cop?'

'I don't carry handcuffs, or pepper spray. But should someone turn this park into a racetrack while setting it on fire, you bet I'd prosecute. But prosecuting poachers is almost impossible, you have to catch them with the evidence. Mostly it's Customs or Border Patrol who do the arresting. I just alert them to what's going on.' She stood beside him, with her map spread out before them. 'This area is for rangers only, it's restricted. There are only a few ways to get in here. How they knew about it?' She shrugged.

'Does that mean it's a local?'

Again, she shrugged. 'Not that many locals come up here. I've only shown this area to a few scientists for research purposes, but that was a while ago.'

'What about other rangers?'

'Only my boss and the old ranger know about it. Walt was a nice guy. He'd worked this park for forty years, it was his home.'

'And your boss?'

'The honourable horrible Harold Grimsby. He's more interested in cutting costs, controlling budgets, sending me away to work in other parks. Believe me, I do my best to avoid Harold.' She angled her head as she tapped at the screen. 'Can you follow that track there?'

Stewart adjusted the controls, and the drone effortlessly pitched and rolled with ease. The photographic quality was incredible. 'We had this robot for surgery in the hospital I used to work at, it's the same principle, using the small screen to be our eyes, the joystick as our hands, and the endoscopes—small cameras—to get into tight places. This is a more fun version.'

'Can I ask you something?'

'Sure.'

'Exactly, what did you do to end up out here? You said it was bad bedside manner? I know I've teased you about your bedside manner, but I've seen how you are with Iris and the other patients, you genuinely care for them.' The empathy in her eyes was breathtaking.

'Um …' It was an effort to tear his eyes away, to focus on

the controls with the drone giving him an aerial view of the wilderness.

But it took little to remember the incident that ruined his world. He could give her a list of excuses, but it had been his responsibility. His penance. 'At my old hospital, they presented me with a middle-aged patient complaining of chest pain, looking at a heart bypass because of his unhealthy lifestyle.'

'Which was?'

He spoke while focusing on the small screen as the flickering heat of shame crept up his chest.

'Keep going, you're doing a great job.' She pointed to the video screen. 'Follow that trail.'

The shame disappeared as quickly as it started, giving him the confidence to tell all. 'The patient was a heavy smoker, a regular drinker, who ate fatty foods, and carried a lot of stress. It caught up to him.'

'Did you give him a lecture to clean up his lifestyle?'

'I dished out some tough love. Most of my patients accept it, but not this guy ...' He took a deep breath. 'He was a prominent businessman who'd surrounded himself with a bunch of yes men.'

'You offended him?'

'So much so, he took it all the way to the hospital board, who happened to be his golfing buddies.'

'Rude much.'

'Who? Me or him.'

'Your hospital board. Aren't they there to employ talented doctors to help their patients?'

He didn't want to say it, preferring to let her work it out.

He flew the drone over a rocky ledge that dropped to follow a waterfall. It was an exhilarating free-fall moment as the projected image of the drone tumbled over the edge of the cliff plummeting along with the water in a sheer drop, to expose the ring of water at the bottom of the pool, spreading out like rings on a tree. 'That's cool.'

She peered up at the sky, taking a step back from him. 'If you had access to tech and robots, and this guy was a middle-aged what's-it, you must have been working in a pretty upmarket hospital?'

'The kind that didn't take patients unless they had a certain level of medical insurance.'

'Wow.' Her forehead crinkled as she looked at him, like really looked at him, past his thick skin, through to places he didn't think anyone could see.

'Are you judging me?'

She didn't answer for a long time. 'I'm guessing this hospital was one of the best for hearts and it's to do with your dream to become the best cardiothoracic surgeon in the country?'

'Correct.' Yet he felt foolish telling her that.

'Those kinds of places would need funding from some bigwigs like your grumpy patient.'

Again, he nodded.

Scooping up her water bottle, she took a deep mouthful as if to wash away a foul taste. 'Isn't the medical profession screaming out for skilled surgeons? Then they do this to you, when you were only trying to help the patient. Would you go back to that hospital?'

'I've applied to be a part of their cardio-specialist surgical team, it's my dream job.' Even if that hospital was a cavernous den of dirty in-house politics, it gave him the opportunity to achieve his dream. 'I've told no one in town I've applied for the job.'

'Everyone knows you're leaving, even though they're trying to convince you to stay.'

'I can't stay. I'm still under contract to my old hospital in Melbourne.'

'How?'

'I'm part of some government deal to cope with the doctor shortage in remote regions. It's like how rich lawyers have to take on so many pro-bono cases a year. I got sent to Woop

Woop.'

'There has to be more than that stopping you from cancelling the contract.'

'My old hospital paid a huge chunk of my medical studies. I'll have to pay it back with penalty interest if I breach their ironclad contract that my mother's lawyers couldn't get me out of.' He wished he could burn the damn thing, hesitant about signing another contract again.

'Uni fees suck, I get it. How long before you're free?'

'According to my contract, I'll have two weeks left when I go back, then it's up for negotiations.' But who'd want to employ him after being kicked out to the land of red dust and sandflies.

'And with you applying for that heart specialist's surgical team …' She narrowed her eyes at him.

'They'll see I'm keen for the job.' He felt like he'd gone and disappointed her and went back to the screen, steering the drone over a large clearing. 'What is that?'

'Brumbies.' Her soft smile grew as she sidled up closer. Again, her aroma was like his personal brand of pheromones weaving around him. He inhaled deeply. 'Aren't they beautiful?'

Alice was beautiful, too.

But he didn't say it, focusing on the small screen showing a herd of about a dozen horses grazing in the grassy field. 'Are brumbies allowed in the park?'

'Shh, don't tell anyone.' Her smile matched her eyes. 'That's our little secret.'

Little? It was a herd. 'But they're wild animals? Introduced?'

'We call them ferals. It's a term that pretty much covers all of the introduced species, from cane toads to wild cats to hard-hoofed animals that causes damage to our delicate wetlands.'

'Hard-hoofed?'

'Water buffalo, brumbies, wild pigs, plus the millions of

cattle that roam this region.'

'Aren't you all about saving animals.'

'I try. According to the local Aboriginal elders, those brumbies have been here since the first explorers. They were here before the pigs, buffalo, and the first herd of imported beef moved into the neighbourhood in the early nineteenth century.'

'You're like this walking, talking reference guide for outback animals. Are you sure you aren't a tour guide?'

Again, she tapped the ranger's patch on her sleeve. He had to laugh.

Then her eyes caught something on the video screen. 'Go back.'

He steered the drone around.

'There. That's where they're getting in.' She pulled her map closer.

He zoomed in over the crushed grass, weaving around an area filled with large boulders. 'What do you want to do?'

'First, we'll clear this mess up, and scout for more,' she said, pointing to the area where they'd found the bird net. 'Then we'll set up that camera facing this area, to get an idea of their vehicle.'

'Only one camera?'

'You've seen how many cameras are in the park on your TV set during your lunch break.'

He chuckled. 'Beats watching some daytime soapie.'

That's when it hit him. It wasn't some story on the television screen. This was real. A pulsing, breathing, living world full of life that surrounded him.

It made him take in the details, the layers in the colours in a world brimming with life. He never truly understood her passion, and her protectiveness of this place until now.

He might not have his dream job yet, but this was Alice's, making him more determined to help her. 'So how are you planning to use your cameras, then?'

'By controlling the narrative of their story.'

Fifteen

Stewart raked up birdseed, hauled trash, slung ropes, helping Alice destroy the poachers' traps. The level of personal satisfaction he'd felt setting those animals free had been incredible. Maybe even better than watching a happy, healthy patient leave the hospital.

When they'd cleaned up the traps they got back into the ute and Alice drove to the tarmac road where the poachers were turning off to get into the restricted area.

'What's the plan?'

Alice rolled out her map across the dashboard. 'I have cameras set up on either end of this road, plus at these points, and back at the area where they set up their traps. This is my only blind spot.'

'Do you have any more cameras?'

'I wish. I strategically set these cameras to cover the main areas to help pinpoint the poachers. The plan here is to block off their access, so they'll only use the one road in. That way they'll pass the signs that clearly state they're entering a restricted area and can be charged under Federal national park laws.'

'But it's a local park, isn't it?'

'The international conservation class ratings allows for this area to come under Federal laws. One of the things they sent out as part of a congratulations pack were those restricted signs.'

'You're setting the poachers up?'

'Building a case. It's hard to prosecute poachers. I have

cameras set to capture any vehicle passing those signs when they enter those restricted areas.'

'Why have restricted areas, when parks are meant to be a public space for people to use?'

'Mostly rejuvenation and habitat protection for endangered species, like the water birds' breeding grounds I showed you, at the billabong this morning. There are also a few Aboriginal sacred sites in this park too, where even you aren't allowed to go.'

'Why not? I'm a nice guy. Everyone loves the doctor.'

She shook her head, her laugh so sweet it matched her smile. 'Nothing to do with your profession, it's your gender. It's women only for secret women's business.' Her eyes narrowed on the dirt track the poachers had created, then she rummaged through the back of her ute and pulled out a thick wide rope.

'What are you planning to do? If you put a log across this road, they'll know you found their stash and they might run. It's what I'd do if I got busted.'

'Me too. That's why I want us to make it look like a natural diversion.'

'How?'

'By creating a small avalanche.'

'Won't that restrict your access?'

'They made this track, not me. It needs to be blocked, otherwise I'll have four-wheel drive enthusiasts crashing this area too.' Her scowl was ferocious and her eyes full of fire—it was sexy!

'Hey …' He raised his dirty palms. 'I love that you're passionate about this, but I'm here to help.'

'Sorry, not aimed at you.'

He squeezed her arm. 'I get it.'

'Good. You'll drive.'

'What?'

'I need you to drag that big boulder. I'll tell you how …' She used the heavy snatching strap to wrap over a boulder.

She then tapped her pocketknife on the other rocks and crevices to scare off any critters camping between the rocks.

Stewart gingerly climbed into the driver's seat as Melody poked her head out of her baby carrier. 'Yeah, I'm driving the beast.' The ute wasn't anything flash, it was a workhorse the way it climbed over rocks, riverbeds, churning through red sands and mud plains. Now this. But Alice had just handed over her tools, treating him like an equal as they worked together. He'd never been this dirty in his life, and for once the dirt and sweat didn't bother him. Not even on his hands.

Alice jogged up to him. Now he understood her trim figure. Her job was hard yakka.

Using her shirt sleeve to wipe the dirt and sweat from her face, she leaned in to change the gear. 'You'll drive in low gear.'

'How slow are we talking?'

'Snail-pace slow. I want you to pull, slowly.'

'Aren't we disturbing the natural habitat?'

'Those boulders fell from the sandstone cliffs. This prehistoric landscape is always changing.'

'I have to admit this part of the park reminds me of planet Mars.' A patch of barren red soil and boulders.

'We get mild tremors out here when the tectonic plates shift. A wedged rock cracks under the pressure, or pebbles sink into the soil from the wet season rains. They move. But today, I only want a few to roll over the poachers' tracks.' She tapped on the outside of his driver's door. 'Get ready …' Her arm was in the air as if starting a car race. 'Go …'

He released the clutch, balancing the accelerator. 'It's not working.'

'Give it a little more gas.'

The engine roared through the cab, giving off some serious grunt, making little Melody hide back inside her pouch.

The wide rope tightened, creaking with tension.

'Slowly … It's coming …' Alice walked backwards,

alongside him as he steered. 'It's coming.'

He felt it pull. Then the rope twanged.

'Stop.'

It felt like it broke. He leaned out the driver's window watching the heavy boulders tumble as if a giant was playing marbles, spilling right across the track. They completely blocked the area, creating a makeshift stone wall.

'Well done, Stewart. Well done. Just park it on the road, please.'

Didn't that boost his ego to no end. He parked the ute, while Alice deftly rolled up the rope and tossed it into the back.

'Grab a leafy branch.' She lifted a large fallen branch from the base of a gum tree.

'What for?'

'To hide our tracks. You can use your neck gator for this.' She covered her mouth and nose with her neck gator. With her hat shading her eyes she looked like a bush bandit. With her big leafy branch in hand she swept at the tyre tracks in the sand, stirring up the dust, removing all traces that they'd ever been there.

Doing the same he worked alongside her. 'You don't do housework, but you'll sweep a paddock?'

Her tinkling laugh made him smile behind his mask.

Leaning back against the side of the ute, guzzling down the water, they admired their handiwork. Covered in dirt, he couldn't stop smiling, nudging his mischievous team leader's side. 'You clever cookie, you've really set them up.'

'That's called controlling the narrative.'

'So said the bookworm.' He'd never been an adventurous guy who got dirty, but he'd been enjoying himself helping Alice. It wasn't the job, the scenery, it was the company. 'So, where to now? I could do with a shower or something.'

'I've got just the thing.'

Sixteen

'Now this is the life.' With a beer in one hand, Stewart sat chest deep in the rock pool of warm mineralised water and smiled.

All day Alice had watched his smile deepen, his shoulders loosen, and his stance straighten. He was no longer hunched over, with that deep-in-thought expression, carrying the burdens of the hospital's patients.

Stewart walked just like his father.

'I'm really feeling like a caveman.'

'You're what?' She laughed, soaking in the warm water, the steam invigorating for her pores, clearing her sinuses. She sipped her cold beer, its citrus and hoppy malt flavours the perfect remedy for washing down the dust from their day.

'After playing with boulders, now this. I approve of this rock pond—'

'Hot springs.' She leaned her back against the rocks, her feet floating as hot water bubbled from the ground. 'It's better than any fancy day spa, right?'

'I agree. And the view's amazing.' Stewart nodded at the scenery that effortlessly spread below them, giving them an expansive view of grassy plains and gentle sloping ranges that blended with the curve of the horizon, making it the best place to watch the sunset.

'Are we camping here?'

She nodded. 'I'm not moving until morning.' She didn't need to take Stewart back to town now that he was getting with the program. She really liked this side of him, not the stressed guy striding through the hospital corridors.

'How many tents do you have?'

'I use the roof top tent. You'll have the other tent.'

'I'll probably fall asleep from exhaustion after today.'

'The open air and sunshine will do it to you, especially if you're not used to it.' His skin was tanned as if he'd been on some summer holiday. 'But you'll be making dinner.' She pointed at the fire pit, ready to go.

'I can't cook.'

'It'll be easy, I'll help. The matches are sitting on the table, waiting for you.'

'I can take a hint.' He dragged himself free from the water, his body glistening and far more defined in muscle than she'd ever imagined. He was wearing just a pair of shorts, and she didn't know where to look—but she just couldn't look away.

He used a towel to dry his blond hair, which flopped everywhere, giving him a boyish look.

This was a bad idea.

'We'd better fix up Melody before you play with fire. The wallabies will start showing up at sunset.'

'I see.' His smile gone and the mask slipped back on. It was his doctor's face, and he was back on the job. 'So how do we do this?'

It was Alice's turn to drag herself out of the hot water. Wrapping a towel around herself, she rummaged under the passenger seat of the ute to remove a small package. 'Once you put this tracker in, we'll let Melody do her thing.' She held up the capped syringe. 'It's new technology they've used on koalas, even on bison in the states. Dad is excited to trial it under our hostile outback conditions. He's put one in Mum's dog so they never lose him, and Mum's dog is smaller than Melody.'

'Where does it go?'

'In the back of her neck. I've got these wipe thingies for sterilising and numbing the area. But I hate doing it.'

'I'll do it.' He took the syringe from her hand, his fingers warm and clean from soaking in the hot springs. 'You get the patient.'

Alice didn't want to.

'Alice?'

'I've broken a rule.'

'What's that?' His patience in waiting for her response was unnerving. She had to answer.

'I got attached.' To both the wallaby and the doctor. Even though she always knew she'd be letting them go, it strangely felt like a family, when it shouldn't.

Melody was a wild animal being returned to her home, where she'd be happy.

Even though Stewart was only her temporary housemate, they were fast becoming friends. Where each day her feelings for him grew, when she'd been trying so hard to stop them, she just couldn't help it.

Slipping into her workboots, she trudged towards Melody and scooped her up. 'I've got your favourite greens, baby girl.'

'I doubt she'll understand my warning that this may sting.' Stewart cleaned the back of Melody's neck area, then applied the numbing gel. 'We should have done this back home.'

'I've been …'

'Putting it off.'

She nodded.

He gently cupped her cheek in such a tender moment she struggled to speak.

'I get it. Your level of care for creatures great and small is a genuine wonder, Alice.' He gently kissed her temple, to whisper in her ear, 'Hold Melody tight.'

She winced as if he was injecting her and not the joey.

'There, all done. Here's the rabbit food Alice was daring to bribe you with.' He held up a posy of spinach and kale to the wallaby. 'Most mothers have lollipops for their kids, my father keeps a stash in his office.'

She put the wallaby down where it moved around as if nothing had happened.

Stewart struck the match and lit the fire pit. 'It's been a while since I've lit a fire. My mother used to have a fireplace, I was always begging Benjamin to let me light it.'

'Is Benjamin your brother?'

His smile fell, as did the shine in his eyes.

'Sorry, not my business.' She started to move, but he grabbed her arm, stopping her.

'Benjamin is my stepfather.'

'Is he a doctor, too?'

'Yes. Head of surgery at …' He paused, taking a deep mouthful of his beer while staring at the flickering flames. 'The hospital I'm going back to.'

'The heart specialist's team?'

He nodded. 'Go on, you can say it … Getting the job because of my stepfather.' He didn't seem impressed about it.

'But you're qualified, aren't you?'

'Absolutely. It's my dream job. But …' He sniffed at the scenery. 'While I've been stuck out here, the other applicants have been practising various forms of cardiothoracic surgery daily. Me?'

'You do surgery, right?'

'More than I care to. From repairing broken bones, nerve damage, and stitches.' He arched an eyebrow at her, his eyes falling to her row of stitches, now a faint red line on her side. 'No scarring. I'm a god.' His voice echoed as he raised his beer to the open valley.

'Smart-arse.' It was impossible to stop smiling when he was like this.

As the night air cooled, she dragged their chairs closer to the fire he was tending. With the hot springs on their right, the ute behind them, the sunset started its evening show. As the logs crackled and sparked in the fire pit, the smoke curled like a whispering white snake vaporising into the sky, it was the perfect place to share stories around the campfire.

'Did you decide to become a doctor because of your stepfather? Or your father, Thomas?'

'Both and neither.'

She looked at him, confused, as he dropped back into his seat and took a deep pull of his beer. When he didn't say anything else she changed the subject.

'I always wanted to do this. Be a ranger.'

'You said you had a lifelong apprenticeship.'

She smiled at the open scenery free from people, politics, and peer pressure. 'Best childhood ever. Admittedly, these days it gets lonely not sharing it with anyone, but I love it.' She was grateful to Stewart for coming out here and that she'd found the courage to share it with him.

He winked at her. And somehow it put her lungs into knots, sending goosebumps—the size of freaking goose mountains—to break out across her skin. How could one wink do all that?

She slipped on a dry shirt, wrapping it around herself, then kicked up an unlaced boot and crossed it over her other knee. In a towel, a khaki shirt, and boots, she was definitely dressed to impress a guy who had her tucked so deep into the friend zone, they may as well name it another layer deep in the earth's crust.

Again, why was she bothering? Stewart didn't have some invisible power over her, pulling her strings like some lovesick puppet. She knew this, she was a smart girl. They could be friends. And just friends. Right? 'Did you always want to be a surgeon?'

He sighed, slumping deeper into his chair, to stare at the fire pit. 'No. Not really. Not that I can remember if I wanted to be anything else, because once I'd decided surgery was for me, that was it.'

'What helped you make that decision?'

'I was ten when I chose to become a heart specialist.' He spoke so slowly, quietly, the words laced with sadness. 'It was when my brother died.'

'I'm so sorry.' She reached out and patted his forearm. He looked at it like it was a foreign object, making her pull away.

But then he caught her hand. His long fingers turned it over to trace the lines on her palm, sending sparks of warm electricity through her bloodstream, to prickle over her scalp in a wave of pure pleasure. Heaven help her if she was reacting to him like this over a simple wink and the touch of his hand, she'd positively die if he kissed her.

'I've told no one this. Not that it's a secret ...' Sandwiching her hand between his, he squeezed it, then let it go. He leaned forward, his elbows resting on his knees, scrubbing hands over his face. 'My brother died from complications related to tetralogy of Fallot, ToF.'

'What's that?'

'It's a birth defect that interferes with the blood flow through the heart.'

'How old was your brother when he ...'

'Ethan and I had just shared our tenth birthday.'

'You're a twin?'

'Was.'

'Oh, my word ...' She practically melted onto the ground, to crouch in front of him, low enough to meet his eyes and see the pain. Now grasping his hands, she didn't care if she was breaching boundaries, she had to console him. 'Twin grief must be so much deeper than grief, like losing a soulmate. It must have been devastating at that age.' No wonder Stewart didn't do birthdays.

His frown deepened but his eyes were cold and empty, laced with pain. 'We shared everything. We shared a room together, went to school, did sports, swapped clothes, toys, and did everything together. Then, suddenly, he was gone. I felt cut off.'

He put some distance between them, to start pacing on the other side of their campfire, running fingers through his damp hair. His voice wasn't just quiet. It was vulnerable.

Exposed. And full of heartache. 'The thing was, Ethan's death was preventable.'

'How so?'

'Ethan's heart condition was never detected, but the signs were there. Believe me, I know the symptoms now, but back then, my father knew them too.'

'What happened?'

'We were playing soccer. It was our weekly Saturday game, and my mother was there watching, with a spare chair next to her that was always empty.'

She tilted her head with confusion. 'For?'

'My mother always took a spare chair, hoping our father would show up at our games. But he never did. Thomas preferred business lunches, golf games, or time at the hospital dealing with his other patients as chief of surgery. If my father had bothered to show up, like he'd promised, he would have been there to save Ethan.' His hands curled into fists, his eyes dark, with brows knitted he glared at the valley.

'If my father had bothered to talk to Ethan or listened to my mother's concerns. Or me …' He tapped his chest. 'I told Dad that Ethan was short of breath. I told him that Ethan's lips would go blue. But Dad ignored me, even telling me I was imaging it. But I knew …'

His head dropped, his voice even lower. 'All Doctor Thomas Mannen needed to do was listen to Ethan's chest for the murmur. To conduct a five-minute scan to see what was wrong. He did it for strangers all the time, but he never did it for his son.'

'Do you really believe that?'

'If he'd bothered to play doctor for his own son, my brother, Ethan would have never gone into cardiac arrest in the middle of the muddy soccer field, where he died, lying under that miserable autumn rain.' Stewart raised his head, his red-rimmed eyes potently blending pain with anger. 'That is why I went into cardiology. It's why I didn't see my father for twenty-two years.'

Alice hated seeing anyone or anything hurting and took quick strides to hold him. She didn't care if he pushed her away, not when he looked like he needed a hug. She wrapped her arms around him, his head resting on her shoulder, his arms wrapped around her waist, and he held her. She wanted him to know that he wasn't alone anymore.

Seventeen

'Will Melody be okay?' Stewart lay beside Alice on a thick picnic blanket. With the handheld GPS controller on night mode, the small red dot represented the joey grazing in the small valley about twenty metres ahead of them. Crickets chirped, stars shone above them, and with the delicate wildflower fragrance and crushed grasses surrounding them it would almost be romantic, if she wasn't so worried about Melody.

'We have to remember this is her world. We're the guests.'

'But she's a baby. And that's a big world out there.'

'I agree. It's why I plan to watch her from my rooftop tent tonight. I'm hoping she'll make friends enough to leave with the mob at sunrise. She'll be safe here. We're deep in the park, well away from any roads, stock routes or crocodiles.' Yet it still worried her, with that tightening pull of sadness within her heart getting stronger.

She peered through the grasses that gave them a grand view of the valley floor. Their camp was on the rise behind them, with a glorious sky filled with an endless galaxy of stars above them.

'Watch. Watch.'

'What?'

'Shh … She's there. The wallaby that lost her baby. The one I'm hoping will be Melody's new stepmother.' She slapped her hand over her mouth to stop speaking, to stop herself from calling out some motherly thing about talking to strangers. This was harder than she'd expected.

With enough moonlight to watch Melody, they saw the joey turn in the ute's direction, then back to the larger wallaby slowly approaching her.

As fear and excitement bristled over her scalp, Alice grabbed Stewart's hand and held it tight. This was it, the make-or-break moment.

The mother wallaby leaned down, nose twitching, as Melody lifted her nose higher. A lot of sniffing went on, a nudge, a shuffle of positions like a dance in the grass, then the larger wallaby nibbled at the grass close to Melody.

'What is she doing?' Stewart whispered, 'I'm not expecting them to hug it out or anything, but …'

'It's like having a coffee date. Those first introductions when you have a meal, it's the same deal. They're eating, getting used to each other's company while being completely aware of each other.' Like she was fully aware of holding Stewart's hand, while they lay on their stomachs on the blanket in the middle of the open field. She should be letting go of him, now Melody was making friends. Shouldn't she?

'I get it. I never had much luck on first dates, especially out here where all they talk about is farming and cattle musters. I had a rating system with Marcus on how long a date lasted before she started talking cattle. I gave up.'

'I gave up dating, too.' She pulled her hand free. 'But you? Come on, you must've gone on lots of dates?'

'Mostly blind dates.'

'At the pub?'

'Train station, coffee shop, pub, hospital cafeteria.'

'Oh, how romantic!' She smirked.

'Not like you reading romance as your fix.' He arched an eyebrow at her. 'Is that why you read so much romance, because you've given up on dating?'

'Most guys feel their masculinity is threatened because of what I do in my job. And in my job, I'm the bad guy.'

'I'd believe it.'

'Really?' She screwed up her nose, rolling over to lie back on the blanket, and stare at the stars. 'Well, I'm sorry. It's what I do and who I am.'

He lay on his side, his elbow bent, resting his head on his hand. 'You've got to admit, your independence is both impressive and fearsome. You're like this land warrior.'

'Hmph. I don't think so.'

'You're very protective of this place and its inhabitants.'

She shrugged. 'It's worth protecting.'

'I can see that. But you shouldn't give up on dating.'

'Yeah, why's that?'

He was so close she could follow the curve of his thick eyelashes, with the heavy air bristling with electricity between them.

'Even though you're a thousand times more intelligent than most of the men in this town—which would put a lot of them off—you're far too precious to be alone.' Unexpectedly, his lips brushed against hers. 'But I like smart women,' he said with his voice low and tender.

He. Kissed. Her.

Stewart, the Hot Doc, kissed her.

Lips to lips.

With lips as soft as his hands. He kissed her.

Alice's mind tripped over as if sliding into the daydream she'd enjoyed many times before. Now it was her reality. Why should she resist when she could sink into the slow slide of his mouth against hers that was so tender, yet completely conquering. It was better than she'd ever imagined.

She kitten-purred as their kiss deepened, her hand sliding over his shoulders as his tongue swept forward in dominating delicious swipes, to tango in tender play. It ignited all her pleasure nerves to pulse inside, lighting her up as if she was being kissed for the very first time.

No one had ever kissed her like this.

She wanted more. Needed more. Right then and there.

His chest pressed against hers until there wasn't a whispered breath of room between their bodies. Her fingers brushed through his hair, with their lips perfectly flush and aligned, kissing her brain quiet to forget the cordial conventions of friendship, with a desire to be wild and mindlessly free.

He tugged off the band holding her braid to release her hair. As his fingers smoothed the strands, a deep, rumbling sound reverberated from the back of his throat. It had to be the sexiest thing she'd ever heard in her life.

His fingers slid into her hair to playfully tug at her head, breaking their lip lock, leaving her to gasp for air to the sound of her hammering heart.

He pulled back, as his heart thumped against her hand where she'd scrunched up his T-shirt. His warm breath brushed her cheek as he softly stroked her temple. Hovering above her, he was beautifully framed by the celestial galaxy of twinkling lights above him, and, for a moment, he truly looked like the prince among the stars.

There, his gaze held hers, locking it so she couldn't look away.

'You know I'm leaving.' His voice low and rough, and the way he looked at her was full of lust and desire. No one had ever looked at her like this.

She couldn't speak, just nod.

'And we're friends?'

That was no friendly kiss, buddy! She fought with her frown, to again nod.

'I don't want to mess up a good thing ...' He swallowed, his pink tongue brushing over the lips she wanted to kiss and have kiss her.

She couldn't take it. Grabbing his T-shirt, she pulled him closer. 'Just shut up with your diagnosis, Doctor, and enjoy the moment.'

With a flash of a smile, their mouths met in a rush of air and a groan of delight. And when the heat turned up, there was nothing perfect or tender about their grasping, grabbing, fumbling fingers. Not when his mouth claimed hers, while weaving a newfound magic with his tongue.

May the stars above help her, she wanted this. This was her dream come true.

Even though he was leaving—tonight they had time to make enough memories to last a lifetime.

Eighteen

'Are you in any rush to get back?' Alice steered the chunky ute, raising a tornado-like storm of red dust behind them. Music played in the background as the endless scenery constantly changed past his window, but their conversation flowed without any awkwardness to it.

Stewart sat higher in the passenger seat, checking out the clock on the dashboard. It was just after one in the afternoon. 'No. I'm not in any rush to return.'

Alice arched an eyebrow in surprise.

'I can't believe I said that either.' Stewart chuckled. Normally he was all about the hospital, never venturing off the asphalt. Now, here he was in a place where he hadn't seen a bitumen road or another soul—except Alice—in two days. The beautiful, resourceful, and amazing Alice.

'I'm glad to hear it.'

His knuckles tenderly brushed her soft cheek. 'Thank you for this. It's the most relaxed I've been in a long time.' What a morning they'd had, enjoying breakfast at the hot springs watching the sunrise. Then out exploring the park as if on his own private safari.

For morning tea, they discovered a herd of water buffaloes that he helped Alice count for her data reports while sitting on the roof of her ute, with coffee in one hand and binoculars in the other.

Then a short trek down the road, they headed deep into a red stone gully filled with caves and rock art. Alice made him carry a garbage bag to collect any rubbish and clear out any obstacles along the path as they hiked to a secluded waterfall where they swam before an early lunch.

It had been an adventurous outback holiday crammed into two extraordinary days. He'd never experienced anything like it. Or anyone like Alice.

'Good. You deserve it.'

His fingers twirled with the fine strands of hair that had worked free from her braid, where her hair was like silk.

And this—being together—it just worked.

He couldn't explain it. All that awkwardness was gone, replaced by something comforting. Whatever this was between them, it was the easiest thing in the world.

She was also a friend who was damned sexy underneath all that khaki. Getting a taste of that passion under the stars, in their personal hot tub, then the roof top tent, and at the waterfall—he was becoming addicted to the great outdoors.

'Can we sneak in another camping trip before I fly out? To check on Melody?' He held up the GPS tracker, where the little red dot represented the larger-than-life wallaby, now with her new family.

Just like that, Melody hadn't even looked back, climbing into the pouch of her new stepmother wallaby and was gone.

No hug. No goodbye. Nothing.

At least he'd been there to share the tender moment with Alice, holding onto each other, as they watched the big mob of wallabies, along with their little joey, disappear deep into the scrublands. He imagined it was how a parent felt watching their child attend their first day of school. But Melody had left to become part of a big family that easily accepted their latest addition.

'Maybe I'll take you on the boats and go fishing. I've always got space when they run fishing competitions, and maybe the locals won't scowl at me so much if you were on board.'

'Do you fish? Or check their catches?'

'Both. Mainly I do regular runs on the waterways searching for illegal nets. I'll take you up to the flood plains and show you the freshwater whiprays. They're the *only* freshwater stingrays in Australia, so unique to the Northern Territory that little is known about them. They're so majestic the way they fly underwater, and they're friendly too. You'll love them.'

'Done.' How could anyone see Alice as the bad guy? It was ridiculous.

Alice took a left down an overgrown dirt track, driving alongside a rambling, broken fence.

'Are we still in the park?'

'On its edge, this is the park's firebreak, and that's the neighbours.' She pulled up in a small clearing. They got out of the ute and he followed her along a winding path that ran up a small hill where the fence lay broken.

'Your neighbour has issues with their fence.'

'Cattle and buffalo break it all the time. I can only do so much without any funding for repairs.'

Coming out of the canopy of trees and into the sunshine, he had to blink at the bright sunshine, adjusting his baseball cap. 'What is this place?'

Alice stood on the hill, hands on hips, her smile was truly glorious as she took in the view. 'Mine. All four hundred square kilometres.'

'For what? Farming?'

'No, this is going to be an animal sanctuary. And you're the only one I've ever shown this to—except for the drone images I've shared with my parents.'

'How come?'

'I thought it was fair, considering what you told me last night about your dream job and about your brother.'

'Yeah, but … Is this why you were so desperate to stay in town when I put in your sutures?' Alice could work anywhere with her credentials and passion. 'I've been trying to work out why someone with your skills would want to work out here.' She wasn't stuck like he was, on a contract with the devil.

'I wasn't using you. I was quite prepared to live in the tent. But I've always wanted a large land mass to preserve, one that wasn't dictated by policy and government say-so.'

'You're making this into a zoo?'

'An animal sanctuary. It's got the same landscape, the same flora and fauna as the park, but it'll be a place free from tourists.' She took a step further, looking over the land like it was a multi-faceted precious diamond filled with a unique colour, clarity, depth and sparkle—when all he saw was dirt.

'Remember those brumbies you spotted in the park?'

He nodded, trying to understand her vision. The broken fence wasn't helping.

'I'm planning on bringing them here. This valley is filled with enough grazing feed for a hundred brumbies, easy.'

He narrowed his eyes, trying to see her vision of horses extending their long necks as they grazed in the slender grasses that shifted with the breeze as their tails flicked away some pesky fly. As he did, waving at the annoying fly in his face. 'When?'

'Soon. I don't want my boss finding out that they're there. He'll order a culling when he does. I've just been waiting on the deeds to this place to start planning. My parents helped me, and Iris, she's been an amazing help too.'

'What's this got to do with Iris?' His favourite ninety-four-year young patient who loved reading romance novels that came with content warnings.

'Iris sold her house. It's been on the market since she learned she couldn't go home after her accident.'

He squeezed her arm to reassure her. 'Iris is well taken care of.'

'I know. And I begged Iris to keep the money from her house sale, refusing to accept it. But Iris, the cunning thing, contacted my parents who created a trust account for this place. I had no idea it was happening until the other day, the day I got the deeds. Iris said it was my housewarming present, and it'll go towards the infrastructure this place desperately needs.'

'Like what?'

'Fencing for a start.' With her boot she kicked at the broken fence.

'How come you didn't say anything to me?'

'As much as I'd love to pop the champagne and shout it out to the world, I can't.'

'Why not?'

'If my boss, the honourable horrible Harold, found out about this place he'd find some excuse to get rid of me.'

'Isn't he all about conservation, too?'

'Harold would call it a conflict of interest and ship me off to another park. But I love this part of the country. This environment is so dramatic. One day it'll be a dry dust bowl, then six months later an inland sea, with a mild winter to a hostile heat for summer, with days like this that make up for it ... The old owner of this property was never a farmer. He was some guy in Adelaide who bought it as a cheap investment property, because property near a national park is considered prime real estate.'

'Out here?' He rubbed his neck, sniffing at the dry dust while looking over an empty mass of land, struggling to picture suburbia and all that went with progress and people. When this place looked completely untouched.

'I think the guy was hoping it'd be a popular place for tourism. But with Kakadu National Park down the road, thankfully, most of the tourists skip this park.'

'I've never been to Kakadu. But I've been to Elsie Creek National Park.' They shared a smile. 'Tell me more about this place.'

'Well, um ...' She swallowed, nervously tugging on her shirt's collar. 'I know it'll be a lot of work, but I'll want a rehabilitation area dedicated to injured wildlife. Mostly, it'll be a place where I won't have to cull animals for being who they are. I'd let those brumbies roam free with the wallabies, like Melody, and whatever other animals wanted to stay in a safe environment.'

'How did you even come up with the idea?'

'I'm just like you, Stewart, when you were a boy deciding to become a heart surgeon. This,' she said, pointing to the landscape, 'is the dream I've had since I was a little girl. My parents helped build a sloth sanctuary in Costa Rica. They go back every few years to volunteer, and that's what started it for me. Then there was the Elephant Nature Park in Thailand, and the many other amazing animal sanctuaries out there. My parents went to those places as part of their studies, while I studied the parks themselves, to learn how they started, and saw the amazing things being done there. I want to do that here. Dad says it's my legacy.'

'No way …' He slowly shook his head in awe at Alice and at the land that spread out behind her further than the eye could see. 'So, you'd actually live here?'

'Eventually. It'll take a few years for that to happen. But it's finally started, and this land is twice the size of the national park next door.'

He slung his arm over her shoulder and kissed her cheek. 'I'm proud of you. But you look prouder of yourself.'

'I am. It's been a long time coming. Look, the reason I'm showing you this is that I know you'll get your dream job as that specialised heart surgeon.' She gently jabbed him in the chest as she said, 'You will be one of the best heart doctors in the country. I have faith in you that you'll do it. So don't ever stop believing in your dream or give up when challenged, because dreams do come true.' She wiped at the tear trickling down her cheek, as she smiled over the land.

His heart melted, fully and completely opened as if to breathe fresh air for the very first time. 'This is a big dream.' For the pair of them, but the encouragement she gave him was overwhelming, he had to hold her back to his chest.

Static came over the two-way radio clipped to Alice's hip.

'Elsie Creek Ranger, this is Elsie Creek Police. You there, Alice?'

'That's Porter.' Stewart recognised the voice. 'He's still Acting Sergeant while Marcus is away.' Porter sounded worried. Although, the guy was under this constant cloud of stress ever since Marcus went on leave.

Alice pressed the button to the radio's microphone. 'Alice here. Go ahead, Porter.'

'Is the doc with you?'

She handed the radio to Stewart.

'Stewart here, Porter. What's up?'

'Mate, I'm sorry to do this on your day off, but there's a situation at the hospital.'

'What's going on?' Couldn't the hospital cope with him being away for a couple of days?

A police siren screamed in the background as Porter spoke, 'The ambulance has gone to meet a jillaroo who's been bitten by a snake at one of the local cattle stations. Jenny's busy with Verily, who's gone into labour. And I'm bringing in a ringer who got ripped up by a mad mickey bull during the muster from another station. He's pretty banged up, Doc, and your dad can't make it here until dusk. How far away are you?'

He arched a questioning eyebrow at his personal tour guide.

Alice's voice was clear and calm, but her eyes were determined. 'Tell the hospital we're on our way. ETA forty minutes.' She was already moving, her hair flying behind her as stones tumbled under her boots, heading back to Elsie Creek.

As he raced after her, the responsibility of his job slammed into him, that feeling of contentment as if on a holiday now long gone. He should have never left.

Nineteen

In record time Alice parked her ute by the main doors of the small hospital.

'Thank you.' Stewart kissed her cheek and was out the door to be met by a nurse holding out a chart. With head down, shoulders stooped, he listened with a focused determination as he disappeared inside.

With no Stewart or Melody for company, the emptiness of the cab seemed loud and uninviting. Alice didn't know whether to stay or go.

'Five minutes.' She'd visit Iris, then she'd get back to work.

Her boots echoed down the hospital's corridor, the brush of cool air-conditioning a welcome reprieve. Coming from the other end was Porter, hoisting his police belt higher on his hips, looking as stressed as he'd sounded on the radio.

'Hey, Alice. Thanks for bringing in the doc.'

'No worries. Are you okay?' She pointed at his blood-splattered shirt.

'This is from that kid I brought in, barely nineteen, ripped up by a bull.'

'Sounds awful.'

'I forgot how dangerous mustering cattle can be. I'd rather hand out speeding tickets and have some irate speedster shout at me, than play cowboy.'

'How are you coping without Marcus?'

'Being a man down makes it a challenge …' He scratched at his scruffy chin, the beginnings of a beard. 'Honestly, it sucks.'

'Marcus is a smart man. He wouldn't have left you in charge if he didn't think you were capable.' She patted his shoulder in a friendly manner, hoping to boost his confidence.

'Hey, thanks.' He even managed a slight smile. But his eyes read: *finally, someone gets it!*

'So, what do you know about poachers?'

Porter shrugged, tucking his thumbs into the thick police belt loaded with his gun, pepper spray and other gadgets. 'Animal poachers?'

'I've got a couple in the park. Stewart and I brought in their traps.'

'Want me to put them away as evidence?'

'I'd appreciate that. I'm sending some of the seeds away for analysis.' Her mind was already drafting her official report. 'Is there any chance you could start an official case file for me?'

'Sure.'

'Thank you.' She checked her watch, noting she was still on the clock. 'I'll visit Iris first, then I'll drop those nets off at the station.'

'I'll be there, getting changed.' He pointed at his shirt, heading towards the automatic doors that slid open as a few women walked inside. 'I'll even put the kettle on for you.'

'Sounds good.' She wouldn't mind one of Stewart's coffees right about now.

'Hi, Porter,' greeted the three women walking inside.

Alice recognised the amber-haired Kat, who was a regular hiker of the park. Beside her was Karen Kimble, the mother of seven children, and Tess, the long-legged postmistress. All of them were carrying flowers, fruit, and other soft furnishings. The sort of things she'd brought in to help make Iris comfortable.

Tess stopped to give him a small wave and a smile. 'Haven't seen you around lately, Porter.'

'Busy.' Porter kept walking, juggling his car keys in hand with the doors closing behind him.

'What's going on with you and Porter?' Karen asked Tess. 'Lover boy was all over you, begging you to date him. Didn't Porter quit smoking and shave his beard off for you?'

'Looks like he's growing it back,' said Kat, tossing her thumb in Porter's direction.

'Come on, let's see how Verily is doing.' Tess walked faster down the corridor, giving a curt smile to Alice, heading in the other direction.

'Hey, Alice, have you still got that baby joey?' asked Karen Kimble. 'You could take it to the school and give a talk to the children.'

'I'm sorry, I released her back into the wild last night.' There was a sharp tug on her heart, the way a string pulls on a kite in heavy winds, missing Melody. 'Gotta go.' Tugging her ranger's hat lower, she rushed past the women, in her dirty khaki grunge towards Iris's room. How was she attractive to a big-city-surgeon?

She pulled up fast, to forget all her thoughts, as if reality was slamming her in the face with a heavy-duty iron skillet, at the sight of the poor Iris trapped in her bed wearing an oxygen mask.

Twenty

'*I'm dying, aren't I?*' whined the young jillaroo brought in from the cattle station due to a snakebite.

'You're not dying,' replied a pretty blonde in half-laced purple boots and a summer dress. 'You've had the antivenene and you're at the hospital where they can stop you from dying.'

'Like you would care? Driving here at a break-neck speed that could've killed all of us.'

'We did that to save you,' piped in the young guy. 'After what you did to Sienna, that poisonous snake should have ripped your arm from your body.' He leaned forward, wagging his finger at the girl on the bed. 'What you did was wrong wrong wrong.'

'Everyone, take a breath.' Stewart approached the three people arguing in the emergency room. 'Make way, please.'

The blonde and the young guy stepped back as he weaved towards the girl on the bed.

'HI, I'm Elliott, and that's Sienna. We're the heroes. Especially the rally-racing babe that drove us here to save *that*.' He screwed his nose up at the patient. 'Annie.'

'Hm-hmm…' Stewart unwrapped the bandaged tourniquet from the patient's arm with a nurse assisting to clean up the wound of four distinct puncture marks in her forearm. 'What happened?'

'Annie hid a snake in the station kitchen's storeroom to attack Sienna. Instead, it bit Annie, who screamed the house down, and we saved her by shooting that antivenene stuff into her veins.' Elliott dumped the antivenene kit onto the bed. 'We should have left you on the side of the road and let you walk.'

'*I'm sorrreeee.*' Annie's high-pitched wailing bounced off the corners of the room, making them all cringe.

'Okay, Elliott, we all know Annie's sorry.' Sienna patted her off-sider's arm. 'And, as something I never want to repeat, we were told to bring in the snake because we don't know what type of snake it is.' Sienna dumped a black garbage bag on the floor with a shudder.

'Well done.' Stewart pulled out his phone and tapped on Alice's number. 'Our local park ranger will identify it.' Any excuse to talk to the lady while they prepped his other patient for surgery.

'Ranger Meadows speaking.' Alice's voice was so flirty and feminine, triggering flashbacks of their intimate time together that made him drop his head and hide his smile in front of the patients.

'Alice, it's your favourite doctor.' Her giggle only made him smile more, turning his back on the three newcomers.

'Stewart? I thought you'd be in surgery by now.'

'I will be shortly. I have a patient suffering from a snakebite. They've brought in the snake. Can you identify it for me?' According to the notes, someone from the station had called and said it was a non-venomous python. Even though the patient wasn't showing any pain, no nausea, no laboured breathing, no weak pulse, or rapid heart patterns as the usual symptoms of a snakebite, she had also been injected with antivenene.

The puncture wounds were clearly visible, but there was no swelling or redness in the area to show a foreign toxin making its way into the patient's blood system.

But he needed actual confirmation from a source he could trust to advise him of the snake's venomous nature.

'Sure, text me a photo. Head and scales. Then I'll call you back.'

'Thanks, rabbit.' Closing the phone, he opened the garbage bag. 'Did you bring the snake's head?'

'Yeah, it's in there.' Sienna opened the bag wider on the floor, displaying what was left of the snake. 'There.'

'Great. Hold it there.' He took a few snaps, texted them to Alice, and could only wait. Like he was waiting on test results on his other patient, who was stable and being prepared for extensive surgery. 'When did you give Annie the antivenene?' He picked up the kit, checking the vials weren't out of date.

Sienna glanced at her phone. 'Three-and-a-half hours ago. It took that long to get here.'

'Where from?'

'Danbunnan Station. Do you know it?' Elliott asked.

Stewart shook his head. 'And where did you get this kit?'

'It belongs to the Snake Whisperer.'

His phone rang. It was Alice.

'Do you recognise the snake's breed?' He asked Alice over the phone.

'*Antaresia childreni.* Otherwise known as a children's python. They're harmless and not known to attack, where they'd rather run than get hurt. So if that snake bit someone, it was trapped, or being hurt. And from what I'm seeing, your photos are evidence of animal cruelty, *Doctor.*' Alice's voice was terse. For someone who fiercely protected animals, he'd just sent her photos of a snake ripped to shreds.

He frowned. 'Our local ranger has confirmed it's a children's python, which is a non-venomous snake.'

All three newcomers visibly sighed with relief.

'But she wants to know what happened to the snake and if this is animal cruelty. She's not happy, and you're on speaker.' He held up the phone as the three newcomers shifted back with widening eyes.

Sienna spoke first. 'I went into our station kitchen's storeroom to fetch some cereal for Annie. When I was leaving, that's when I noticed the snake curled up behind the door. I couldn't get past it, I was trapped, so I screamed and that's when Annie came inside to help me.'

'Why is the snake covered in white powder?' Alice's stern voice was calm and clear over the speaker with a level of professionalism to it. Hearing her like this, she was such a beautiful bad-arse, it made him hot under the collar with his lips threatening to sprout into a smile.

'It's flour,' replied Sienna. 'Annie knocked over the flour bucket when she lost her balance when the snake bit her. She was trying to capture it.'

'But it was Annie who dumped the snake in there in the first place to scare Sienna silly.' Elliott made stabbing motions at Annie seated on the examination bed. 'You stole it from Josh who saves snakes! Making Sally, the world's greatest cattle dog, a murderer of snakes, and now we'll all be going to jail for snake cruelty, because of you.'

They were all speaking at once.

'STOP.' Stewart waited a heartbeat before proceeding. 'So, not animal cruelty?'

'A cattle dog did that trying to save me and Annie.' Sienna sighed at the bag holding the snake. 'Poor thing, I feel sorry for the snake. It would've been a horrible way to go.'

'Did you hear that?' He said to Alice over the phone.

'Yeah.' Her sigh was heavy. 'Sadly, it happens. I'll let you go.'

'Before you go, Alice.' He turned his back on the others in the room and lowered his voice. 'I don't like snakes in the house.' Considering the lady rescued animals.

He could hear her frown.

'But I'm okay with turtles.'

He hoped her silence meant she was giving him one of her soft smiles.

'I'd better go check on PP then.'

'Thanks, talk soon.' Pocketing his phone, he pointed at Sienna and Elliott. 'You two, make yourselves scarce. Nurse, can we get an icepack on the bites to reduce any bruising on the patient and I want her on an IV. We'll start Annie on a course of fluids.' He lifted the patient's very bony wrist, checking her vitals. He wasn't really worried about the snakebite, it was the patient's overall condition that was bothering him more.

'I'm dying, aren't I?' Annie's tears highlighted the dark rings under her eyes and her severely sunken cheekbones. Her skin was sallow, and there was no muscle or meat on her bones, she was a living skeleton.

'Annie, you're not dying. The nurse will clean up the wound and I'll be running some blood tests. Nurse, when Dr Mannen Senior arrives, have him conduct a physical on Annie before joining me in the OR. Have Annie admitted.'

'Yes, Doctor.'

'Why?' Annie sat up on the bed.

'I want to be sure you aren't reacting to the antivenene medication.'

He pulled back the curtain and walked out into the corridor. He looked left, then right, spotting Sienna leaning against the wall. 'Where's your offsider?'

'Bathroom.'

'How long has Annie been like that?'

'She's anorexic, isn't she?'

'At this stage, I'm conducting a diagnostic assessment. What can you tell me about Annie?'

'The station's head stockman and I have been monitoring Annie's eating habits for a few weeks now. She'll only eat tiny amounts, then throws it up. Her drastic weight loss has been happening for about seven weeks, before that, she was fit and healthy.'

He tapped on the tablet to order some tests to ensure there wasn't any other underlying medical issues impacting Annie's health. 'Is Annie still working?'

'Until yesterday, when Annie fainted in the cattle yards. She was having today off sick. The head stockman made Annie an appointment to come in tomorrow for a check-up because the boss wanted Annie to have a physical before she returns to work.' Sienna stepped closer, the concern clear in her voice. 'What they do is dangerous with those huge cows. And apparently, Annie was manning the gates.'

'I don't know what that means.' Although he'd had a patient, Eskie, who had extensive hand surgery for getting his hand caught in some gates pushed by cattle.

'Elliott had to explain it to me, too. Apparently, the gate controls the flow of cattle through the barricades that they'll use for loading them onto trucks. Yesterday, they were working on cleanskins. Ferals.'

He lifted his head from the chart at the word Alice used. 'What does ferals mean to you?'

'Cattle who haven't seen a human. They're wild, feral, and big. Their hoofs alone are four times the size of my boots.' Sienna pointed to her half-laced purple boots that weren't the normal standard of footwear worn on the stations. 'The way Elliott explained it is that where Annie fainted, if she hadn't closed the gate in time, they would have trampled her to death.'

'Which is why your boss is asking for a medical clearance before she returns to work.'

'Jake Cullen is a smart man.' Sienna nodded firmly, with clear admiration in her voice for this guy.

'Do you know of any reason why Annie would want to lose weight?'

Sienna shook her head. 'The head stockman and I both agree that Annie is not eating enough to effectively perform her duties as a jillaroo during a muster. And yet, here I am, the station's relief cook, hired to feed these people …' Her brow flitted from a frown to one of sorrow as she stared in the direction of Annie's room.

'You can't force a person to eat.'

'I know.' Her sigh was heavy.

'Are you both staying in town? That's not meant as a pick-up, it's just in case I have further questions about Annie's condition.' Sienna was an attractive blonde, with light blue eyes. Normally, he'd flirt a little, but not today. *What's going on?*

'I'm planning on it. I'm not driving back to Danbunnan in the dark in my toy-car that's smaller than the cows. Have you seen the wildlife that's out there?'

'I have.' A fast and recent introduction to a world without walls, patients, but lots of fresh air and sunshine. He rolled his shoulders as if pushing away a touch of claustrophobia from being indoors again.

'Got any recommendations on where to stay?'

'The pub, I guess. Is it true Annie used that snake to set you up?'

'Yes. Halfway here Annie confessed to putting the snake in the storeroom as a prank. Along with a whole heap of other garbage you wouldn't believe. Elliott thinks that Annie was sabotaging my job, trying to get me off the station.' Her frown was cute. But her sigh was sad as she glanced around the place. 'I guess she won, right? We rushed to town, believing it was a poisonous death adder or something.'

'Pranks don't involve live snakes. Which is cruel. The ranger isn't happy about this.' He'd hate to see Alice angry, because she was a strong woman who wouldn't hold back.

'Do we need to call the police? It's serious if you've mentioned sabotage.' Stewart pointed to the main doors giving him a clear view of the police station, where the ranger's ute was parked beside the police patrol car. *Why is Alice parked over there?*

Sienna shrugged. 'I'll talk to the boss first. See what he wants to do.'

Jenny approached in her surgical scrubs. 'We're ready for you, Doctor.'

'Sienna, I'd appreciate it if you kept us informed over anything relating to Annie.' Stewart left with Jenny, heading for the operating theatre.

Jenny handed him the case notes for the patient. 'I'll be

assisting you in the operation until your father arrives.'

'I thought you were busy with Verily and the baby?' He flicked through the paperwork.

'Braxton Hicks. I've sent Verily home. If that's okay with you?'

'Maternity is your department, Jenny. I'm just your backup.'

'But I'll need to organise an extra bed for Verily's room in the maternity ward when she comes back.'

'Why?'

'Alex not only brought in Verily's bag for her and the baby, but he also lumbered in with his swag, quite prepared to camp in her room.'

It made him grin, before his smile fell as he looked over the chart of his latest patient. As he scrubbed in, his phone on silent, sitting on the nearby bench it displayed a text message that read: *'I don't like snakes in the house either, Doctor. Good luck with your surgery. A.'*

The simplicity of Alice's text made him pause. He wanted to hold her, to brush his cheek against her silky hair, to just breathe her in and let the world slip away as their hearts beat in unison as if they were one. Alice—the mere thought of her was making him feel whole again. And he hadn't felt like that, not since …

'Doctor?'

Stewart frowned, shaking his hands over the sink, his focus back where it always belonged—on his job. *Three weeks to go.* 'Okay, let's put this cowboy back together.'

Twenty-one

Stewart called her rabbit! *Rabbit?* Asking for help to identify a snake and he drops the one simple word *rabbit.*

As she steered down the town's main street, Alice peeked at her reflection in the rear-view mirror, brushing hair away from her ears. She didn't have rabbit ears or buck teeth. So why rabbit? Was it because she grew what he called rabbit food? Or was it payback for making him wear a T-shirt with a bunny on it?

Alice parked her ute at the rear of the small town's hardware store. It sat across the road from the mighty pub that towered over the corner, on the main road of Elsie Creek. She'd been at the police station getting the ball rolling on the poachers. Then home to a very quiet house to unpack. Normally she wasn't home this early, and would have relished the extra hours to read, but the silence of sitting in that house without Melody or Stewart had her snatching her ute keys and walking out the back door.

As the local police were short-staffed, she could at least do some of the footwork, making this place her first stop. She might find nothing, but it was a start.

The feed store was like a fast-food drive-through, but these people did it for stock feed. Customers would drive inside the shed through one roller door, load up their utes, then drive out the other end. Its deep shade had Alice removing her sunglasses as she stepped inside, only to flinch as a large white ball whizzed past her.

Thwack!

The ball got caught in the blue net wrapped around a black tyre, swinging off the raised roller door.

'Oh, so sorry, I am.' The young woman rushed forward, wearing a softball glove on one hand as the other scooped the ball out of the net.

'It's Speedy, right?'

'I is, I am. And that's Cecil. He's a pet, not a wild animal, you know. Cecil's our softball team's mascot.'

'I know who Cecil is.' The large water buffalo came towards her, dropping its head to press gently against her belly for a tickle behind his ears. His particular sweet spot was the tip of his ears, where his wiry fur was softest.

'Hello, Cecil.' The pampered pet wandered the streets as a mobile billboard with words written in chalk along his black sides. Today's message read: *Verily's gone into labour*. On the other side: *Live boxing, tomorrow night*. The chalk colour matched the bright blue ribbons wrapped around his tail and blunted horns.

'Is Cecil eating your food?'

'Hiding in the shade, he is. Cecil prefers the flowers the Flynn brothers are trying to sell in their hardware store.' Speedy giggled. 'Sorry about the ball, I am.'

'All good. Did you get the nickname Speedy for throwing fast balls?'

'I wish. But as my coach, who is a world champion, she tells me I'm getting better, I am. And you're …' Speedy pointed with the hand hiding inside the chunky softball glove.

'Alice.'

'Cool. Don't tell the bosses I threw that softball. I'm supposed to hang the tyre on the tree. Just that this time of the day the sun isn't good. You'd know, with your skin, you would? Our coach, she makes us wear sunscreen. She's having a baby, you know.'

'Verily?' Alice struggled to keep up with this conversation

at the speed Speedy spoke.

'That's her. Gone into labour this morning. Everyone's waiting for it, they are. Everyone's stocked up on chalk to write on Cecil's back. Here, you take some too ...' From her pocket, Speedy pulled out some large chunks of street chalk.

'I'll be okay.'

'Nah, you live here.' Speedy grabbed Alice's hand and dumped a handful of chalk into it.

Wow, a gift from a local, she couldn't say no. 'Thanks.' Alice tucked the chalk into her top pocket.

'Now watch this ...' Speedy wound her arm like a sideways helicopter propeller, and let the ball rip, throwing it underarm. It wasn't fast, but it landed in the centre of the tyre's net. Speedy gave a small jump of joy. 'I did it. Did you see it? Did you?'

'Well done, Speedy. I couldn't do that.'

'Verily's been running a coaching clinic for softball pitchers, she has. We had players come from all over to learn. Do you play?'

'No. I know nothing about softball.' Alice craned her neck at the pallets of assorted stock feed. From hessian bags of horse feed, cow licks, feeding hay, to tinned dog food. There were flea and tick solutions, heart worm medications, calf-milk replacers, including formulas she used for wallabies and possums. It was all here, where Alice was hoping to find a certain seed mix on their shelves.

'You know, for years and years and years, I couldn't even chuck the ball. My pitching was so bad, the ball never even made the distance from the pitching mound to the home plate.'

'You're throwing a long way now.'

'I am. Did you see?' Speedy's smile was wide and infectious, as she bounced on her toes, all jittery.

Plucking the ball from the net set around the hole in the tyre, Speedy skipped back to the scuff mark made on the cement, ready to pitch again. 'You should come. Verily taught me. She's a world champion who holds a world record.'

'I didn't know that.'

'If Verily can teach me to throw, she can teach you. And this year, we're hoping to win more than one game. You should come, you should.'

'Won't Verily be busy with the baby.'

'Verily's got Molly and the rest of the women on our team eager to help. And of course, Alex. He's like the big brother, and he's my cousin, he is. Does that make Verily's baby my second cousin?'

'Not sure.'

Even Cecil lifted his head up from his ear rub to shrug. Then plonked his head back against Alice's belly for more ear rubbing.

'Alright, big fella. You can go suck up to someone else.' It's a good thing her khaki ranger's uniform blended well with dirt and buffalo hair.

'I should ask Molly if that makes us related when the new baby arrives.' Speedy pulled out her mobile phone.

'Before you do, Speedy, I'd like some help.' Alice dragged out the plastic evidence bag she had in her cargo pants' pocket. Courtesy of Porter, it was a proper police evidence bag that held some of the poachers' seed mix. 'I'm wondering if you stock this kind of seed?'

Speedy examined the bag. 'We do, we do.'

As Cecil meandered out of the shed, Speedy skipped to the row of floor-to-ceiling shelving. Still wearing her baseball glove, she pulled down a plastic bag. 'It's the wild birdseed mix. Do you want some?'

Alice compared the seeds to her sample, it was the same variety and seed blend mix.

'I might collect a bag of this stuff later.' Alice took a photo with her camera phone. 'While I'm here, where can I find the grass seed and a sprinkler.'

'Inside the hardware store.' Speedy pointed with her floppy softball glove to the internal adjoining door. 'The

Flynn brothers will show you, they'll tell you where to get some good topsoil if you need it.'

'Sounds good.' It might be a long shot, but Alice had to ask. 'Speedy, who buys this birdseed?'

'The wildlife carers like Flo and her ducks, which is usually Rigsy bringing Flo in on their shopping dates. You know Flo, don't you?'

'I do. Is there anyone else?'

'Um …' Speedy tapped her chin with her softball glove. 'There's Bella.'

'Who's Bella?'

'Bella runs the local hemp farm. Her theory is if she throws out the birdseed when we play softball, the birds will go there instead of going near her hemp farm when she's planting her seeds. Bella does it every softball season, she does.'

Alice arched her eyebrows, trying to work out the logic of a totally illogical statement.

'But now the coach looks after the sportsgrounds, she's always telling Bella off. But Bella says it's tradition, she does. So the coach has her chucking out her birdseed on the outer field.'

'Are you talking about Verily as your softball coach?'

'No, Agnes Picket. Verily is our pitching and fielding coach. Agnes was our first coach, and now she's co-coach and our batting coach and caretaker of the sportsground, she is. When you come to softball practice, don't let the looks scare you off. Or her shouting. Agnes is always shouting coz she forgets to turn her hearing aid on, but she's really nice and will do anything for anyone, she will.'

'I didn't say I was going to play.'

Speedy shrugged. 'What else are you gonna do after hours? It's where most of the real women hang out for fun — that's what Kat calls us. And as Tess says, it's a place where there's not one glue gun or knitting needle in sight. Tess hates arts and crafts, which is funny when her grandma owns the craft store next to the post office. Do you do craft?'

'No.' She was barely keeping up with this conversation.

'Me neither. This is my craft now.' She held up her softball in her glove. 'I'm gonna be the best softball pitcher for our team this season, I am. Verily calls us dust princesses, even got a song, we do. Or is that a poem?' Again, she tapped her chin with her softball glove. 'Do you want to hear it? Do you?'

Speedy looked so excited, Alice hated to disappoint her. 'Sure?'

Speedy brushed down her shirt, cleared her throat, holding her softball glove to her chest, she lifted her chin high. *'Our helmet is our crown, our shirts are our ball gowns, and the field is our castle, where we never leave the playing field cleaner than we arrived. We are the good girls who steal, playing all our bases freely, sharing a love for diamonds—except you'll find ours waiting for us in the dust* … It's good, isn't it?'

Alice double blinked. Then blinked again. For the girl in khaki who didn't own any ball gown, and regularly came home covered in dust, it hit home.

Now that she'd put roots down in this town, buying her property, would it be so wrong to try something new? To do something other than sit at home alone every night, to try and make a connection with the people in this town so they didn't see her as the bad guy?

'When do you practise?'

Speedy's smile widened. 'I'll write it down, I will.' She skipped to her counter.

Alice shook her head. How did she get talked into this when she was here for work? 'Speedy, does anyone else buy that wild birdseed?'

Speedy rubbed her temple with her softball glove. 'There were these three guys who bought out all we had. I had to order another pallet, I did. I just restocked that shelf for Bella to do her seed thing for *our* softball season.' Speedy held out a piece of paper. 'Times, dates, and coaches' phone numbers.'

'Um, thanks ...' She still wasn't sure if she would show up. 'Do you remember what those guys who bought the seed looked like?'

Again, Speedy shrugged. 'Just three guys in this white van. They paid in cash, they did.'

'When?'

'A couple of times.'

Her stomach dropped so hard Alice wanted to throw up. Were those poachers blatantly making this a regular run in her park! 'What kind of white van?'

'It's like the van we use for the hardware store, we do. But different. It's just white like a tradesman van, it is?' Speedy pointed to the car park, where the hardware store's brown van stood in the shade of the shed.

Alice looked around for any cameras, something that may help build her case. But she found nothing.

Come on, it was a feed store for animals.

'Would you remember the van if you saw it?'

Again, Speedy shrugged. 'No. But I know they drove to the pub from here, they always do.' She pointed with her glove to the towering building that lived across the road. 'Everyone goes to the pub, they do.'

'Not me ...' But now Alice had no choice.

Twenty-two

'I hope you're not here to tell us off for over-feeding Karma, Missy?' The grey-haired grouch tugged on his retro trouser braces so hard they twanged before landing with a thwack on his shoulders. All he needed was a bow tie to complete the look with his swanky fedora. It would be a good look—if he wasn't scowling at her.

Oh, joy, pick on me, the bad guy.

'Hello to you, too, Billy.' Alice nodded at the pub's yardman, and caretaker to the large crocodile that only had three claws, and a body armour full of battle scars as a testimony to the predator who was nearly a hundred years old. 'Karma looks good.'

Three sharp spiky strings of wire ran across the top of the eight-foot meshed fence containing a plush palace that came with a personal lap pool, perfect for a retired man-eating beast. 'The barbed wire is new. Is it me or is the fence taller?'

'Had to. The long-lost Peddler climbed in there while on some freaking treasure hunt.' Billy leaned his shoulder against the chain mesh, poking up the brim of his funky fedora. 'All the fellas in the pub chipped in after that. We even got sensor lights and cameras.'

'For the pub?'

'Nah, the croc. Them fellas love Karma.'

'Are they still making Karma bet on every football game?' A lot of locals won a stack of cash based on predictions Karma made by jumping for meat.

'We only let Karma jump on special occasions. Like the

boxing bout tomorrow night.' He pointed to the rear of the pub where a length of green lawn led to a group of men building a boxing ring.

'The last time I was here, they were building a rodeo ring.' Back when she got hassled by various cattle station owners for not opening the stock routes sooner. Duh, she did that for their safety.

'So we're not in trouble?'

'No. I'm here about something else. Who manages the cameras?' Because they were angled towards the car park area that may show the feed store's driveway.

'The publican.'

'Is she in?'

'Where else is she gonna be? Come on through, Ranger.' Billy opened the door to the front bar.

'You can call me Alice.' The scent of hops and other assorted ales greeted her as she removed her hat and sunglasses. Expecting wall-to-wall cowboys, she was surprised by the large empty room of tables and chairs. There was no one here except a blonde lady seated at the bar. 'Where is everyone?'

'They're saving themselves for tomorrow night.' Billy plonked on the stool at the far corner of the bar and nodded at the barmaid, known as Mean-Rene. 'Is the publican around?'

'Is there an issue with Karma? You're not gonna revoke our permit, Ranger?' Mean-Rene, the scary front bar manager, crossed her heavily inked arms over her chest. In a leather vest, Mean-Rene looked like someone who'd manage an outlaw bikers' bar, not an outback pub frequented by cowboys.

'Nah, the new ranger wants to talk to the publican, is all,' said Billy.

'Alice, please.' It's why she didn't visit this place. Come on, she wasn't the bad guy. And she wasn't a cop either, but she was here hoping for a lead to give to Porter, given he was swamped by a desk loaded with paperwork. The Acting Sergeant wasn't coping very well with Marcus away.

Mean-Rene gave a stern sniff, before disappearing through the door behind the bar, and soon returned. 'She's coming. What'll you have?' She poured a schooner from the beer tap and placed it on the bar mat in front of Billy.

Alice glanced at her watch. It *was* knock-off time. 'Schooner, mid-strength please.' Hey, she'd drunk in bars in various airports with her dad, wearing goofy T-shirts that were the perfect tool for striking up conversations with strangers. She'd drunk in swanky bars, in some very fine five-star tourist resorts near some famous national parks. She was also a grown-up who could walk into a pub anywhere and order a drink. She just preferred not to in this town, where they scowled at her like she was the bad guy. *Oh, the joy!*

'That'll be our shout for the new ranger, Rene,' said the publican, entering through the bar's back door.

'You're the boss lady.' Mean-Rene placed the schooner in front of Alice. 'With compliments of the management.' She even curtsied, but the scowl remained.

'Thanks, but not necessary.' But then Alice *had to* sip while under the glare of Mean-Rene. 'It's the best beer I've had all day. Thanks.' And it was. Cold and crisp.

Satisfied, Mean-Rene nodded, flicked her black hair over her shoulder, and went to the other side of the bar.

'It's nice to see you off the clock, Ranger.'

'Alice.'

'Samantha. The old ranger, Walt, he'd come in at least once a week. You? How many times?'

Alice didn't want to admit it. 'This will be my first beer here.'

'I thought so.'

'The new ranger—' said Billy.

'It's Alice. And I've been here three years now.'

'I'm known as *the publican*, and I've been here all my life.' Samantha poured herself a beer. The publican was younger than Alice, wearing jeans and sneakers, her blonde hair in a loose bun. But she had an underlying aura of someone who carried a lot of business-like responsibility.

'Alice is interested in our security cameras,' said Billy.

'My upgraded security system, that my punters paid for,' said Samantha with a wry grin.

'Do you record your security vision?' Alice asked.

'We only had them installed last week.'

'How long do you plan on keeping the video recordings? My CCTV footage goes straight to the cloud, and it's held for two years.'

'Why?' Billy asked.

'We're a public space. Universities use it for wildlife research, and the police for certain things like missing person searches. Being a pub wouldn't you—'

'Listen, Missy, we're not in the big city. This is Elsie Creek. And we live upstairs.' Billy pointed to the ceiling. 'We'd hear it if anyone broke into the pub.' Then his stern expression softened as he meekly mumbled, 'except when that long-lost Peddler jumped in with Karma.'

'Why the interest in our security system?' Samantha asked.

'Excuse me, Ranger?' The woman who'd been sitting at the other end of the bar approached. 'Sorry for interrupting, but were you talking to the doctor at the hospital over a snake identification earlier today?'

Alice barely nodded. How did this look—a government employee having a beer in a bar!

'Did you bring in that jillaroo with the snakebite from Danbunnan Station?' Samantha asked.

'Yes. I'm their relief cook, Sienna.' She held out her hand all business-like making them shake it as if in a boardroom about to start business negotiations.

'So how is your boss, Jake Cullen?' Samantha casually cradled her schooner of beer like a coffee being drunk in the office.

'Good. Busy with the musters.' Sienna sat next to Alice, putting her drink on the counter.

'I'm surprised the black prince isn't in town,' mumbled Billy. 'That lad would clean up in the boxing bouts tomorrow?'

'Prince who?' Alice asked.

'Jake Cullen, he's the owner of Danbunnan Station. It's one of the oldest and largest family run cattle stations in the area,' explained Samantha. 'The Cullens were considered royalty in the cattle industry.'

'I've heard of Danbunnan.' Alice's little sanctuary was nothing more than an ink mark on a map, compared to the sheer size of Danbunnan Station, which was over two-and-a-half million hectares. It was bigger than some European countries she'd visited.

'I started at Danbunnan Station a few months ago and I know nothing about cows.' Sienna then grinned. 'I didn't know Jake could box, but he did punch a door clean off its hinges.'

'That lad was one of the very few who got banned from this pub …' Billy poked up the brim of his fedora. 'First time when he was fifteen, I reckon. Jake and that larrikin Cowboy Craig were hustling pool at one of our rodeos, and it ended up in a bar-room brawl. That Jake walloped men older and bigger than him, too, and ended up spending the night in the lock-up for his troubles, until his family bailed him out.'

'Is Jake still banned?' Sienna asked the publican.

'No. That was back in my mother's time as publican. I have no problem with Jake or Cowboy Craig, who's a regular.' Samantha sipped from her beer.

'Well, I wanted to apologise to the ranger, and to ask you about snakes. Wild ones.' Sienna swivelled on her bar stool to face Alice. 'We've got this young jackaroo, Josh, who would be the perfect little brother, he's that sweet. Everyone loves him. He's also our snake whisperer, rescuing injured snakes that he returns to the wild. It's his hobby.'

'Don't he get bit?' Billy slid his thumb beneath his retro suspenders to make them sit higher on his shoulders as if to turn up his hearing.

'No. Josh has been doing it for a while. He even has his mother making him these special snake bags.'

'So how did you end up with a snake in the storeroom?' Alice asked.

'This sounds like an interesting story ...' Samantha pointed her beer glass at Sienna. 'I'll shout you the next drink if you share.'

'Deal.' Sienna held out her glass for a refill and explained all, since there were only four people in the bar, with Mean-Rene rummaging around in the coldroom.

'So, my reason for approaching you, Alice,' said Sienna. 'We weren't cruel to that snake, and like I said at the hospital, I felt sorry for it. And, if I know Josh, he'll be absolutely gutted when he learns what happened to that snake.'

'Sounds like a good lad to me.' Billy sipped on his beer, then sat up with a frown aimed at Alice. 'Hey, that jackaroo's not gettin' into trouble capturing wild snakes, is he, Ranger?'

'Danbunnan Station is private property. Besides, the children's python is commonly bred as pets because they're so calm, and in the Northern Territory you don't need a permit if they're legally obtained.'

'Well, alright then.' Billy mumbled over his beer, with Sienna sighing with relief for this jackaroo named Josh.

'If this jackaroo is saving snakes, and if he wants to, I can get him the correct permits to cover him,' Alice suggested to Sienna.

'Why would you wanna do that for?' Again, Billy burred up, giving her the evil eye.

'Because I'm always looking for potential wildlife carers. Having a snake wrangler I could call on—I'm all for it and will help them any way I can.' She stared him down because she was not the bad guy.

'Well, alright then.' Billy's grey eyebrows disappeared

beneath his fedora, his shoulders stooped as he focused back on his beer.

Samantha rubbed her forehead, giving a low chuckle. 'Careful, Billy, you're getting as grumpy as your brother, Mickey.'

'When are you returning to the station?' Alice asked Sienna.

'Tomorrow, after we see what happens with Annie at the hospital.'

'I'll give Stewart—'

'Who?'

'Doctor Mannen, the doctor who called me from the hospital to identify the snake.'

'He was hot,' Sienna said with a grin.

'Aren't you living with him, Alice?' Samantha asked.

'We're housemates.' Yet, after their trip to the park, was that all they were?

'That's right, your house got trashed by white ants. How the heck could you let that happen, Missy?' Billy pointed his half-empty beer at her. 'Everyone knows you've gotta bait your houses, especially when we've got white ants that build truck-sized ant mounds out here.'

Alice rubbed the bridge of her nose to not snap at the old man. Her old house collapsing was not her fault. 'Sienna, if you swing by the hospital in the morning, with a cup of coffee for the doctor as his delivery fee, I'll give Stewart a snake wrangler's kit. It'll have some paperwork for permits, and a professional antivenene kit for this Josh.'

'Really? Like he'll be legit?'

'Sure. Once Josh is registered, I can hook him up with some universities who may pay him to collect data. Some of those places supply equipment too, like the GPS tracker I'm trialling on this wallaby to learn about their habitats and lifestyle.' She unclipped her phone and swiped to the app. 'That red dot ...' She pointed to the small screen, showing Samantha and Sienna. 'That's Melody. She's an agile wallaby.

We found her a foster mother.'

'Lot of effort for roadkill,' mumbled the grouch in the corner.

'The university is conducting a study, hoping to find a solution to limit their cousins interfering with the farmers' crops down south. But for me, to be honest,' she said with her voice softening, 'I want to monitor this wallaby. She could hardly walk when I found her, and I've been her foster mother for a while. But she's good now.'

'*Hellooo*?' Someone who looked like a supermodel fresh from the catwalk had entered the bar. Lowering her large sunglasses, her narrow nose lifted as she inspected the room. 'My husband is looking for a place to plug in the chords for ringside lighting?'

'Billy?' Samantha nodded at her yardman.

'On it, boss lady.' Billy gulped down his beer, tapped his hat at the women, and was out the door.

'What'll you have?' Samantha asked the woman who looked like a polished movie star.

'I'll have champagne, please. Rene, the darling, put a bottle on ice for me already. Is this the ladies' lounge?'

'It seems like it.' Samantha poured a glass of champagne. The ice rustled in the bucket as she returned the bottle. Then went back to her seat in the corner, where she picked up her own beer.

'Thanks, darl. I'm Krissie.' She waved her long nails at them as if playing an air piano. 'What are we talking about?'

'Snakes,' replied Sienna.

'Mmm, so men? I love talking about men. Especially when they're all hot and sweaty, thumping their chests like cavemen in a ring with all that testosterone. Are you all coming to the fight tomorrow night?'

Alice chuckled behind her beer, shaking her head.

'No, I'll be safely back on the station,' said Sienna, sharing the laugh.

'I'll be the one hoping to control the testosterone.'

Samantha pointed at the barmaid entering from the coldroom. 'With Rene leading the charge, she's my muscle.'

You'd think Mean-Rene would take offence. Instead, she lifted her heavily inked arms and gave a bicep curl, showing off her lean muscles.

'That's why we have the ring girls, darl.' Krissie pointed her manicured nail at Mean-Rene. 'And you, Rene, would make a wonderful ring girl. The boys love a bad girl with ink.'

Mean-Rene arched a manicured eyebrow. 'My hubby would love that. *Not*. I'll be stocking the mobile coldroom and sorting out the eskies for tomorrow, boss lady. You right to …'

'You go. I'll watch the bar.' Samantha leaned back, sipping on her beer. Pretty chilled for a publican.

'What's a ring girl?' Sienna asked Krissie.

Alice was wondering the same.

'They're the sexy gals who enter the boxing match, holding up the boxing round numbers in between bouts. That was me …' Krissie daintily patted her high hair. 'But now I'm married, the hubby likes to keep me to himself and hires other girls. They'll be here tomorrow.'

'Anyone we know?' Samantha asked.

'Not unless you follow rodeos, they're coming in from Mount Isa. Real buckle bunnies.'

'Good. My patrons will approve.'

'My husband thought so, too.' Krissie sipped her champagne then placed it on the bar mat, which she patted down as if smoothing down a tablecloth in a fine dining restaurant. 'So, are any of you ladies married?'

Samantha shrugged, Sienna shook her head, and Alice just sipped her beer.

'You're kidding me. How? When you're in a town flooded with cowboys.'

'I'm not looking for anything,' said Samantha sternly.

'Ditto.' Alice wondered how fast she could drink this beer

and bolt.

'What they said.' Sienna tossed her thumb in their direction.

'Oh, puh-leese, don't tell me you're all broken hearted? Just so you know, I've had my heart ripped out, stomped on, and kicked to the curb by many a loser. Until I found my man who spoils me rotten like a kept woman and I'm not afraid to say so. Mind you, I work pretty darn hard to keep my man happy. And he keeps me happy. So, now it's your turn. You first.' Krissie pointed a long nail at Sienna with a look that said she wouldn't stop until answered.

'Fine. I was cheated on in ways I struggled to comprehend.' Sienna shuddered, taking a deep gulp of her drink.

'I'm so sorry, darl.' Krissie daintily patted the back of Sienna's hand. 'You do realise that it's probably for the best?'

'How? When I then end up falling for a guy I can never have.'

'Ooh, dilemma.' Krissie's eyes widened so much her false eyelashes blended with her eyebrows.

'No dilemma. Because it's not happening.' Sienna crossed her arms over her chest, end of conversation.

'Oh-kay. Your turn.' Krissie pointed her polished nail at Alice. 'The girl in khaki. Why so much khaki?'

'I'm a park ranger.' Normally she'd be patting her patch on her sleeve, but not with her short unpolished nails she hid under her khaki-covered thighs.

Samantha said to Alice, 'Did you know my grandmother helped create that park?'

'No, I didn't.'

'Grandma and a few other women helped the local Indigenous women protect their sacred sites from development. Danbunnan Station had a hand in that, too, through Annabelle Cullen. That would be Jake's ...' Samantha looked at Sienna for the answer.

'One of Jake Cullen's great-aunts.' Sienna sat up with an

excited wriggle on her bar stool. 'I've been reading up on Danbunnan's history, it's fascinating stuff. And if I remember correctly, Annabelle Cullen married a Phillip Kidman.'

'Is that any relation to the movie star Nicole Kidman?' Krissie asked.

'No, he was the son of the cattle king, Sir Sidney Kidman,' replied Samantha. 'The guy owned over sixty stations at one stage. None as big as Danbunnan Station, and he had his eye on Danbunnan as the prize jewel of his empire, but the Cullen's weren't budging. Yet the women cleverly used the Kidman and Cullen political connections to form the Elsie Creek National Park in …' Samantha looked to Alice.

'It's been a national park since 1968,' said Alice.

'Is it worth looking at?' Krissie asked. 'Kakadu was just enormous, and full of people you had to shoulder your way through to see the exhibits.'

'Elsie Creek NP has some gorgeous gorges, waterfalls, hot springs and its only down the road—wait, don't go, it's only for locals. Right, Ranger?' Samantha hid her sly smile behind her beer.

Alice drank her beer, swallowing her need to agree.

'You know, they set up a trust for that park. Every year, the local women would run a fundraiser for the park in the old tea house rooms.' Samantha pointed her beer to the window with a view of the train station sitting on the other side of the train tracks. 'Sadly, that's one of the downsides for closing those tea rooms. But, if anyone's interested, it's a museum now, with some great works from local artists.'

'Oh, I'm in.' Sienna raised her hand as if taking a vote. 'After being stuck on a station for months, I need to appease my shopping withdrawals.'

'What happened to that trust?' Considering Alice now had one for her own property.

'The old ranger, Walt, used to manage it to ensure the place never closed.' Samantha narrowed her eyes at Alice. 'You know anything about it?'

Alice shook her head.

'Which explains why the ranger's house has gone to rack and ruin.'

'If I'd known …' She wouldn't be homeless.

'What happened?' Sienna asked, with Krissie nodding beside her.

'White ants ate out the floor of the ranger's house. It's elevated, and it left poor Alice dangling in the air. I heard the Hot Doc rescued you.'

'Stewart did.' Her hero, with kisses that made her hum and her body bend like putty in his hands. He really was a god of lust. But she couldn't tell him that. Or these women.

'Not only did the Hot Doc rescue our fine ranger from the rubble of a fallen house, he then stitched her up. How many did you get?'

'A dozen.'

'Then the doctor lets Alice move into his house, because you were worried about losing your spot in the park.'

'That's true.' Alice groaned, rubbing her forehead, feeling the dirt under her fingertips. Stewart did mention their living conditions would become a topic of conversation in this town, she just didn't expect it to be repeated in front of her.

'I heard you took Stewart to see the park. I hope he liked it?'

'Stewart did.' *I think.* 'He was talking about trying to sneak in a fishing trip before he left.'

'Good.' Samantha then leaned in closer. 'We're hoping he'll stay. Apparently, the town's mayor is trying to marry his daughter off to the good doctor.'

'An arranged marriage! That's terrible.' Sienna scowled over her drink.

'Most of the single women in this town would gladly line up to be the Hot Doc's bride,' said Samantha.

'Does that include you, darl?'

Samantha scoffed, shaking her head. 'Stewart's too cocky, clinical, and blond for my taste, but the man has some serious skills. He's performed miracles in our little bush hospital. I saw Eskie's hand.'

'Who?' asked Krissie.

'Eskie. He's this stockman who got his hand crushed in the drafting gates. We were expecting him to get evacuated to some big-city hospital and not see the guy for months. We couldn't believe it when Eskie strolls into the bar a week later, hand all stitched up and happy he can wriggle his fingers. When, by rights, he should've lost some feeling. The punters were calling it a miracle.'

'Good to hear our jillaroo, Annie, is in excellent hands at the hospital.' Sienna raised her drink as if toasting to the good doctor.

'Why is a surgeon that skilled working out here?' Krissie asked.

'Stewart won't be here for very much longer.' Alice sighed, watching bubbles rise in her beer glass.

'Stewart leaves in a few weeks, and most of the people in this town have been doing what they can to keep him,' explained Samantha. 'Is it true that Stewart is still under contract with his old hospital?'

Alice nodded. It was a reminder to stop pining for the guy, even if it was too late. Kind of like Sienna, who had fallen for a guy she couldn't have.

But Alice wasn't in love. Mind you, she'd never been in love to compare. But Stewart was leaving. And so was she, emptying her beer in a few mouthfuls.

'Another one, Alice?' Samantha picked up the empty glass.

'No, thanks. Can I ask if you've seen any strangers around?'

'Hello, that'd be me?' Krissie lifted her champagne glass in the air as if making a toast.

'Oh, me too.' Sienna playfully clinked her glass against Krissie's with a giggle. 'This is my first time in town.'

'How about three men driving a white van?' Alice

pointed to the windows facing the feed store behind her. 'They bought some wild birdseed across the road, before coming here.'

'When?' Samantha asked.

Alice shrugged. 'I'm just chasing a long shot.'

Samantha's eyes narrowed at Alice. 'Is it something to do with the park?'

Alice nodded. She didn't want to say, and it was too early to point fingers.

'Talk to Luke in the bottle shop. The guy has this uncanny knack for knowing who drives what. Tell him I sent you.'

'Thanks.' She slipped on her hat. 'Sienna, I'll leave the paperwork and antivenene kit for your jackaroo with Stewart to take to the hospital.'

'Brilliant. It'll be the perfect morale boost the guy needs. Thank you, Alice. Now I'll need to find something to make the rest of the crew happy.' Sienna swivelled on her bar stool to face her neighbour. 'Krissie, do your buckle bunnies have posters they could sign? I've got a stockman who'd love one.'

Bunnies. A reminder of Stewart calling her a rabbit. Considering rabbits were feral, she couldn't take the nickname as a compliment.

'Sure, darl. Come, take your pick.' Krissie jumped off her stool, then pointed her long nail at Alice and Samantha. 'Now, you two ladies, don't be all work and no play, when it can be so much more funner when you find yourselves a good man. When you do, hang onto him, spoil him, and he'll never leave you, and then he'll spoil you back. As for you, darl,' she said, hooking her arm through Sienna's, 'let's talk about this guy you can never have.' Krissie waved and led Sienna out into the beer garden.

Samantha waited a beat after the door closed. 'Do you have poachers in the park?'

'We tore down a stack of traps yesterday. Birds mostly.'

Samantha's face fell with concern. 'I'm so sorry to hear that. Talk to Luke, and I'll tell the rest of the staff to keep an eye out. We'll be discreet. And as punishment for Billy being rude to you, I'll make him go through the CCTV footage we do have.'

'Thanks, I appreciate it.'

'Hey, we live here, and that's our local park, too. Even if you are only a visitor.'

'I'll be living here permanently, too. I mean …' Alice took a sharp breath and revealed her secret. 'I just bought the land next to the park.'

'To do what?'

'Create an animal sanctuary, a safe place for those brumbies not allowed in the park. I hate it when they do their animal culls.'

Samantha's eyebrows raised.

'Don't worry, I know I'm the bad guy around here, so I'm not telling too many people. Besides Stewart, I've only told you. I'll be getting proper fencing, so the farmers won't have to worry about the wildlife wandering on their stock routes or interfering with their properties.'

Samantha gave Alice's forearm a friendly squeeze. 'That is incredible.'

'Do you mean that?'

'It was one of the reasons why my grandmother got so involved with the park in the first place, she wanted to save those brumbies.'

'Really?'

'My grandmother made Walt, the old ranger, look after them too. I know a lot of people who'll back you if you do. They'll even lend a hand in getting them out of the park, as long as those brumbies go to a good home.'

'They will. Once I get the fencing done.'

'I can round up a bunch of drovers who'll gladly volunteer to do it. Hey, the Station Hand himself will do it.'

'Ron?'

'You bet. And I know the name of some good fencers who'll do it cheaply for you, too.'

'I thought the locals hated everything except cattle.'

'Wild pigs. Definitely. Water buffaloes they may have issues with when they had that TB scare back in the day. But most of the old-school stockmen have broken in a brumby or two in their time. Your sanctuary will be a wonderful addition to Elsie Creek. When are you going to announce it?'

'I've got to get it past my boss first. He's not impressed with me, not after the house.' She hadn't even emailed her boss about the poachers, trying to avoid the backlash, preferring to look for answers she knew the honourable horrible Harold was going to ask. She'd do it tomorrow.

'I'll keep your business quiet until you're ready to go public. And don't worry about the locals calling you the *new* ranger. They do that because they don't know you. My advice, Alice, don't be a stranger. There's no harm having a beer once a week to say g'day. They're just looking for a connection, that's all.'

Alice looked around the bar, in a town where the locals chose to create a national park they could enjoy. It wasn't picked by some politician in some office in parliament to make themselves look good. They cared about the park, like she did. 'I might just do that.'

'Who knows, you might find someone to date.' Samantha winked, sharing that wry grin.

Alice shook her head. Why bother with cowboys, when she'd been with Stewart, who was exactly the top-shelf, A-grade, el-primo male she'd always thought him to be. Except he was leaving.

Unless she spoiled him the way Krissie suggested?

Twenty-three

Inside the small operating theatre, machines beeped steadily indicating a healthy heart, even if the patient's stomach was spilling in a mesh of blood and organs across the operating table, that Stewart was busily putting back together.

The operating theatre doors opened, and with gloved hands raised, Doctor Thomas Mannen walked in. 'I'm here.'

Stewart nodded at his father.

'Is this the ringer who danced with a mickey bull?'

'I have no idea what you just said, Dad.' Considering his father had come from a land of peak-hour traffic jams, suit and ties, boardroom meetings and golfing dates, he doubted anyone from the city who knew the senior Doctor Mannen would recognise Thomas today.

'A ringer is the Territory's name for—'

'I really don't care. Suction … The bull's horns just missed this patient's liver.'

Thomas inspected the wounds. 'He's very lucky.'

'He is, considering we've got a punctured lung, perforated bowel, and four broken ribs.'

'Hmm … Reckon he'll make it.'

'Once he's fully recovered, he can ride that bull if he wants to.'

'If it hasn't ended up as today's steak, already.'

Stewart winced, not minding Alice's stance on vegetarianism.

As they worked on the patient, Stewart asked, 'Did you

check on the young snakebite patient?'

'Annie, yes. Anorexia is hard to diagnose medically.'

'I'd like to send her to Darwin for further evaluation. They have a psych team, and they can give her the results of her blood tests there.'

'Agreed. Will we be doing a patient evac on this guy? Maybe two for the price of one.'

'I'd rather not move this guy until he's stable, but I've got more of his blood type being brought in from Katherine to keep us going until we can send him on the evac.'

'What did that cost us?'

'Saline. We have a surplus.'

'Good.' Thomas gave a curt nod, while busily suturing the patient.

They worked in silence for a while, only asking for the tools needed as they operated.

'Alice took me to see Elsie Creek National Park,' Stewart said to his father.

'Really? You don't do dirt, son.'

Stewart frowned. A few weeks ago, that may have been true, but he'd done a lot with Alice, getting dirty with her from the moment they'd officially met in her collapsing house.

'Alice talked me into it. She said I had to see Elsie Creek National Park before I leave. I'm glad I went.' Seeing the park, the way Alice showed him, was incredible. It hadn't been a monotonous voice rehashing the same speech on some tour bus. He'd been privy to a unique world, with his own pretty terrific tour guide.

'Alice would've shown you the best places.'

'She did.' Stewart finished on the last suture, perfectly tying it off. *Snip*. 'And we're done.'

'Your stitching has always been extremely neat. I remember you doing stitches on oranges when you were a kid.'

That was the first time his father had ever mentioned

something from their past.

Returning his tools to the tray, he gave his recommendations for post-op treatment to the nurse and headed for the scrubbing room.

His father followed, stripping off his gloves and surgical cap. 'How long before your contract ends here?'

'Three weeks.'

'You should take off a week earlier, to settle in before you start at your next job.'

Stewart narrowed his eyes at his father. 'Why?'

'We'd owe you that, at least, based on the overtime you've done for us.'

Stewart lathered soap over his hands and arms then washed them under the cool stream of water gushing from the tap. He wouldn't mind another soak in the hot springs. Maybe he should invest in a hot tub—which he couldn't. Not in his apartment, and not here in this town when he was leaving.

Could it be real? A whole week knocked off away from this place of penance.

Then one thought came at him hard, as if whacking him over the head, sending a shock wave down his chest to squeeze his rib cage with fire. It was the thought of saying goodbye to Alice.

Idiot. He should never have started anything with Alice. Sure, he'd warned her, but he'd somehow forgotten to warn himself.

'Take two weeks if you want it,' said Thomas.

'I'll think about it.' What would he do with the time off? The only time he'd had a holiday was the past few days with Alice. A jam-packed tiny window of time filled with memories, where she'd effortlessly shared everything with him. How she'd skim her fingertips along his shoulders to comb though his hair. The way her mouth curved when she smiled, through to the laugh that had him dying to hear more. There was her intelligence, her skills, her confidence in the great outdoors, and her gentleness at finding all his buttons to peel back his walls. He should have never let her in.

They were friends. Just friends. So this was good. 'I'll take that week.'

Thomas nodded. 'I had a phone call yesterday, it was from your mother's husband.'

'Benjamin?' Stewart elbowed the lever to turn off the tap and shook the excess water free from his hands.

Thomas nodded, washing his hands in the next sink. 'So you applied to be on his surgical team?'

'I did. Did Benjamin call you for a reference?' He dried his hands with a towel.

Thomas nodded.

Stewart sat hard. 'Why? I didn't nominate you.'

'I am your senior.'

'You're rarely here for any of my surgeries.' Stewart oversaw the ordering, the budgets, the bartering for equipment, ran the clinics, and did the patient rounds, because Thomas was never here. Thankfully he had a great team that supported him. A team that was much smaller than his old surgical teams back home, who helped him run an entire hospital that looked after an area bigger than Melbourne's entire regional area.

Thomas dried his hands on the towel, tossing it into the waiting bin. 'Benjamin asked if you were qualified enough to be on his surgical team.'

'Of course, I am. I've always wanted this, ever since Ethan—' Jeez, a name he hadn't spoken of in years, now twice in two days. 'You had better not have screwed this up for me. How you got involved is beyond me, when you haven't been a part of my life for over twenty years. You should not have that power over it now, especially when I want this job. No, I deserve that job. Period.'

Thomas sighed as he sat next to Stewart. 'I know more than you realise, son. Your mother kept me updated on your school reports, photos, you name it. Then when you became a resident of the hospital, Benjamin updated me regularly, too.'

Stewart arched an eyebrow at his father. 'How well do you know Benjamin?'

'We were first-year interns together.' Thomas sat back, crossing his arms over his chest with his legs stretched out before him. 'In fact, Benjamin rang me asking permission to take your mother out on a date. We'd been divorced a year by then, but, as a friend, he had to ask.'

'I didn't know that.'

'We didn't want you to know.'

'Why?'

'Because you hated me. I don't blame you, because I hated myself, too, especially for being so ignorant of my son's health condition.'

'Is that why you walked out on your family?' Stewart's teeth gritted, remembering that god-awful day. His father gone, not long after his brother had died, leaving him with an empty soul filled with that foul taste of heartache. It was the day he'd put his childhood aside and picked up the medical books his father had left behind in his empty home office.

'As a doctor, and a father, I'd failed in the worst possible way.'

Stewart wasn't ready to forgive the man, either.

Then he realised something. 'You had me transferred here.' He thought it had been nothing but the rottenest of luck that he'd ended up out here. Only to discover his senior, his boss, was his estranged father. If he didn't have such an ironclad contract, he would've quit and run back to the airport to catch the first plane, train, or cattle truck out of here.

He stood and glared at his father. 'You would've known what was going on with the board. That's how you had Benjamin send me here.'

'Your mother had a hand in that.'

'Sure, Mother can be meddling, but not this. It was you

who had the sway with the hospital board, you used to play golf with them.'

'Priscilla wanted me to keep an eye on you.'

'How? When you're never here.' His father would rather mismanage his time to leisurely cruise around in his van, like some nomad, travelling to outback communities and cattle stations under the guise of medical clinics.

'Because you're managing this place so well, I don't need to be here. I told Benjamin they were idiots for letting a surgeon with your talent go.' Thomas pointed to the operating room empty of staff. 'In my day it didn't matter how appalling a surgeon's bedside manner was, not when they made up for it on the table.'

Stewart inhaled deeply to push down his anger, while his voice was cool and controlled. 'So, you didn't ruin it for me with Benjamin?'

'I told them that the skills you've learned here from the wide range of trauma surgeries is impressive. Look at today's surgery on that young man, who is expected a full recovery. Young Eskie, who had his hand crushed in the drafting fence, was a miracle. Your surgical performance rate and your survival stats, considering what little staff and equipment we have, is impressive.'

'It's not cardiothoracic.'

'We haven't done that kind of surgery in a while.'

'You didn't tell Benjamin that, did you?'

His father's silence was his answer.

'Gee, thanks, Dad.' Stewart shifted to the other side of the room, barely containing his anger.

'In Benjamin's hospital you know you'll be competing with the other surgeons trying to make a name for themselves, and a lot of the time you'll end up just assisting and not being the chief surgeon. But that's where you have to ask yourself, will you be wasting your skills as a specialist or are you better off sticking to trauma? Because we both haven't done any open-heart surgery in a while.' Thomas leaned over and rapped his knuckles on the wooden door jamb. 'Not that I want to.'

'I'm qualified for that job. Period.' He deserved it.

'Listen, son …' Hands on hips, Thomas stood before Stewart. 'Do you really want to go back to fixing up rich businessmen's hearts who'll never remember your name? Or do you want some kid who'll show off his scars to his friends speaking your name?'

'I might be a smart-arse who brags about his surgeries, but I never did this for the fame.' He'd done this for his brother, it was always about his brother. Only to discover he'd been played by his parents dictating his career path.

Well, he wasn't a kid anymore, this was his life and his career on the line. Period.

'I'm not like you, who does it for the fame and public recognition. You always did that. If it wasn't to brag to your cronies back in the hospital or give some speech in front of Mum's cocktail crowd, it's here. This town may see you as a hero, but back home, we know you left because you were ashamed your peers never looked at you the same way after you stuffed up with Ethan.' His teeth gritted, and he leaned forward. 'And that was all your fault.'

Thomas sat hard on the bench seat.

Holding the door open, Stewart paused to look at his father. 'You know, you never said sorry. Not once did you ever say sorry about not being there to save Ethan.' And he let the door swing behind him.

Twenty-four

Alice strolled into the pub's bottle shop, her second drive-through store for the day, where music blared from the speakers. It's where she found Luke feeding the ribbon-wearing water buffalo a bunch of flowers.

'Oh, hey, it's the new ranger. On foot.'

'Hi, Luke. And hello again, Cecil.'

Petite flower petals scattered across the buffalo's black lips like confetti, as he pressed his forehead gently against Alice's belly, demanding another ear rub.

'I see you found Cecil's sweet spot.' Luke tossed the flower stems into the bucket full of flowers. 'Here for some red wine?'

'I'm good. Samantha said you were the man to ask if you remember three guys in a white van, coming from the feed store.'

'Strangers?'

She nodded while rubbing the soft tips of Cecil's ears. 'All I know is they were in a white van, like the hardware's van, and may have visited a few times?'

Luke eyes squinted into the distance as if digging deep into his memory banks.

Then he started nodding as his smile grew. 'I remember. It was an old white tradies van, a Ford Econovan, with a roof rack carting nets. It had three guys who bought three cartons of beer, ice for their esky, and a bottle of rum. One of them had a thing for the chilli beef jerky, he cleaned us out.' He pointed to his wall of fridges, where a small counter held a display of chips, beer nuts and jerky.

'What sort of nets were they carrying? Being a keen barra fisherman, you'd know.' She'd met Luke on the water a few times over the years, he was one of the rare ones who bothered to smile and chat with her.

'That's why I remember those guys. I was worried they'd use that net to block off the rivers.'

Alice arched an eyebrow.

'Don't stress, Ranger, they weren't here for the fishing. They were carting a much finer net than fishermen use. They were crop nets.'

'Is that like a bird net?'

Luke nodded. 'I asked them about it, and they said it was to cover some crops to protect them from the birds.'

'Like what?'

'Rambutans. Carambolas mostly. I know a few farmers who net their crops from birds. My grandma has me annually hauling out nets to cover our fruit trees. Our net is much finer, it's like an anti-aphid net to stop insects.'

'I didn't realise there were so many types of nets. What was this net like?'

'It wasn't one net, it was an entire roll of netting material, about the average crop roll size, which is about six by a hundred metres.'

Her stomach squeezed as if sucker punched. How many more traps were out there?

Cecil raised his head to sniff at her chin. She had to step back from the potential tongue lick from the beast. But it helped lift the mood.

'Did they say where they were going with that roll of netting material?' *A freaking hundred-metre net.*

'Nope. But they weren't any commercial farmers I know, they were just passing through.'

'Next time they do come through, any chance you could get their number plate for me? Please.' Then she could pass it on to Porter at the police station.

'If we're talking nets, and you doing what you do, Ranger, are you worried about poachers in the park?'

'I'm just doing some digging, that's all. But I'd appreciate it if you kept an eye out.'

'Consider it done. Hey, did you find those whiprays I was telling you about?'

'I did, thank you. That's five areas you've told me where they are now. We've got a healthy population.'

'Like you said, Ranger, they're a good sign our waterways are pristine. Those whiprays are now my lucky charm for fishing. Just don't tell anyone about that spot, coz that's my new secret fishing spot.'

'All good. Did you speak to your grandmother about Cecil visiting Iris at the hospital?'

'We visited Iris yesterday …' He exhaled heavily, shaking his head slowly. 'Iris didn't look good, but she asked my grandma to write out a eulogy. So Gran's been up all night, pressing her black clothes, planning funeral wreaths already.'

'Iris said you guys were close?'

'Iris was our neighbour for a long time, she was always at our family functions and Christmas, but how she was yesterday …' He patted Cecil's back with long, slow strokes. 'Gran made sure we said our goodbyes.'

Alice gazed at the sky, while the buffalo lapped up his head massage. Did she take her drone out and scour the park for more poaching traps? Or did she complete the last request for a ninety-four-year-young friend?

She didn't want to say goodbye to another dear friend, not when there was a hole in her heart from saying goodbye to a little joey.

But Iris was on limited time.

'Is it too late to do it now? So Iris can watch the sunset with Cecil.'

Luke's smile grew across his deeply tanned features. He was a popular guy among the locals. It was easy to see why, with his handsome smile full of fun and mischief. 'Want me to load Cecil into the trailer? You can drive him there, right now.'

'Yes, please.'

'Where is your ute?'

'Over at the feed store. I'll be right back.' She bolted across the road, dragging out her phone.

'Hi, Alice, you've got perfect timing. I've just finished my surgery,' said Stewart over the phone.

'Was it a success?'

'Normally this is the part where I'd tell you I'm a genius ...' But he sighed heavily, with a level of sadness in his voice. 'It now depends on the patient. He's stable, but not stable enough to send him to the ICU in Darwin just yet. So, I'll be on call tonight.'

What's new, the guy was always on call. 'You're not feeling guilty for having a day off, are you?' Because he didn't sound happy.

'No. Although, it feels like decades since we were soaking in those hot springs. I could really handle them about now.'

Hmm? How could she remedy that? Should she try Krissie's tactic of spoiling the guy?

'What are you doing? Why do you sound out of breath?'

'I'm running to my ute.'

'Where are you?'

'In town. I'm loading Cecil onto a trailer for sunset. For ...' She didn't want to say it.

'Do you want me to get Iris ready?'

'Could you, please?'

'I was going to suggest it. I saw her earlier. You'd better prepare yourself, Alice. Iris is in the final stages of organ failure.'

'What does that mean?'

'Her body is shutting down. And we have to respect her wishes for the *Do Not Resuscitate* order.'

She fumbled in her step, as her heart ka-thumped slowly,

as if full of sludge and heartbreak. 'How long have we got?' Her throat was tight, with tears threatening to form, as she fumbled with her car keys.

'I can't answer that. But I can get Iris ready.'

'Thank you. I'll see you soon.' Back in the driver's seat, starting the engine, she nodded at Speedy eagerly waving with her softball glove, standing alongside the Flynn brothers closing the hardware store.

Alice drove the ranger's ute across the road, then around the back of the pub, where Billy and Luke were loading Cecil onto a low car-trailer with secure rails along the sides, making it perfectly safe for carting around a buffalo.

On the pub's back lawns, under the shade of the palm trees, Krissie and Sienna sat at the picnic tables, holding up their champagne glasses in a wave. Behind them stood the boxing ring, with ringside seats being built by a group of men who'd paused to watch.

Alice hated being the centre of attention while reversing up the trailer, before effortlessly hitching it onto the back tow ball of her ute.

'You're quick, I was going to help with that,' said Billy.

'Not my first rodeo.' She plugged in the trailer's lights, trying to avoid the grouch.

'Give my best to Iris for me?' Billy removed his fancy felt hat, putting it over his heart. 'It's a sweet thing you're doing, Alice. Really sweet. And I'm sorry for being a grump earlier.'

Did Samantha, the cagey publican, have a chat with Billy already?

'I'm not the bad guy, Billy.'

He gave a meek shrug. 'You should meet the real bad guys, the outback mafia.'

'Who?'

'Billy's talking about the Triple Js,' said Luke, shutting the trailer's cage door shut. 'They're also known as the *knights of the round card table*. They meet regularly at the hardware store to cheat at cards.'

'You're welcome to join us, Alice.'

'Thanks, Billy. I might one day when I've got time.' But she was running out of time today. 'We good?' She asked Luke.

Luke hoisted his bucket of flowers into the back of her ute. 'Cecil's ready to roll.'

'Thanks, guys.' Back in the driver's seat, the powerful diesel engine didn't miss a beat, towing a hefty twelve-hundred-kilo water buffalo down the main street of town.

Cecil's ribbons flew, with his head raised, wearing a wide smile like a cattle dog lapping up the wind in his face. Cecil was quite the spectacle.

Except the locals frowned at her, the park ranger, towing their favourite water buffalo. They looked at her like she was stealing Cecil for all the wrong reasons—especially when water buffaloes weren't allowed in the park.

Oh, joy, I'm the bad guy again.

Twenty-five

With a bucket of flowers in one hand, Alice led the water buffalo onto the hospital's helipad, which sat at the back of the tiny bush hospital.

Seated in her wheelchair, Iris pulled down her oxygen mask. 'There he is.'

Cecil snorted, forgetting all about the flowers, to suddenly skip and wag his tail like an excited puppy. He rushed towards the frail woman wearing a beanie, with her favourite crocheted blanket over her knees.

'Easy, Cecil.' Alice pushed against the beast, worried he'd hurt Iris.

'He'll be fine, dear. Remember, Cecil visits the school daily to eat the children's lunches.' Iris's wrinkles shifted as she smiled, her eyes sparked to life. 'Hello, my dear old friend.'

Cecil, with his shiny black nose, sniffed at Iris's open hand, then at her beanie, her neck, her arm, down to where the IV was in her wrist. And then he held himself, head down, close enough for Iris to lean forward and hug him.

'I didn't know Cecil could be so gentle,' said Stewart, carrying two coffee mugs. 'Got us a chair and coffee. I know you only have one, but ...'

'Perfect.' Alice held her hands over his. 'It's been a long day for both of us.' He nodded as she took her coffee, and she sipped on the rich, creamy caffeine that flowed smoothly over her tongue and coated her throat. It was sublime. 'Be careful, Doctor, you keep making me coffee like this and I'll be fighting my addiction all over again.'

She sat beside Iris who was tenderly stroking the neck of the buffalo.

'Luke gave us a whole bucket of flowers to feed Cecil.' Alice passed a bunch of daisies to Iris.

'Thank you for doing this for me. You were always so thoughtful, dear. Both of you. At my age I couldn't ask for better friends.' Iris then smiled up at Cecil. 'And you were my daily treasure. Thank you, my friend.' She kissed the buffalo's forehead, his dark eyes looking at her with such a deep sorrow, Alice sniffed to hold back her own tears.

Alice didn't want to say goodbye.

Stewart rubbed her shoulder while sipping on his coffee. They watched Iris feed the buffalo as the sun dropped lower in the large sky free from clouds. Soft shades of pink and pastel orange emerged on the horizon, blending with the lingering rich blue of the daytime sky. It was a serene backdrop, casting a gentle glow over the vast landscape.

'It's a busy place back here at the helipad,' said Iris.

'It's a ground-level view of what I used to see from the old ranger station's house.' It was a great view of the police and fire stations backing onto the tiny airport that was just a runway with a tall tower over its office that stood beside the hangar's curved roof.

'What are the firemen doing?' Stewart pointed across the helipad to the rear of the fire station. 'I didn't know we had that many full-time firemen.'

'We don't. They're the local volunteers, running their weekly drills. It's more of a social thing for those guys, though. It reminds me of a sports practice.'

Behind the fire station, over a dozen locals were dressed in protective firefighting jackets and helmets. Jax, their fire chief, had created an obstacle course where his volunteers started with rolling up the long fire hoses, then moved on to climb ladders, and then drag dummies a certain distance, while racing against each other to beat the clock. Their laughter and jovial shouts carried across the tarmac. As well as the smell of fried onions being cooked on their barbecues by Lucy, Jax's partner, who ran the local coffee van.

A small red plane, with a straw broom painted on its underbelly, flew low and fast overhead with frightening speed, making them sit back in their seats. It stirred up the dust mixed with faint exhaust fumes to blend with the aroma of dry grass. It flew in a wide circle over the town, the train station, then back over the stockyards to land on the runway.

'Iris, that's Monet and her plane she calls Gertrude.' Alice pointed at the small red plane taxiing down the runway. The twin propeller engine stilled, the door opened, and a petite ash-blonde jumped out, wearing a pair of aviator sunglasses that made her look effortlessly cool.

'I know Monet,' said Stewart. 'She's taken me on a few flights for medical emergencies. Marcus told me Monet was a big help to the police at Christmas after that cyclone.' Stewart pointed to the roof of the police station. 'Can you see the roof, Iris?' The police station roof was covered with a comic-book image of a masked burglar being captured by a policeman with a very muscular arm.

'My word, I'd heard about that, that roof ...' Iris could barely lift her arm. Her breathing was shallower and her eyelids were heavy, as if fighting to stay awake.

'That's the strong arm of the law. It ticked Marcus off when he saw that,' explained Stewart.

'Who—who ...'

'Who did it?' Stewart shrugged. 'I think Marcus knows who the culprit was because he stopped searching. He might not have made any arrests, but he's allowed the hardware store to sell spray paint cans again. You should see the other roofs, Iris ...'

While Stewart explained, Alice sat very still. Her lips pursed in a white line. She'd suck at poker.

'Alice?'

She just couldn't face him, preferring to look for a cloud

in the sky, to admire the wildflowers and individual grass blades, right down to the ants.

'Do you know who graffitied the police station's roof?'

'I can't tell you.'

'Why not?' His eyebrow arched.

'You're friends with a cop.'

'Don't you consider Marcus a friend too?'

'Kind of. It's more of a professional business thingy. I haven't had beers with the guy like he does with others out the back of the police station.' Where Porter was currently pacing backwards and forwards, with beer can in hand. Beside him was Tanisha, the vivacious Aboriginal community police officer, wagging her finger at Porter, like a mother to a child.

'We … we … we won't say anything.' Iris melted into her seat, tugging at her crochet blanket of many colours.

Stewart gently placed the oxygen mask over Iris's mouth and nose. 'Have you solved the riddle of who is this town's roof tagger? How come you know when you're always working at the park? And how come no one else knows?'

'No one asked me. But that reminds me, I have a snake kit I'd appreciate you giving to Sienna.'

'Who?'

'Sienna. The pretty blonde who brought in the snakebite patient from Danbunnan Station. There's a young jackaroo out there who rescues injured snakes. I want to help him.' It's what she did. 'I'll leave it next to your coffee machine for your morning rounds.'

'Sure. But you didn't answer our question.' He slid his arm around Iris's shoulders. Both looking at her expectantly.

'Are you ganging up on me?' She gasped in mock horror.

'Spill your secret, Alice. We're waiting.' Stewart wore a comical grin, his eyes bright and playful, while Iris's were dimming, and cloudy above that oxygen mask.

Alice leaned forward and spoke in a hushed tone. 'It was Monet.'

'That Monet?' Stewart pointed to the bush pilot working with Mickey unloading assorted cargo off the red plane, filling up the trailer he towed behind his nifty buggy. 'How did she do it?'

'Monet's got rock climbing rigging she used to climb onto the roof, along with a bag of spray paint cans, and a plan she had on her tablet. It was quite clever, really. Monet marked out the roof like a grid, where she only had to do a small section at a time, as if completing a puzzle. It took her a few hours.'

'You saw her? Where were you?'

'Sitting on the front landing of my old house, hiding behind Penny the money tree, while bottle-feeding Melody.'

As the shadows across the artwork lengthened, they kept a vigil beneath the sun, tipping on the curve of the distant outback horizon.

Then Cecil raised his head and bellowed out a deep mournful cry that echoed like a horn. It was so full of sorrow it made Alice sit up with a cold chill of dread washing over her.

It made everyone in the area from the airport tarmac to the fire station all stop and look over.

'Stewart?' Alice stood.

Iris's hand had gone limp in hers, her head slumped forward.

'No, no, no.' She cupped Iris's cheek. She wanted to gently shake her friend to wake up. 'Iris? … IRIS!'

But Stewart was beside her, pulling her back. 'Let her go, Alice.'

'No. Iris was just talking. She was just—'

'She's gone.' Grabbing her by the shoulders he made her focus on him. 'Iris is at peace.'

As Stewart organised the medical team to attend to Iris, Alice approached the water buffalo. Her vision blurred by the tears, their salt bitter on her tongue as she heaved the air in gulps trying to stop her own wail of pain.

She used her shirtsleeve to clean the black sides of the water buffalo. With the chunks of chalk Speedy had given her earlier that day, she wrote the words she never wanted to write. But it's what Iris had requested in their many discussions:

Thank you, Elsie Creek. I'll miss you all, Iris Rosewood. R.I.P.

'Off you go, Cecil.' She gently tapped his rump to let the walking billboard do his thing.

Cecil's bulky head hung low, as did his tail wrapped in ribbons. His heavy hoof steps echoed as he crossed the helipad where the bush pilot, Monet, stood with Mickey, who'd removed his cap and bowed his head.

Cecil's slow march approached the police station, where Porter and Tanisha stood out front and saluted.

At the neighbouring fire station, the volunteers lined the small road, their fire helmets held against their chests. They stood with bowed heads and waited, watching the buffalo turn right and headed towards the town.

Along main street, the traffic slowed, and the pub became silent as their patrons spilled onto the street, where many men removed their hats and lowered their heads in silence.

The train tooted in the distance as Cecil raised his large head to listen to the rattle of the carriages riding the rails.

The blue ribbons wrapped around his horns drooped, as the words of such sad news made even the breeze become still. With a swish of his tail, he strolled toward the sinking sun on the distant horizon where it swallowed the never-ending outback highway. Elsie Creek may be just a speck on a map, but it was a place that someone as special as Iris called home. It was a place where you mattered, no matter who you were. It was a place where someone as special as Iris was going to be missed.

Twenty-six

Grief sucked. Old age sucked. And her boss sucked.

Still lying in bed, Alice scowled at the message on her phone from her boss telling her to go to Limmen Park, to hassle the fishermen on the Cox River.

'Not going.' She was done playing the bad guy, dumping her phone onto her bedside table.

'Not going where?' Stewart asked, carrying a steaming cup of tea.

'The honourable horrible Harold wants to send me to another park.'

'Is your boss a park ranger?'

'No. According to the other rangers, Harold Grimsby is a seat-filling desk jockey. One who does the barest minimum of work while biding his time for his hefty government superannuation payout. What's this?'

'Tea. Of some kind.' He gently passed her the teacup with its matching saucer. 'I make coffee, so consider yourself lucky because I don't do this for anyone—not my patients, or my staff. But, as you're usually gone by the time I get up, I thought …' He gave an awkward shrug.

She'd never seen the guy do awkward, especially when he was normally loaded with double doses of confidence.

'I feel so privileged. Do you know what tea leaves you used?'

'Nope. It's from the green tin you use in the morning.'

'Green tea.'

'So, I did good, huh?' His smile was brazen. 'I'll admit, I googled the instructions that said to ensure it had fresh boiling water and one of your fancy spoon scoops per cup. You said some teas deserved a bit of ceremony to them. So …' He bowed as if meeting the queen.

The laugh spilled freely from her chest. 'Thank you.'

Stewart sat on her bed. 'Are you going to be okay today?'

Truthfully, she was physically and mentally drained, after being a blubbering mess over Iris passing. Stewart had been there for her, walking her home and never leaving her side. Only to have her cling to him, kiss him, to then tear off his clothes. She'd practically jumped his bones, in a desperate need of something physical and good, to take away the heartache. She needed to feel alive.

But in the harsh light of day, she felt like she'd been a very needy, greedy animal. Dropping her head, the heat rose in her cheeks. 'Sorry about last night.'

'Hey …' He lifted her chin with his fingertip. 'Don't be ashamed, Alice. Last night was amazing.' It said so in his eyes, clear blue and caring. 'Your romance novels have taught you well.'

She spluttered out a laugh over her teacup as he grinned.

Hold on. Wasn't she supposed to be spoiling the man who'd brought her a cup of tea in bed?

Were Krissie's words of bar-room wisdom working in reverse?

She sipped on her tea. It was weak, or as her father would call it, *chatter-water weak*. But Stewart had tried, and she wasn't going to tell him any different. 'Thank you for the tea. No one's ever done that for me.'

'Well …' Didn't his smile just shine.

'Are you off to work?'

'I've got rounds to do. Are you working today?'

'I'm thinking of chucking a sickie.'

'You should take a day off.' He then took a deep breath and announced, 'Like I'm taking the week off before I start my new job.'

'Huh?' Her eyes rapidly blinked as if full of grit. Stewart was leaving early? How many days did they have left?

'I haven't had many days off in this town, and my father's insisting on it. Like I'm insisting that you take the time off. It's called bereavement leave, and you were Iris's personal representative.' He gave her hand a gentle squeeze.

'Does that mean I have to sign papers and stuff up at the hospital?'

Stewart nodded. 'Did Iris make any funeral arrangements with you?'

'All booked with the local church. Iris said she'd planned it all out with her neighbour, Esther, years ago.' She slumped back into her pillow, the burden of grief was mining all the joy in her soul. 'It still sucks … How do you cope when life and death are part of your job?'

'It's why I try so hard to save whoever comes across my operating table. Sometimes you have to let them go, knowing you did what you could. It used to eat me up, too, blaming the doctor, the conditions, my lack of skills allowing patients to pass.' He raked his fingers through his hair. 'It was so freaking unfair. And it is. My mentor told us we had to manage a level of disconnect to keep moving forwards, especially with our jobs.'

'I wish I was like that sometimes, to live in a state of disconnect.'

'No, you don't. Not you.' He gently cupped her face to tenderly brush her cheek with his thumb. 'Too many doctors live like that now, we're so clinical.'

'What does that make me? An emotional mess.' She rubbed her puffy eyes, all cried out.

'The best advice given to me was to acknowledge the loss, then seek the comfort of someone you cared about. Which is what we did last night, together.' He stared at her for a long second, staring deeper than anyone had ever looked, in a way that went past her flaws. Alice wanted to hide under her pillow.

'I've never been like that, not the way I was with you last night, where we both were someone's comfort, Alice.'

Surely not? The guy had been engaged to another woman, the hand doctor he'd mentioned.

'But you must remember, Iris was ninety-four. She was ready.'

'I know. It still sucks.'

'That it does.' He leaned over and kissed her forehead. 'Come find me later if you're staying home today. Say, about lunchtime?'

'Any lunch requests? Or are you going to make me eat the hospital food?'

'Not when I appreciate the flavours from your flourishing totem-pole garden. I'll leave it up to the chef to surprise me.'

'I can do that.' She saw what he was doing, helping her to move forward because that's what the world did, it kept on moving. 'Oh, and don't forget to take that snake kit.'

'Now you've got me playing delivery boy?'

'I told Sienna to bring you a coffee for your delivery fees.'

'I've trained you well. But you still can't touch my coffee machine. Wouldn't want you getting addicted.' He winked at her before leaving the bedroom.

For some time, she remained sipping on her tea. Did she dare crack open the cover on a book and avoid the day?

Dragging herself out of bed and into the kitchen, she flopped into the chair at her desk, and lifted the lid of her laptop.

In the nearby fish tank, PP the pig-nosed turtle was pigging out on a plump strawberry, to look up at her before chowing down on some tender celery leaves. Stewart was spoiling the turtle too.

She tapped out an email message to her boss:

To the honourable horrible Harold Grimsby …

Dear Dickhead,

I wish to inform your small monkey brain to shove your

request—to go play the bad-guy in another national park—up your pompous posterior! As the Chief Park Ranger for Elsie Creek National Park, I will be remaining at Elsie Creek National Park and will no longer be available for you to pimp me out for last-minute work orders. Instead, I'm taking a few days' personal leave because of the unfortunate passing of a wonderful member of my family.

Iris was family. She was Alice's first friend in Elsie Creek, who would have had a good giggle over Alice's email.

Even though her finger hovered over the send button, Alice wasn't stupid. She hit delete, then tapped out a very brief email. It was none of Harold's business what she did in her personal time.

In the living room, she flung back the curtains to flood the room with light. The sky was a soft blue at the beginning of a glorious new day, but she just wasn't feeling the joy with Iris gone.

Melody, the wallaby, was back where she belonged, and Stewart would soon leave to live on the other side of the country. All of them were leaving her alone. They were disconnecting from her.

But she also understood a gift when she saw it. Her time with Iris had been truly amazing. So too with Melody. And Stewart was still here.

Stewart who'd seen her at her worst, covered in dirt and sweat in the park. He'd rescued her from a falling house, to then stitch her up and allow her to move into his house. Even though she'd tried to avoid him that first week, it was impossible when he'd check on her stitches while she'd been at her most vulnerable. He'd listened to her rambling nonsense as they walked Melody along the sides of the road under moonlight. He'd held her at her blubbering ugly-crying finest, where she'd revealed parts of herself she didn't know existed as they lay tangled in her sheets, communicating to each other in ways that didn't involve words.

Alice wasn't afraid to fall in love. She was just afraid that no one would fall in love with her and her flaws.

After the past few weeks sharing a roof with the guy, it was impossible to stop picturing a future of waking up beside him every day for the rest of her life. Life was precious, it was a gift, and so was Stewart.

Maybe she should heed Krissie's suggestions about spoiling the guy so that he'd never leave. But now that Stewart was leaving a week earlier, Alice had limited time left to convince the man who had her heart to stay.

Twenty-seven

Stewart peeked at the name flashing on his phone's screen as it rang.

'Hello, Mother.' With phone pressed to his ear, he strolled down the hospital corridors and headed for the nearest exit, to blink at the harsh daylight bouncing off the helipad. He hadn't been out here since Iris had passed.

'Hello, darling. I'm just letting you know the cleaners have finished, and the windows in your apartment look absolutely stunning.'

'You're at my place?' He hadn't thought of the place, not with so much happening this past week.

'I had to inspect their work. Are you sure I can't talk you into a painter? Or some soft furnishings, something —'

'We've had this discussion before, Mother. No. Period.'

'When are you flying in?'

'Um ...' He hadn't even booked his flight. 'I've been busy.'

'I'll arrange it. Tell me how to get you out of there.'

'Charter plane to Darwin, then a direct flight to Melbourne, please.' He was used to his mother doing it for him. Not that he wasn't capable, it just made her feel better.

'Now, I'm having a few friends over for your welcome home dinner.'

'Who?' He didn't have friends in Melbourne anymore, not since they'd ostracised him. His supposed friends avoided being seen with someone who'd upset one of the hospital's major donors.

'Benjamin, of course.'

'Well, you are married to the guy.'

'And darling Olivia.'

'Liv, huh? You know we broke up, Mother.' They both didn't think a long-distance relationship would work when their relationship revolved around the hospital. His entire relationship with Olivia was medicine related, it never involved camping trips, totem-pole gardening tips, or learning how to grow grass.

That's right, he had a lawn.

And liked it.

Rather than sit around and grieve for Iris, Alice had him digging dirt and spreading grass seed late into the night. They'd both been covered in dirt, exhausted, yet filled with pride, sitting back, drinking beer, admiring what they'd done.

With his first coffee of the day, he'd step out the back door to inspect his little dirt patch, where new shoots poked through the heavy dew. Then at sunset, he'd admire the way the sprinkler would softly rain like liquid diamonds over a bare patch of raked dirt Alice had brought home in one of her many trailers.

Sure, it might be nothing more than a fine layer of lime-green hair across the topsoil, but he never thought he'd get a kick out of lawn, considering he'd grown up in an apartment, without a garden. Now they had two, a high-tech totem-pole vegetable garden and a lawn. Even though Alice was growing the grass for future wallaby rescues, he had visions of making it his own private putting green.

He tapped his head to wake up. He was meant to be making arrangements to leave, not thinking about lawn.

He was also trying to distance himself from Alice. But he couldn't, not when it was so easy to be with her. Finding himself crossing whatever distance stood between them, be it the corridor, the kitchen, the car park, just to share the same space as her. They were two halves making a whole that made perfect sense to him. And he was leaving.

Alice knew he was leaving.

They both knew it was impossible for him to stay.

He also couldn't ask her to come with him, not when she was following her dream, while he chased his dream job. Alice understood that.

Yet, they were acting as if he was staying.

Alice kept making his meals, leaving *'eat this, drink that'* notes in the fridge with strange doodles that made him smile. For dinner he'd been helping her, learning how to cook, even taking turns to stack the dishwasher. Even though they had no Melody to watch over, they still walked the road at night under twilight and talked.

'When are you expected at the hospital?' His mother asked over the phone.

Stewart looked back at the building he'd practically lived in since his arrival, then kicked a stone across the deserted helipad. 'I'm having a break.' It had been a slow day. Missing Iris, who he would've shared morning tea treats with, made by Alice who usually worked away from sunrise to sunset.

Yet, Alice had taken the week off to organise Iris's affairs.

Did he dare go home to share lunch with the lady?

'I'm talking about Melbourne, darling.'

'I can escape this place in eight days, where I'm hoping to front the hospital's CEO and start work.' There's no way he'd be able to sit around moping for a week in his apartment. He wanted to show those who'd judged him wrongly that he was worthy of that job—*if* he got the job.

'Hmm, you'll need travel time. Time to settle in and time for dinner with me.' Priscilla's voice was pre-occupied, as if jotting down his travel plans in one of the small notepads she always kept on hand.

'So, Mother, is it true you pulled some strings to send me here, to have Dad watch over me?' Who he hadn't seen since his dummy spit.

'Did Thomas tell you that?'

'Dad also told me how you'd keep him updated on what I

was doing. Is that true?'

For a woman who could effortlessly play her part as the perfect hostess at her many fundraising functions, controlling conversations with a cocktail glass in one hand, while speed texting in French with the other, Priscilla went considerably quiet.

'Mother …'

Her sigh was long and loud. 'Don't hate me, darling. I only wanted you to be safe.'

'I get that.'

'Even though Thomas has his faults, he is your father. Are you two talking yet?'

'Nope.' And he doubted that bridge would mend in the days they had left. 'Benjamin was more of a father to me. And this is where you tell me about the job.'

'No.'

'Come on, Mother. Who helps you hide your secrets?'

'Only my shopping secrets, which comes with some silly lecture like last time.'

'You'd bought a hundred tea towels—when you've never washed a dish in your life—making me hide them in the attic with the other things you bought for charity.'

'The accountant said I needed to. I kept the receipts. Oh, I must get Lucella to deliver those goods to the charity store. Benjamin will have my head if he sees them.'

'You don't have to do it, Mother.'

'Darling, when you live with superheroes who perform miracles on people, you try to do what you can to help those who need it.'

'I know.' His mother may seem like a socialite snob to some but, underneath, Priscilla really was a softie. Who was also really good at changing the subject. 'I haven't got the job, have I?'

'I'm trying, darling, but Benjamin is in a bit of a pickle.'

'How so?'

'It's that pesky CEO who's saying you haven't done as

many open-heart surgeries as the other applicants. You may have to start back at intern level.'

His jaw ticked as heated anger crept up his spine. The nail-scratching BS politics of the hospital he was returning to was already beginning. It was something he hadn't missed about that hellhole of judgement and dictatorship. But he'd grind his teeth until he had none left just to get this job.

'That's ridiculous.' Why should he play at an intern's level when he was practically a CEO running this place?

'Benjamin says the same, and he is trying, darling. Your father's report told of the many wonderful things you've done. Olivia explained that hand surgery you did on that young man. She said it was impressive work. Maybe you should work with Olivia.'

'I want cardio. Period.' It was always cardio—to have no child suffer the way his brother did.

'I know, darling, I know. They haven't made their decision yet, so I have my fingers crossed. A girl from my Pilates class knows a tarot-reading white witch, and she's going to do some candle magic wish for you.'

'Seriously?' He laughed at the absurdity of it. Reminding him of Alice's money tree she called Penny.

'I know, but it's all in good fun.'

Jenny waved at him from the hospital doors.

'I've got to go, Mother.'

'Okay, darling. I love you. I can't wait to hug my boy, which will be soon.'

He smiled at the phone, missing her too. 'What's up, Jenny?'

'Do you feel like doing an outpatient call?' She held up the chunky medical backpack as he followed her down the corridors towards the main entrance that was the hospital's hub.

'What about the ambulance?' Through the closed glass doors of the main entrance, he could see the ambulance parking bay was empty.

'It's gone to meet the transport from Darwin hospital. They're bringing back your patient from ICU.'

'The one ripped up by the bull?'

Jenny nodded. 'Oh, and we're finally getting that ECMO machine you ordered on that transport.'

'Seriously?' He'd ordered the heart-and-lung-bypass machine the first week he'd arrived. A clear demonstration of how few open-heart surgeries he'd done when the ECMO was one of the essential tools. No wonder they weren't jumping at the chance to give him the specialist's job.

'Your father is out at Avallon Downs checking on one of Dustin Must's retired station hands complaining of chest pains. Thomas has decided to give all those retired stockmen a medical check-up. He won't be back until tomorrow.'

Typical of his father to find an excuse to stay away.

'You know I'd love to go on this outpatient's call—' Jenny held out the pack to Stewart with a bottle of water.

'Why aren't you?' Because Jenny was usually the first to race out the door, with a medical kit under her arm.

'Verily's waters have broken. She's on her way in.'

'Which leaves me.' The guy who didn't go anywhere unless it was absolutely necessary. The last time he did this was on an outback treasure hunt with Marcus. He hoisted the heavy pack over his shoulder. 'Where am I going?'

'This gentleman will show you. Their friend is hurt at their campsite in the park. Sadly, you'll be on your own, as Porter is out on patrol, Jax is managing a brush fire, and with Alice on bereavement leave, I didn't want to bother her.'

The main doors of the hospital slid open and Alex rushed through with a red-faced Verily holding her belly. Following them was the entire softball team and their entourage of children wearing assorted coloured tutus.

Leading the charge was the scary mono-brow coach, wearing fluorescent green board shorts, a chunky chequered red flannelette shirt, with long brown and yellow football socks, complete with black thongs. It was Agnes Picket. 'THE

BABY IS COMING. I REPEAT THE BABY IS COMING. THIS IS NOT A DRILL, PEOPLES.'

'*Agnes!* This is a hospital and not a softball field,' said Jenny. 'Verily and Alex, this way. Everyone else stays in the waiting room or goes home.'

But they all wanted to stay, talking at once.

'Are you the doctor?' A guy appeared at Stewart's shoulder.

'I'm Doctor Mannen. Are you taking me to the patient?' The place was pandemonium. There were softball players and kids in tutus everywhere.

'I'm Blackie. My mate Vinnie's in the car park waiting for us.'

Stewart hesitated. He knew Alex wanted him to stay and help with the baby. But Alex was busy with Verily who was huffing and puffing the Lamaze breathing techniques along with five other women, with the corridor filling with patients and visitors.

In his old hospital he wouldn't even be assigned to the maternity ward, he never went near it. Jenny knew what she was doing, no one would miss him if he ducked out for a bit. After all, he was leaving in a matter of days for the job he'd been training for his whole life.

It was a reminder to not make promises to patients who'd forget about him the minute the hospital's front doors closed behind them. And he would soon be returning to that revolving door of patients in a city where over five million people lived. 'Where's the patient?'

'Shina. Shane. When we first met him, the brudder had a black eye, so we called him Shina. This way, Doctor. Thanks for doing this.' Blackie led him into the bright sunshine, the heat of the day washing over them. 'You get the privilege spot. Air-con's good back there. And the man with the plan and the van is Vinnie.'

Stewart nodded at the driver as he climbed into the back of the white van, the door closing behind him. The lock came down and the driver peeled out of the car park.

'Where are we going?'

'The local national park,' said Blackie, from the passenger seat. 'Have you been there?'

'Once. Why couldn't you bring your friend in with you? You've got plenty of room in here to lay him down.' Even if it was full of assorted cages.

Blackie winced a little, scrubbing nails through his scruffy hair, while Vinnie pushed up his sunglasses and kept driving. 'Shina's got the type of accident that people may ask questions over.'

'Like who?'

'The police.'

'I'm a doctor.' He tapped the medical kit to make his point, the way Alice would tap the patch on her ranger's uniform sleeve.

'And park rangers.'

'What about the ranger?' Stewart frowned, surprised at how defensive he was over Alice. He gave the cages a closer look, to discover tucked in the corner behind his seat sat a large bag of birdseed.

No. It couldn't be. He couldn't have been that stupid.

Vinnie lowered his sunglasses at Stewart. 'Get comfy, Doc, because Shina has a bullet wound you need to fix.'

Twenty-eight

Alice parked her bulky work ute in the driveway and slid out of the cab. Juggling her keys in hand, she wove her way around the totem-pole garden brimming with assorted fruit and vegetables. The strawberries were particularly fragrant, red, and plump today, but she couldn't be bothered plucking one.

In through the back door, she dumped her bag on the chair in the kitchen, before flicking open the laptop sitting on her desk. There were a few emails from the honourable horrible Harold she didn't want to deal with, as well as from the university. Closing the lid, she ignored them all.

She looked at her latest book, sitting on her coffee table beside her favourite reading chair. She just couldn't find the energy to pick up a book and plonk herself down, like she normally did at the end of the day.

Because it wasn't the end of a working day.

Grief was an energy-sapping, mind-numbing vacuum. Made worse when she'd been listening to a lawyer with the drollest monotone. Only three people were requested to the reading of the will, where she'd found herself seated with Cecil's owner, Esther and her sparkly tiara, and her grandson, bottle-shop Luke. Alice had nearly fallen asleep with her eyes open—which Luke did—until the lawyer mentioned the money. It had Esther coughing so hard they had to get the octogenarian some water.

Because Iris was loaded.

And that generous, sweet soul, had given the bush

hospital a sizeable donation, with a request to build a garden for inpatients to enjoy. Iris also asked that a stash be set aside for her neighbour, Esther, to run some *secret sister project*—sealed inside an envelope that the lawyer gave to Esther who only stared at it with tears.

But what surprised Alice more was the sizeable chunk of change Iris had set aside for her new wilderness park. Iris had given her so much already, Alice was going to build a monument to her friend.

Out of habit, she flicked on the television set, which displayed the CCTV footage of the park, where the entire screen was divided into squares to show the many angles of the park.

She flicked on the kettle, opened the fridge, and just stared at it for who knows how long.

'This is ridiculous.' She had no energy, no excitement, no passion for anything lately—except to spoil Stewart. Oh, and PP, happily doing laps in his fish tank.

Her phone rang. Dragging it out from her pocket, it was her father calling. 'Hey, Dad.'

'Hey, Gumnut. Gotta sec?'

'What's up?'

'It's Melody's tracker. Have you looked at it lately?'

'Um, no. Why?' She lifted her laptop lid and tapped on the keys. 'No way. Melody's fifty kilometres away from the hot springs.'

A wallaby rarely travelled more than twenty kilometres in a day. But a wallaby carrying a six-month baby the size of Melody, wouldn't make half that distance. And that wallaby troupe normally stayed within their five-kilometre region where they flourished. Something had gone wrong. 'When did that happen?'

'According to the kid babysitting the project, middle of the night. Do you think an eagle has Melody? Because she's stopped in that position for a while now.'

A huge lump started to form in her throat, Alice struggled

to swallow. She couldn't handle any more bad news about something she cared about, not this soon after Iris passing. 'I hope not.'

'Me too. I know it's not a good time, but could you …'

'You don't need to ask, Dad. I'll call you as soon as I know more.' She slipped on her uniform, loading up the radio, plonking her hat on her head, then stuffing her work bag.

Alice turned on the handheld GPS tracker, then spread the park's map across the kitchen table to get an idea of the area Melody was in.

A crackling chill of ice ran down her spine, sending an electrified wave of shivers across her skin. *The poachers are back!*

Alice grabbed her laptop, dropping into her rocking chair, she tapped on the keyboard to get eyes on the area from that camera they'd set up. She hadn't had the TV on in days, not since Iris's funeral.

The TV displayed smaller square images of the park. The area where she'd found the poachers' nets with Stewart was clear.

But then something moved.

She zoomed in closer, tapping a few buttons to make it take up the entire space on the television screen.

There was a guy lying on a blue tarp in the shade. Behind him were cages of various birds and animals. Did they have Melody? Where was his vehicle?

Now standing before the large screen TV, she brought up every single camera she had on the park to scrutinise each square, showing a different area of the park. A few cars were parked by the waterfalls, a car was parked by the hiking trails picnic area. Regular traffic.

Then a white van peeled past one of the cameras.

Horrified, her eyes widened as she watched a young guy get out of the van to unlock one of the iron gates blocking a restricted area.

'They have a key!'

Bile burned the back of her throat, and with trembling fingers, she dialled the police station.

The recorded message came on: 'You've dialled Elsie Creek Police. As our operators are currently busy, please leave a message and we'll get back to you. In case of an emergency, please dial triple zero.'

Friggin' ferals!

The officers had to be out of range, which meant they could be anywhere in the thousands of kilometres that made up their outback region. While she managed only two hundred square kilometres of that territory that those pricks were stealing from!

The anger pricked at her skin as she watched the van pull up into the clearing.

The she gasped, dropping onto her haunches as if someone had pulled the floor out from beneath her.

It was Stewart, climbing out of the van, and at gunpoint. He stared at the camera with a pleading look. Pushed in the back, he was forced to head for the deep shade of the trees.

She rubbed her temple with eyes glued to the big screen TV, hoping this was a horror movie trick of the mind. But the time stamp on the big screen showed it was real-time.

And time was of the essence.

Without a thought, Alice ran, slamming the back door behind her.

Twenty-nine

'You're lucky the bullet went straight through and missed the major arteries, but you've lost a lot of blood.' Stewart bandaged up the patient's thigh, applying pressure over the wound. 'How soon can we get you to the hospital? I can clean that wound more thoroughly and apply some sutures. I'd like to start you on a course of antibiotics because you're at risk of getting infected.'

'Told you, Vinnie—we should have taken Shina in.' Blackie shook his head, assisting Stewart by holding up the IV bag, while Shina lay on the blue tarp.

Nearby, Vinnie dropped his cigarette butt into the dirt and ground it under his boot. 'Are we done?'

'Look, just drop Shina and me at the hospital. I won't say anything. I'm not a cop, I'm a doctor.' Hoping he'd proven himself by staying calm while focusing on his job, trying to ignore the handgun tucked into Vinnie's belt.

'It was an accident, Vinnie. I'll tell the cops I was hunting for pigs, that's all.' Shina then said to Stewart, 'I tripped over my own feet, and I had the gun on me.'

'Don't forget the part where you screamed louder than the gunshot, scaring off every bird for the next hundred k's.' Vinnie scowled. 'This trip was for Blackie, man.'

'I'm getting engaged.' Blackie grinned, shifting the saline bag to his other hand. 'I promised my girl a ring. But she's got expensive taste. You know how it is, Doc?'

'Um, sure?' If he kept playing nice, perhaps they'd return

him to the hospital, where normally he was the hero, not the hostage. 'My ex picked her own ring.'

'So has mine,' said Blackie. 'She's also told me what she wants for the wedding, and that's big bickies.'

'And we're all gonna sit in a knitting circle when we're old and grey telling our story to the people in matching jumpsuits in this place called prison, if we don't move.' Vinnie glared at his offsider. 'We need to fill our quota. All we've got is a dozen birds and a dumb wallaby and a joey.' He tapped his boot against the cage where the agile wallaby cowered in the corner with its back to them. 'But I know of a place where we can fill our order. I haven't scoped it out yet, but I've been told it's worth it.' Vinnie pulled out the map.

'What is it?' Blackie leaned in for a closer look.

'Apparently, it's some exclusive breeding ground for some very fine waterbirds. We're talking eggs. No squawking feathers. Just the eggs and chicks. Easy as, mate.' Vinnie traced his finger along the map. 'Here.'

'Can we get there in the van?'

'There's a ranger's track that runs through to a gate, and we have the golden keys to this castle.' Vinnie grinned like a predatory wolf, holding up a set of keys with a National Park Ranger tag on it.

Stewart recognised the tag from Alice's car keys. It was the same tag found on the gate keys he'd used on his first trip to this park with Alice. Did Alice lose her keys?

He had to do something.

'Your friend needs to go to the hospital. His blood loss and potential infection is putting him at risk of losing that leg. The soil here has melioidosis, it's killed people.'

Blackie stabbed his finger in the air as if pressing an invisible button a dozen times. 'Hey, Ning-bat's uncle had that Nightcliff gardener's disease and lost fingers, just from a nick while he was gardening. And Florida's girlfriend had that backpacking friend who skinned her knees on that camping trip only to die a week later.'

'Am I gonna die, Doctor?' Shina's eyes were wide with fear. They stood out against his pale complexion.

'Let's get you to the hospital so that doesn't happen.'

'After we've finished this job.' Vinnie scooped up the cages and loaded them into the van.

'Blackie, you gotta get us out of here. I'm too young to die. And not like this.'

Blackie squeezed Shina's shoulder. 'Don't worry, brudder. I promised I'd find you a doctor, and I did. I'll get you there safely.'

'You'll want to hurry,' Stewart said. 'The longer we wait, the higher the risks your friend has for infection.'

'Blackie …' Shina gripped onto Blackie's leg.

'Okay, stay cool, brudder. I'm onto it. Here, take this, Doc.' Blackie handed the saline bag to Stewart, then approached the van. 'Listen, Vinnie—'

'Grab the end of this roll, will ya?' Vinnie pointed to the large roll of white net.

It was the same netting material Stewart had helped Alice cut down. It stood alongside a dozen cages. One cage held rainbow lorikeets, another some black cockatoos, and cage with a few lizards that Vinnie was loading into the van.

Blackie helped load the roll of net onto the roof rack. 'We need to get Shina help.'

Vinnie tied down the roof rack's cargo. 'I know, man. I get it. But we need to finish this job. It's just a detour on our way out.'

'It'll take a few hours to set up the nets.'

'Not if we're collecting eggs. We just walk along the billabong.'

'This is croc country, mate.'

'Not this far inland, and it's the dry season, and it's a billabong. It'll be easy. Look, if someone hadn't found our nets, we would've cleaned up, and be long gone by now. And Shina wouldn't have tripped over his own two feet and shot himself like that. But we've only got a handful of wildlife that's not even gonna cover the fuel costs.'

'Do you think the ranger found our nets?' Blackie asked Vinnie.

'Doubt it.'

'How can you be so sure?'

'Because Ranger Meadows would've submitted some fancy report into their ranger's system letting everyone know to watch out for poachers. Instead, my cousin's told me that the ranger's been on bereavement leave these past five days, then she's being shunted off to Limmen Park for a week to hassle fishermen on the Cox River. The park's ours, boys.'

They knew everything!

His teeth clamped so tight they were going to snap from grinding, Stewart peered through the trees' canopy. It took him a while to find the camera he'd helped Alice put in that tree.

Alice, baby, please be there to call the cavalry.

Thirty

'Friggin' ferals!' Alice threw the phone onto the empty passenger seat, with no one answering at the police station. She'd even tried the radio, but they were all out in the communities. She had the satellite phone to call for help, but the nearest town was over four hours away in either direction.

She was on her own.

Alice checked Melody's GPS tracker, it hadn't moved. But the cameras' last frozen scene on her laptop showed the poachers were packing to leave.

But where?

Dragging down the map from the visor, she pulled it open across the dashboard, glancing at the road she'd driven along twice a day for three years. She knew this park's story like the pages of her favourite book.

Think.

Alice wasn't a cop, feeling like a lame one-woman army on a rescue mission. She cared for Stewart in such a deep way, she'd die for the man. He was a part of her family, and she'd do anything for her family, even if the odds were against her. All she could do was try and come up with a plan while keeping her foot on the pedal to save Stewart.

The hill came in sight, and she slammed on the brakes. The ute skidded in the dirt. With her binoculars, she scanned the scenery, searching for a solution. Something.

It was a typical scrubland with large ant mounds jutting out like mini sandblasted pyramids across the red soil plain.

Stewart said it reminded him of the surface of Mars.

She checked the GPS. Melody's red dot showed they were on the move just on the other side of the hill. But where were they going?

Again, she checked her map.

As she'd blocked off their access with Stewart, they only had one way into that area. The bad news was the road broke off into three areas. With only one way down that hill.

She didn't want them to know she was here, because if they did, who knows what they'd do to Stewart? And she didn't want them in some high-speed chase, not with him and Melody in that van.

Slipping on her work gloves, hat on her head, she grabbed a thick rope and her shovel, and climbed the hill. Dressed in khaki, she could blend with the wilderness, they'd never see her coming. It was time to change the narrative.

Thirty-one

Stewart sat cross-legged on the van's floor, with the patient, Shina, stretched out beside him. The van's engine whined and groaned loudly as it inched its way along the bumpy track.

'Hold on,' called out Vinnie.

The van lurched to the left, then landed with a jerky thud to the right. The cages in the back fell, with birds screeching.

'Ow.' Shina wailed, his face screwed up in pain as both Stewart and Blackie pulled the cages off his leg.

'I'll sit on one.' Stewart tried to rearrange the back of the van. He paused at the sight of a baby wallaby poking its head out of the adult wallaby's pouch, its ears scanning, its nose twitching.

'Melody?'

The little joey pushed out of the pouch and Stewart opened the cage. Melody bounded straight into his arms, the same way she used to greet him every day after work. 'Are you okay, Melody?'

'What the hell?' Vinnie scowled in the rear-view mirror, slamming on the brakes.

'Let them go,' Stewart demanded.

'Why? That's my rent money you're holding.'

'This joey brought a lot of joy to many patients.' Including himself, and now she was trembling in his arms. 'Let Melody go.'

'Not gonna happen, Doc.' Vinnie lifted his handgun in warning. 'You should be more worried about yourself.'

'Whoa up, Vinnie! The doc's been good to us.' Blackie held up his palms as if trying to instil calm.

'Put it back in the cage, and focus on our friend first, Doctor.'

Stewart didn't want to, but the way this van was straining to make it through the terrain, it might be safer in the cage. 'Sorry, Melody. Stay in there for a bit. I promise I won't leave without you and your new mother.' He put her back in the cage, then used a large rag to cover it. He'd seen Alice do it while explaining how it made them calmer.

He hoped that by now Alice had noticed Melody's tracker. When Alice knew she'd go nuts.

That thought brought a new wave of deep fear to sucker punch fire into his guts. He didn't want Alice out here, or anywhere near these guys.

Stewart scowled at his kidnappers, putting himself between the wallabies and the poachers as the van lumbered and lurched its way through the potholes, pits, and gravel that made up this track. It struggled with the terrain that Alice's ute cruised through as if on a flat freeway.

He looked for something familiar to give him an idea of where they were, but he was clueless.

With each minute passing, so did the hope of being rescued.

He couldn't count on anyone at the hospital noticing he wasn't back yet. With Jenny busy with Verily in the birthing suite, it could be hours before anyone noticed.

'Aw crikey, when did that happen?' Vinnie slowed the van down and pulled on the handbrake. Resting his arms on the steering wheel, he shook his head at the three-way intersection where fallen rocks and trees had blocked two of the roads, leaving only the skinny track on the right.

'The rocks move all the time,' said Stewart, his voice louder than intended.

The two men swivelled around from the front seats to face him.

'On my tour, the ranger told me they get tremors out here, and one small pebble could've sunk from the rains, or cracked under the weight and the rest will fall.' Was that clever, khaki-wearing, warrior queen controlling the narrative?

Vinnie looked over his map, then shifted the van into gear. 'We're in luck, boys. According to the map, that skinny track will take us directly to the billabong. It's just there.' He slowly nudged the van through the tall grass.

'I can't see nothing through this long grass. Isn't that ranger meant to look after the roads?' Blackie pointed to the window showing nothing but light brown grass with white spear-like seed heads taller than the van.

'This is one of their protected areas, not open to the public, so I'd say she uses her quad through here,' replied Vinnie.

'Spear grass is a bugger. You've gotta be careful it doesn't get into the vents and into the air filter.'

'Why do you think I'm crawling? We can walk faster than this.' Only for the van to drive into a patch of thick red sand, the wheels suddenly sinking deep as if falling into a shallow pit of concrete. 'Bulldust.'

They were stuck.

'Everyone out, except you, Shina.' Vinnie opened the van's side door. 'You too, Doc.'

'What do you want me to do?'

'Push. Blackie will help you. And before you think about doing a runner, you'll get lost in that long grass and end up wandering in circles for days before you find a proper road, let alone another human being.'

They couldn't even see the treetops. It was like a world of grass, taller than corn stalks. It reminded him of a scary horror movie that involved bad things happening to people in cornfields. 'I'll help push.'

Stewart took the right corner of the van, with Blackie on the left. With Vinnie up the front, they pushed the van through the sloppy, sandy soil until the van got traction. Then they were back to nudging down the grass, that scratched both sides of the van, until Vinnie steered them into a clearing.

'Where did the road go?' Blackie sat higher in the passenger seat.

'It should be here.' Vinnie traced his finger over the map, his nose close to the page as if he needed glasses.

Shina groaned. 'I don't feel so good, Doc.'

Stewart put his hand against the patient's temple. 'He's got a temperature, guys. Your friend is deteriorating.'

'You'd better not have gotten us lost, Vinnie.' Blackie stabbed at the air between himself and the driver.

'It's just here. According to the map, the billabong should be right here.' Vinnie tossed the map onto the dashboard. Gripping the steering wheel, he lurched the van forward, pushing down the tall grass, only to suddenly tug on the handbrake. The van's tyres skidded beneath them as if sliding on ice before jerking to a stop with a splash.

'I knew it was here.' Vinnie smiled widely, pointing at the view through the front window.

They were parked among the tall reeds and vivid green grasses that grew along the edge of a billabong that was as big as a lake.

'This place is huge,' said Blackie. 'Shina, there are flamin' birds everywhere.'

It took Stewart a while to realise they were at the back end of the billabong. Directly on the other side of the small rise where Alice had made him breakfast. The place Alice called Mother Nature's birthing suite.

Why did she direct them here?

'I've never seen so many waterbirds in one place,' said Blackie, eagerly looking through the front window.

'Me neither.' Vinnie put the van in reverse, but the tyres spun as if they were bogged again.

Blackie opened the passenger door and jumped out, his

boots squelching in the mud. 'You moron, you drove us into the mud.'

'I couldn't see it with all this grass.' Vinnie jumped out of the driver's seat, his boots landing with a splash. 'Just great.' He was in water up to his ankles, soaking the bottom of his jeans. 'Blackie, find some sticks or something to shove under the tires.' Water sloshed as the grass brushed his hips. He held on to the side of the van to get to the back.

'How bad is it, Vinnie?' Shina asked.

'We're bogged good.' Vinnie leaned down out of sight. 'Wish I'd brought the winch this trip.'

'Oi, Vinnie, check this out.' It was Blackie waving madly with a wide grin, having created a path among the lush, thick grass that grew in the water like reeds. 'Eggs. A big mob of em, just here.'

'I'll get the bag. You stay put, Doctor.' Vinnie warned with a wave of the gun. Each step sloshing deeper into the water as he waded through the grass towards Blackie and disappeared out of sight.

'I'm sorry about this doctor, I really am.' Shina was lying in a pool of sweat. 'Go. Open that door and run.'

He wanted to run and take Melody and all the animals with him. But where would he go? But he was also bound by his ethics to never leave a patient in need alone.

What would Alice do in this situation? She was his fearless wilderness warrior, who was at home in this sort of setting.

An almighty scream ripped through the air, sending hundreds of birds to shriek for the sky. The combined cries were deafening as water splashed and more panicked screaming echoed around them.

'Crocodile!'

Stewart's blood ran cold.

Eggs. Long grass. Back of the billabong. Dammit. They were in the middle of the crocodile breeding grounds.

Thirty-two

L ying on the roof of her khaki-coloured ute, blending in with the scenery, Alice watched it unravel through her binoculars. She followed the roof of the white van as it fought its way through the long grass, past the bulldust, to then get bogged in the mud.

She hadn't expected them to drive the van straight into the billabong itself. *Idiots.*

Her radio crackled with feedback. She turned down the volume and climbed off the ute to crouch behind some boulders.

The birds were now settling on the far side of the billabong after those horrific screams. But she couldn't tell where they came from, as the thick grasses that formed a floating mat they called *croc grass* hid everything.

'Elsie Creek Police to Ranger Meadows. You there, Alice? It's Porter. I got your message about the poachers.'

'Alice here,' she whispered through the radio's microphone. 'I'm in the park, and I've got the poachers in sight. They have Stewart.' Her heart pounded with fear for Stewart.

'Isn't Stewart with Verily, who's gone into labour?'

'The poachers are holding Doctor Stewart Mannen hostage with a handgun. I've only seen one gun. There are three men. One poacher is injured, he's in the back of the van with Stewart. The other two are in the billabong somewhere.'

'Where is the van?'

'It's bogged, right next to a massive crocodile nest.' It was risky going anywhere near those nests, knowing how extremely aggressive those man-eating beasts were when protecting their young. 'Look, Porter, I'm not some gun-toting cop, I'm a ranger. Please, tell me what you want me to do.'

'Keep an eye on them while I organise a team with what resources I have. You be careful, Alice, and stay back. We'll handle this.'

She chewed on her bottom lip, desperate for some way to see inside that van. All she needed was to see Stewart, for him to poke his blond head out of that van so she could signal him. Something. This was her family.

Thirty-three

'Blackie? Vinnie? What's going on?' Shina sat up, his sweaty shirt sticking to him, as perspiration beaded on his forehead. 'Can you see them, Doc?'

'I'm not walking out there. That's crocodile grass, they nest in that.' Remembering all his lessons from Alice.

'Use the front window. You'll be safe up there.'

Normally, he did nothing as extreme as this, not until he'd met Alice.

Grudgingly, Stewart scrambled through to the driver's seat, knelt on the seat, and leaned out into the wilderness. The sun bore down on him, the breeze cooled his cheek, the fresh briny scent of mud and water was refreshing. But he couldn't see anything, only the billabong, birds, and tall grass.

'Here, Doc, I'm here!' It was Blackie, waving from high in a tree only ten metres away. 'There's a crocodile right there. Right. Bloody. There.' He pointed, while squealing at the massive crocodile lying in wait at the base of the tree. 'Get Vinnie's gun and shoot it.'

'I don't know where Vinnie is.'

'VINNIE! Where are you, brudder?'

There was silence.

Stewart climbed back inside. The front tyres were underwater and sinking deeper into the mud. There was no way he'd be able to drive it out of here. 'I need to find help,

Shina. Blackie's in a tree trapped by a crocodile.'

Shina lay back in defeat.

When the side door ripped open, he had to blink a few times, expecting Vinnie.

'Alice?'

'Hi.' Her red hair was in a thick braid, her ranger's cap shaded her green eyes that were full of concern. Her lip's parted, her eyes widened, and it was one of her full blossoming smiles that almost knocked him on his arse.

'Oh, rabbit.' He jumped over the seat to hold his heroine. The feel of her in his arms had his blood pressure soaring, as that invisible connection to capture and crush his lips against hers was irresistible.

Alice was the first to push back. 'Let's get you out of here. Porter is on his way. Where's Melody?'

The cage behind him rattled.

'She can hear you.' He pulled back the cover.

'Come here.' It didn't take much, and Melody was nuzzling into Alice's arms, the happy tears were real at this reunion.

'HELP! Please, dear God, help.' Vinnie wailed. It was pitiful.

'Where are you, Vinnie?' Blackie hollered, climbing higher in the tree.

'That mongrel croc got my leg. I'm on these rocks, man, I can't climb. Doc, help. I'm bleeding.'

'I'm so sorry to do this, Melody, but this is croc country. Can you ...' Alice turned to Stewart.

'I'll put her in the cage.' Stewart hated doing it, too, but knew it was for a reason. Strangely all the animals had calmed down as if they knew they were in danger of the crocodiles, or that their khaki warrior queen was here to rescue them all.

Like a leaping rabbit, Alice used the roof rack's ropes to climb onto the open window of the driver's door, to scout the area. 'I see him. They're both trapped, but they're safe *if* they don't move.' She jumped down. 'The Awesome Jawsome has the one they called Vinnie cornered. I'm guessing that's Splash that has the other guy in the tree.'

'That's Blackie in the tree,' said Stewart.

'It doesn't matter, because Dash is still lurking around somewhere close. So we've gotta move.'

'We can't leave them here, Alice.'

'Why should I rescue them when they kidnapped you, Melody, and those birds? They don't deserve it.' Her voice was firm, powerful, but it also exposed her level of hurt. She'd come to his rescue.

'I'm sorry, I'm really sorry,' Shina wiped at the tears and sweat. 'We just did it for easy money, that's all.'

'Shina needs medical help. So does Vinnie. And I never walk away from a patient.' It was his code of ethics. A promise he'd made himself he couldn't break for anyone.

'Are you kidding me?' She was furious, with fire in her eyes, stomping away from them.

'Where are you going, Alice?' He followed her.

'To bring down my ute so I can drag that sinking van. But I will not save those idiots in the billabong, not until Porter gets here. Letting them stew in the face of a man-eater will be a good lesson.' She unclipped her radio as she followed the track up the hill. 'Elsie Creek Police, National Park Ranger Meadows here.'

'Go ahead, Alice.'

'Porter, can you send the ambulance, and I'll also need someone to bring my airboat from the back of the doctor's house.'

'Have you got them, Alice?'

'I do. Doctor Mannen is safe.' Even as she scowled at him in her anger, he rushed to hold her again.

His hand cupped her beautiful face, their eyes locked, and his heartbeat clipped its rhythm in his chest. It was nothing compared to the flash of emotions crossing her face. Alice saw and understood so much, hoping she understood him now. 'Thank you, Alice. You're my hero.'

'I'm not the bad guy.'

'You never were.'

The radio again barked into life. 'Alice, have you got the doc nearby? I have a message for him from the hospital.'

She handed him the radio.

'Stewart here. Go ahead, Porter.'

'Jenny just called. There's an urgent issue at the hospital. She needs you back. ASAP.'

'Verily had just gone into labour when I left,' he said to Alice. 'It's why I came out and not Jenny.' Thank goodness, or Jenny would have been stuck out here.

'So, who are you going to save first, Doctor?'

Thirty-four

'Why can't we chain this idiot to the roof rack or make him sit in the back? Why does he have to be in the cab with us?' Alice angrily shifted through the ute's gears, barrelling down the dirt road. The red dust cloud behind them was enormous. Flying over the bumps of a cattle grid, to take the wide sweeping turn, to then bounce up onto the asphalt road heading for the town of Elsie Creek.

Stewart sat in the passenger seat, with the poacher lying on the back seat.

With the van dragged free, the caged wildlife were safe and out of harm's way for now, leaving the other two poachers at the billabong. The crocodiles weren't budging, they were the best guard dogs anyone could ever want. She couldn't help the poachers without risking her own life.

But instead of returning those poor animals to their regions, Stewart had made her help the idiot bleeding on her back seat.

She might not have handcuffs like the police, but she had plenty of plastic cable ties to strap the thug to the rack that ran above the windows, even if Stewart complained.

'I'm sorry,' Shina mumbled.

'You say another word, mate, and you'll be kissing my elbow for what you did.'

'Alice, calm down.' Stewart tightened his grip on the handle above the passenger door.

'Don't tell me to calm down. They were going to steal

from that breeding ground, which has been undisturbed for years. And they had a key! Hey, how did you get that gate key?'

'Vinnie's cousin,' whimpered Shina. 'Harold something. He works in the office.'

'Harold Grimsby?' It couldn't be.

'That's him.'

Not the honourable horrible Harold? Her foot pulled back from the pedal as her jaw fell, suddenly ill to her stomach.

'I thought they had your keys,' said Stewart.

'Mine are all there.' She pointed to the clips she kept on the dash, where the keys were rattling softly. 'Where are those keys now?'

'Blackie used them at the gates.'

'Did you see where they went?'

Stewart shrugged. 'Alice, we need to move.'

Alice hadn't realised she'd slowed down so much. Planting her foot on the accelerator, the engine grunted full of muscle, barrelling down the road, churning up the miles as her mind ticked over.

'How many times have you poached from this park?' She gripped the steering wheel, scared to hear the answer.

'Um ...' Shina swallowed hard. 'E-e-every time they sent you away to work in another park, Vinnie would get the call.'

'You arseholes.' She lost it, her fury boiling over as she ripped off her hat and reached into the backseat to slap the idiot over the head. 'That's for Melody, the wallaby. Who we bottle-fed.'

'I'm sorry.' Shina ducked his head, trying to move out of her reach. 'I'm sorry.'

'Alice. Stop it.' Stewart grabbed the steering wheel and her hand holding her hat. 'If you can't keep your eyes on the road, I'll put *you* in the back.'

'Hey, it's my ute. You're the passenger.' She slapped her hat back on her head and continued steering down the road. 'I can't believe you're so calm, trying to save your kidnappers who held you hostage. *You*.'

'Did I say thank you?'

'Don't. Just don't.' She held up her hand to Stewart, trying to ignore him. Especially when he gave her that look that normally had her melting to his every whim. *Not today, buddy.*

'Rabbit, you're doing the right thing.'

'How? When it feels so wrong.' As wrong as being called rabbit, that was a feral pest down south. 'Leaving those birds and Melody and her new mother in that cage to save this moron.' She turned around and said to Shina through gritted teeth, 'You're lucky the good doctor is here, or I would've left you all out there.'

Shina swallowed in fear.

'ALICE.' Stewart frowned at her.

'What?' She shrugged. 'Who else is going to defend the wildlife in the park?'

'I knew you were passionate, but I've never seen you this angry before.' Stewart then said to Shina, 'You are lucky I'm here. But if you say another word, I think she'll kick us both out.'

They drove in silence for a while.

Alice's mind stewed over the situation that just brought up more questions. 'Let me get this straight: my boss, Harold, gets you guys to poach from the park?'

Shina nodded in short sharp bursts.

'How long did you stay?'

'A few days at a time. We were told to stay well away from the tracks so you wouldn't notice.'

'They sent me away—'

'Every six weeks.'

Desperate to control her tongue and her fury for being played the fool, she had to ask, 'How many birds did you catch?'

Shina swallowed. Hard. The sweat beading on his forehead was not from the heat, as she had the air-conditioner blasting cold air to cool her own hot head. 'How. Many.'

'Hundreds.'

'You arsehole.' She reefed on the handbrake, the ute spun around, facing the way they'd come from.

'Alice, what are you doing? I'm not letting you hurt him.' Stewart held his hands out, blocking her.

'I can't believe you're protecting this cretin. Especially after they held you hostage! *You!* It's only because of how much I care about *you* that I'm doing this.' She was livid. Getting out of the cab, she slammed the driver's door so hard the cab rocked. 'I've never been so scared for anyone, like I was when I'd realised you'd been kidnapped.'

Stewart followed. 'Alice, I'm okay now, I'm safe, thanks to you. But we need to keep moving.'

'This part of your ride stops here. You'll be going with them.' She pointed to the fast-approaching red-and-blue lights shifting on the humidity haze that looked like water shimmering on the tarred road. 'I'll be going back to clean up their mess, while you go do what you do, Doctor.'

Porter was first on the scene in his four-wheel drive police ute, towing her airboat, with the ambulance bringing up the rear of their small convoy.

'I brought back-up.' Porter nodded at the passenger climbing out of the police car.

Dressed in military khaki camo gear, complete with bulletproof vest and some serious military-grade weapons, the new guy had redefined military mean in one look.

'Now we're talking.' The relief that she didn't have to do this on her own made it easier to breathe.

Porter did the introductions. 'Alice, Stewart, this is Connor Symes. He's a sergeant from the military Special Operations Command. Marcus uses him as a consultant.'

'Glad to help.' Connor shook her hand, the guy was a wall of bristling muscles that rippled on his arms just by shaking her hand. It was as if a real-life, walking, talking handsome hero had stepped out of one of her romance books.

'Um, hi. Where have you been …' *All my life.*

'On holiday.'

Stewart cleared his throat. 'Alice?'

'What do you care? You're leaving.' On so many levels.

She walked and talked, with sweet layers of sarcasm dripping from her words, she explained the situation to Porter and Connor. 'This is Shina. He's an animal poacher who got a bullet wound in his leg because he accidentally shot himself while setting up traps. It's because of Shina the other two idiots took Stewart hostage.' She flicked open her pocketknife and cut the cretin free.

Connor wasn't too gentle pulling Shina out of the car, with Porter just as mad.

'Shina can't walk, guys.' Again, Stewart defended that cretin, as he collected his medical bags from the back of the ute. The look he gave Alice was foul.

'Go, Doc, we'll talk later. I've had Tanisha on the airways wanting updates, as Jenny wants you there now.' Porter and Connor carried Shina to the ambulance, where Porter handcuffed him to the ambulance bed. 'You're under arrest for kidnapping, trespassing, and —' He turned to Alice.

'The illegal capture and possession of protected wildlife. Including Federal charges for destruction and endangerment of wildlife in a Class 1 protected area. That carries a penalty of ten years' imprisonment for each animal you put at risk!' She was not letting them get away with this. 'And don't let him near a phone or he'll tip off my boss and anyone else involved.'

'Good point,' said Porter. 'You guys good with that?' The ambulance workers nodded, but Stewart said nothing as he climbed into the ambulance.

She didn't expect him to, because they'd clashed, crashed, and were both smouldering over their epic battle over each other's ethics.

So be it, she had her job, and he had his.

'How can we help, Alice?' Porter asked.

'I guess we'd better rescue the other two morons. That's if the crocodiles haven't eaten them.'

Thirty-five

'Are there crocodiles here?' asked Porter approaching the billabong with Connor.

'Definitely. This is why we need the airboat—to get past this croc grass.' Alice had backed the boat trailer to the water's edge and was now unclipping the flat-bottom boat with a massive air-propeller on the back, perfect for crossing flood plains. 'All aboard.'

'Man, I want one of these.' Connor with his dark wraparound sunglasses and his bullet-proof vest, combined with the hefty automatic rifle in his hand, he was the most lethal weapon she'd ever seen in her life.

'Put this on, Alice.' Porter held up a bulletproof police vest.

'What for?'

'You said this guy had a handgun.'

'He did. But I'm sure he would've shot at the crocs by now if he still had it.'

'Which one had the gun?'

'I don't know. Stewart said it was Vinnie, the guy trapped on the rocks. And that one hugging the tree is Blackie. I can't believe we're rescuing these idiots.'

'I agree,' said Connor, helping Alice put on the heavy cumbersome vest. 'Can't we just cruise around for a bit and let 'em sweat it out?'

'Not a bad idea.' Especially when the vest was making her shirt sweaty on her back.

'Normally, I'd be all for it, guys,' said Porter, clambering on board. 'But I have no intention of sitting in a crocodile-infested billabong after dark. Especially when I've got a stack of paperwork waiting for me.'

'I guess that includes me on the paperwork part.' She had the poachers' case file to present that she'd inadvertently been putting off all week. Luckily, as it turned out.

Standing on the airboat's bow, she shoved it off the trailer, using the oar to get them into deeper water. 'Can you guys grab an oar? We're close enough to float over to Blackie in that tree. Their nest isn't far from there, and I'd rather not chop up the croc grass too much.'

Connor pushed down on the oar like they were in a gondola. One push and they were floating. The guy was strong! He turned to Porter and asked, 'You're really struggling with Marcus away, aren't you?'

Porter pushed with his oar on the other side. 'I'll admit, I'm being punished.'

'What for?' Alice asked, keeping an eye on the terrain.

'Because I was more worried about getting Tess to date me, than doing my job. It could have cost me my career.'

'For asking the postmistress out on a date?' Alice shrugged. 'Since when is dating a crime?'

Connor leaned over to Alice and said, 'Porter was delivering a cupcake to Tess at the post office when he was supposed to be watching over Marcus's new lady, who ended up kidnapped.'

Porter pointed at Connor. 'You know, that's one bomb scare, and now *two* kidnappings since you've been back in town.'

'Oi, nothing to do with me, mate. I wasn't even in the state when that treasure hunt was happening. I wish I had been here to help Marcus. It's why I'm here now.'

'I'm so glad both of you are here. Really, I am.' Alice moved to the bow. 'Pick up those oars guys, we've got a five-metre crocodile dead ahead.'

'How did you manage to trap them like this?' Connor

asked.

'I controlled the narrative, dropped a bunch of boulders to send them this way. They were meant to get bogged in the bulldust, not get bogged by the billabong and go egg hunting straight out of a crocodile's nest.'

'I've never seen a crocodile's nest, and I was born in Elsie Creek.'

'How come?' The guy looked fearless.

'I grew up on scary stories about the billabong bunyip to always steer clear of places like these.' Connor tapped on the lethal weapon he had slung over his shoulder. 'How are we going to get that snapping handbag to move without firing my puppy?'

'Easy.' She rummaged through the sack and removed a slab of meat.

'Is that why you stopped on the way? To pick up the roadkill?' Porter covered his nose.

'We needed croc bait.' It was the worst part of her job. Having caught many crocodiles in her time, she knew what they liked.

'Do you get many wild pigs out here?'

'Not if we can help it.' She threw the pork like a discus in the Olympics, it flew surprisingly far, to crash land with a splash. After the scattering of some birds, the water settled, and it floated on the surface. 'Dinner is served.'

'I can still smell it from here,' complained Porter, while Connor shrugged.

'Give it a second,' she said as she washed her hands with her eyes on the water for any predatory man-eaters.

'You know, I've got some concussion grenades on me.' Connor tapped his belt clip that had all sorts of gadgets. 'If you wanna speed up the process. Only gives 'em a headache or scares them off.'

'If we were on the main river area, I'd say yes. But this is the waterbirds breeding grounds, it's bad enough we're disturbing it now as it is.' But she'd remember them for the future.

'*Help me, please. You've gotta help me.*' Blackie waved at them from high in the tree.

'Shut up. You're scaring the wildlife.' Alice wagged her finger at him. 'You're lucky I'm not feeding *you* to the crocs.'

'Man, don't you love that red-headed temper?' Connor chuckled.

'I've never seen you like this, Alice. You're scaring me.' Porter grinned at her.

'There she goes.' Alice pointed at the slowly submerging crocodile as it disappeared completely without a ripple.

Porter spoke in a hushed voice, 'I think's it worse not knowing where that crocodile is.'

'Keep your eyes on the bubble trail and wait.' She pointed at the floating bait. 'We don't want her jumping out at us when that guy starts climbing down the tree. Crocs can jump over six feet in the air to snatch birds from trees.'

'We'll wait. I've seen how high Karma jumps at the pub.'

Connor leaned against his oar, watching the bait. 'So, are you going to ask Tess out?'

'Seriously?' Porter pulled a face at Connor.

Alice unexpectedly giggled.

'What else are we gonna talk about while we wait?'

'I'm not telling you.' Porter frowned at Connor.

'Why not? I remember you were hassling Marcus and Tanisha for dating tips.'

'Is it true that you quit smoking and shaved off your beard for Tess?' Alice asked.

Porter sighed heavily. 'Yeah, it's true.'

'Why, man? The ladies love beards. I've got Que hiding my razors on me lately, preferring my face fuzz.' Connor rubbed at his five o'clock shadow.

It was a good look for the guy, who'd be perfect as a cover model for a military romance novel.

'Why should you change for anyone?' Surprising herself at the words spilling from her own mouth. She sat in the pilot's seat, as her voice gently echoed across the billabong making her listen to herself.

She'd been feeling so self-conscious over her khaki uniform, especially with Stewart, thinking she wasn't good enough because his family was wealthy. In this town Stewart had plenty of women, more feminine than her, vying for his attention, baking him cakes and all sorts. The plot twist was that she'd been doing the same with Stewart's lunch and dinner. *Ugh!*

But Stewart was also going back to the same hospital in Melbourne, where his ex, Olivia, worked where they were friends.

'Alice is right. I was being an idiot, putting my career in jeopardy, risking other people's lives, when I was more interested in my love-life.' Porter's angry voice skimmed across the water. 'And what makes it worse is that Tess never even agreed to date me. I made a fool of myself over a woman, I'll never do that again. If someone doesn't want to be with me, why should I waste my time trying to convince them?'

Connor looked at Alice with an arched eyebrow.

Yet Porter was right. She'd been doing the same thing, trying to convince Stewart to be with her, when he was leaving, anyway. If Stewart truly cared about her, he'd fight to stay and not be so keen to leave for a job in the city.

Then her skin bristled over her scalp as she realised she was also guilty of selfishly trying to distract Stewart from his dream job. It wasn't fair, especially when she had her dream job. Even if it was getting all hot and sweaty, slapping away at mosquitos in the swampy waters, trying to coerce a crocodile away from the poacher trapped in a tree. It was her life. Her story. 'Ready to arrest this scumbag?'

Thirty-six

The ambulance tore into the emergency parking bay. Stewart had never been more grateful to see the squat one-level bush hospital. Yet, part of him wanted to rush back and help Alice in the park.

Alice was hurting in more ways than he'd realised, all carefully hidden under her anger. What she'd said about him leaving was true. But she'd said it as if he was deserting her, revealing how deeply she cared for him.

No one looked at him the way Alice did. The depth of raw and open emotion she'd shown to him, and the urgency to keep him safe was astounding. Alice had gone against everything she stood for just to help him bring in the poacher. To learn her boss was part of the racket stealing animals from the park she was trying to protect was devastating for her. He saw that. Even though she complained in the car, fighting her own anger, Alice drove him to meet the ambulance—for him, while he was trying to help a stranger who'd hurt Alice.

It was his job to help strangers heal. Yet, he couldn't help but think he'd gone and hurt Alice more.

The ambulance's rear doors opened, and his tiny hospital team helped move Shina inside as he quickly worked on their latest patient.

Holding onto her police cap while waving a key and a set of cuffs in her hand was the Aboriginal community police officer, Tanisha, racing to meet them. 'Is that my prisoner?'

'Porter said you'd have the key.'

'I also have strict instructions to re-cuff him, so he doesn't escape, or phone anyone.' The Aboriginal police officer glared down at the patient. 'You're my prisoner now, boy. I don't like poachers who steal from our park.'

'You can watch him in the emergency room, Tanisha.'

Jenny approached, her face as dull as her nursing scrubs, with downturned eyes filled with worry.

'I'm here, Jenny. What's wrong?'

'Verily had the baby.'

'And? The birth went well?'

Jenny nodded. 'It's a girl.' There was no joy in her words, no smile inviting a celebration. And the waiting room was full of people who were silent, with none of that excited energy he'd seen earlier. It was as if the hospital had a dark cloud hanging over it, infecting everyone inside.

'The baby is having trouble breathing. I found a heart murmur, and I've run some tests with what I can do. I, I, here ...' Jenny passed him a chart.

He read over her notes walking down the corridor. 'Where is the baby now?'

'This way. Are you okay?'

'I'm fine, thanks to Alice.' He checked over the reports, his wet shoes squeaking as he walked down the corridor. His lower trouser legs were covered in mud.

His steps softened as he entered the maternity room that was filled with a heavier tension. A few nurses and the parents were standing around the crib.

The baby was tiny.

He greeted Alex and Verily, then borrowed Jenny's stethoscope to check the newborn's breathing as she lay in her special care crib.

'What's wrong with her?' Verily stood with Alex, both clinging onto each other's hands.

The baby's teeny heartbeats were erratic, with a distinct murmur inside her tiny little chest, she struggled to inhale deeply. Her petite lips were brushed with a hint of blue, with her face red and in obvious distress.

He turned to the nearest nurse, his voice low but urgent. 'Nurse, prep for emergency surgery. And get my father in here, now. Fly him in. I don't care how, just get him in here. *Now.*'

'What's wrong?' Alex went positively white, with Verily fisting his T-shirt.

'It's tetralogy of Fallot. ToF.'

'English, Doc.'

'It's a birth defect that one in every two-and-a-half thousand babies are born with.' Including his own twin brother. 'I can and I will save your daughter. Period.'

'How?'

'By performing open-heart surgery. But as her parents, I need your consent.'

Thirty-seven

It was another stunning sunset sharing its canvas of warm and vibrant shades of pink through to pastel orange that stretched across a horizon that went further than the eye could see. Crickets chirped, as birds settled in the trees, Alice carried the heavy cage from the back of her ute and gently placed it on the grassy meadow that ran through this valley like a lush carpet worthy of an oil painting to hang in some museum.

'Okay, guys, home time.' She unhooked the cage and let the door swing open. Then she stood back, like she'd done with all the other cages.

The birds flew fast and free, leaving nothing but droppings and feathers, as they fled to the tree line.

The small lizards she let free near the boulders to scurry for safety.

And the furry little macropods had their special place in this valley, where she crouched in the grass and waited for them to leave their cage at their own pace.

Melody poked her little head out of the pouch, gingerly climbing out with her neck stretched beyond the open door. Her new mother close behind, with their little noses twitching and their ears scanning the area.

'I hope you stay away from strangers, guys.' She gave a weak smile, trying to fight the heartache burrowing into her chest, as the bitter taste of failure flared in her mouth. Her stature softened as did all of her confidence, that was once a steady flame, flickered weakly like a dying ember. How had she let this happen?

She fought the urge to hug Melody one more time. To snatch the joey into her arms, and take Melody home, where she'd be safe.

But Melody was a wild animal. And this was their home, which Alice was meant to be protecting.

The two agile wallabies crept among the blue and pink wildflowers. To then pause and peer around them as if to get their bearings.

Melody then did what any joey would do at her age, she climbed into her new mother's pouch. And without warning, the mother leaped away. Her hopping motion lean and efficient through the grass.

Alice stood, watching the mother wallaby aim for the tree line where the other wallabies had gathered. Her haste triggering their flight instincts to rush for safety, deeper into the trees.

Alice sighed. 'Sorry, guys.' She meant that. This area was supposed to keep them safe and free from people.

Learning that her boss was involved in the poaching from the park, that he had manipulated her, made her feel like the biggest idiot on the planet.

She was grateful to Porter and Connor, who'd made Blackie confess to his crimes before letting him climb down from the tree. Blackie spilled everything he knew about their poaching operation and his involvement these past six months, with Shina only joining them for the last three months.

It was Vinnie who took longer to talk. As the guy in charge, Vinnie had more to lose.

And Alice was not letting Vinnie climb into her airboat until he confessed to everything.

Trapped on the rocks, with a bleeding leg, and a territorial male crocodile blocking them, it still took the threat of them leaving without him for Vinnie to confess that he'd been poaching from the Elsie Creek National Park for almost a year. Using other people's cars so as to not raise suspicion, until he bought his van and enlisted the others to help. Once Vinnie started talking to Porter, who taped the confession on his phone, he revealed their entire smuggling operation.

Porter was determined to stop the smuggling operation, taking command of the situation. Damn, it was like the cruisy boy-cop grew up in the blink of an eye and was a force to be reckoned with.

Porter and Connor transported the two poachers and their van back to town, leaving Alice with the clean-up, before she could even start on the paperwork.

Alice dumped the empty cage into the back of her ute. Sitting on the ute's tailgate, with the valley floor rolling out like a carpet under the sinking sun, she sipped from her water bottle.

Nearby curls of steam rose from the hot springs, its overflow trickling down to the valley below her, as the wallabies slowly left the safety of the trees to creep along the edges of the field.

She'd wait.

She wasn't in any rush.

Even if it hurt to let them go, it was the right thing to do. She had to let them all go: Iris, Melody, and now the one she loved the most, Stewart.

Alice heaved in dry air as hot salty tears trickled down her cheeks at the reality of losing him. She doubled over, pressing her hand to her heart, which had become a battlefield of emotions, shattering like a toppled vase, leaving the flowers to wilt and die. She could hardly breathe.

After Stewart being kidnapped and held hostage by poachers, there was no way she would try to keep him in town now—the real bad guys had made sure of that.

Thirty-eight

For five and a half gruelling hours, Stewart stood at the operating table. His back ached, his feet were numb. Cramps twinged his calf muscles as the strain across his shoulders burned. But he wasn't stopping. He had to do this, to make up for his helplessness in not being able to save his twin brother. It was as if his entire life's training had been for this one moment.

But was it enough?

Tools on the tray. He sighed with his head down, the dread strangling his chest as the burden pressed like hot burning steel across his shoulders.

'I'll go speak with her parents.'

He removed his surgical mask as he made the long and lonely walk down the corridor that felt ten times the distance.

Inside the waiting room people leaned against the wall, slouched in chairs, or were lying across the floor. It was as if the entire town had squeezed into this one space. One by one they lifted their heads, rustling papers, nudging each other, murmuring as Stewart approached the room in his surgical scrubs.

Stewart motioned for the parents to come forward. This wasn't for everyone's ears.

Alex pushed Verily in the wheelchair, hope brimming in their eyes.

'Doc?' Alex's voice was gritty. A two-day growth peppered his jawline, matching the dark rings under his eyes.

Stewart rubbed the back of his neck before crouching

down to speak to the new mother who was being forced to face her worst fears. But not today ... 'She's going to be okay.'

'Really?'

'Your daughter is a fighter, with a strong and healthy heart doing exactly what it's meant to do.'

'When can we see her?' Verily's eyes were glassy, not with sorrow but filling with joy.

'Jenny is moving her into the nursery now. Give her five and she'll come get you.'

'Thank you, Doctor, thank you.' Verily leaned over and hugged Stewart. Alex reached over and bear-hugged them all. He wasn't being left out.

Alex, then spun around and with a fist punch into the air he shouted, *'She's going to be okay. Our baby girl is okay.'* Alex's voice echoed down the hospital corridor, and the waiting room full of people erupted. Cheers, hugs, shouts and whoops of congratulations, and even happy tears were shed. It had the patients, watching from their doorways, join them in the celebrations.

The joyous voices followed Stewart as he headed for the change rooms to get out of his scrubs, to find his phone and call Alice. As to what he was going to say to her, he didn't know.

Pushing open the door, he found his father seated inside. 'Nice to see you finally made it.'

'I stitched up that poacher Porter brought in with his crocodile bite.'

'Vinnie?'

'Yeah. It wasn't much. Alice had worse when she did her side falling through the hole in her house. But you'll be glad to know Vinnie,' Thomas said with a vicious scowl, 'your kidnapper, has been taken back to the police station. Are you okay?'

'I'm fine, thanks to Alice. Why didn't you scrub in? I could have used your help.'

'I couldn't do it.' Thomas shook his head. 'When I realised

what it was … It's the same condition as …'

'Ethan, Dad. You can say his name.'

His father's chin quivered as his shoulders seemed to curl over his chest. 'I'm sorry …' His voice cracked, as his haunted eyes watered. 'I'm sorry to both you and Ethan. There isn't a day goes by that I don't regret it. Every time, even now, if anything remotely reminds me of Ethan's condition, I freeze up or walk away.'

'Is that why you left the hospital? Us.'

Thomas barely nodded. 'I've been carrying that guilt and shame now for over twenty-two years, thinking I could hide from it out here. But this …' He pointed to the empty operating theatre. 'A few things came out of this operation today, son.'

'What's that?'

'I realised that feeling I'd failed Ethan will never go away.' Thomas slowly rubbed the area over his heart. 'But I'm also incredibly proud of you, son. You are a far better surgeon than I ever was, and you are more than worthy of that job in Melbourne.'

Stewart hadn't even been thinking of the job. He'd been solely focused on saving that baby girl, so that another child didn't suffer the way his brother had—and certainly not for brownie points to get some job!

But then, Stewart stepped back a few paces, the cool wall hard against his spine, blinking at the floor. He'd just performed a highly specialised procedure.

'Congratulations, Doctor, on a fine surgery. Be proud of what you did.' His father's hand landed heavily on Stewart's shoulder. 'Now, if you'll excuse me, I'm going to call Benjamin and tell him what you just did, on your own. It's a miracle this town will never forget.'

Thirty-nine

As the town celebrated the success of the newborn's surgery late into the night, Alice and Porter—along with Tanisha, who was making them the strongest bitter coffee—were holed up in the police station. Porter was glad of the company as they babysat Blackie and Vinnie in the cells, waiting for a police transport to take the poachers to court in Darwin.

All night Alice had been busily filling out reports at the small Elsie Creek Police Station as the Darwin Police took down the entire poaching operation. All Porter, Tanisha, and Alice could do was wait for the phone to ring.

And, finally, it did.

Just not the way Alice had hoped.

Her big bosses had called to inform her of dishonourable horrible Harold's arrest in Darwin, charged with illegally interfering and supplying the black market with protected wildlife. She knew that already.

But then they levelled her with the mother lode.

Harold had also been embezzling the funds for managing Elsie Creek National Park. Her. Park.

It stunned her to silence, leaning back hard in her seat, holding the phone to her ear in the open office area of the police station.

The trust fund for the Elsie Creek National Park, which Samantha had mentioned earlier, was gone. In its place was a pile of bills, all under Alice's name. One of them was from the pest guy for applying a termite treatment to her old house twice for a tidy sum of five thousand dollars each visit. The house the white ants ate!

Alice now had to answer to her big bosses, and they had lots of questions she couldn't answer from the police station. She had to go back to her corner desk tucked away in the kitchen in the doctor's house.

As PP the pig-nosed turtle face-dived into a strawberry while wallowing on a soft bed of fresh lettuce, Alice worked at her desk at home, scouring through her electronic work diary. On speakerphone to her superiors, she was being made to answer each false claim to help the prosecution build a solid case to lock up the pariah for a very long time.

Even if the good guys finally had a win—her self-esteem and pride in her job was at an all-time low as the sun rose on a new day.

As she finished up the call the back screen door opened. It was Stewart. He rarely used the front door anymore.

'Hi.'

'Hi.' The distance between them was huge. The last time they'd spoken hadn't been pretty.

'Congratulations on your operation being a success. Open-heart surgery on a baby, that's huge. Have you been celebrating?' He deserved it.

'No. I was sitting with the baby all night to make sure there were no complications. I'm tired. I'm going to take a hot shower, and ...' He paused, sliding his hands into his pockets, and said, 'My mother's chartered a plane for me in the morning.'

Even though her stomach knotted, folding in on itself to become cement, she'd been preparing for this. 'After what happened to you, no one can blame you for leaving town. I'll get out of your hair.' She brushed past him for the door, but he snagged her wrist.

'I got the job.'

'You did?'

'It was just offered to me.' He held up his phone, but he

didn't look happy about it.

'Congratulations.' She patted his arm, trying to be positive for him, even pasting on a smile. 'That's two big wins for you.'

'What did you win?'

'A few tough lessons.' Who knew failure came in many flavours. But she also had to come clean. 'I need to tell you I'm sorry.'

'For what?'

'I've been spoiling you for my own selfish reasons, which was wrong of me. In the beginning, I wanted to spoil you to make you happy. To see you happy truly made me happy. But then I foolishly thought if I spoiled you more, you'd stay.'

'You knew I couldn't.'

She shrugged, more at her own stupidity. 'Here's the real kicker, for a long time I've been secretly crushing on you, watching you walk up and down that road past the old ranger station nearly every night.'

'I-I-'

She held her hand up to cut him off. It was embarrassing enough to admit, but why not lay it all out on the heart surgeon's operating table. 'Being with you these past few weeks has been a fantasy come true. But it was more than that, it felt like a family, a home.' She glanced around at the house that was once a shell, now breathed with a warm familiarity to it.

Whoever said *never meet your heroes* was right. Living with them was worse—it was heartbreaking.

'I now understand why you live in this world of total disconnect.'

He frowned at her. 'What do you mean by that?'

'Dealing with life and death is a big part of your job. You told me that when a patient passes you learned to disconnect, so much so, that I think you've been living that way for a long time, you probably don't even realise it.'

His frown deepened. 'What makes you say that?'

'You said your apartment has less stuff than this place.' She waved at the kitchen counter where his coffee machine sat next to her colourful tins of teas and their favourite coffee mugs.

'I hate clutter.'

'I get it. But you've been so disconnected from people, this town, this empty house that's more lived in than your apartment, that it's become your way of life. The reason I recognise this is because I was doing the same. I wasn't getting involved with the place or the people, until you. And that's entirely my fault, but a lesson I learned through you. I was denying my own happiness by not being a part of something amazing—which is this town and the people who got together to celebrate the birth of a baby. I doubt they'd do that in your Melbourne hospital.'

'No. The waiting room was packed. I searched for you …'

'I had to finish my paperwork on those poachers.'

'I get it.'

'Well, I hope you'll understand when I tell you I won't be here to say goodbye.'

His brow twitched.

'Letting go of Melody and Iris was hard, but letting you go is the hardest thing I'll ever have to do. But it has to be done. You're too good to work here, your skills will help a lot more people in the city, not to mention the pay and conditions would be an improvement.' She bitterly wiped at her hot tears. She'd spent far too much time crying these past few days.

'Alice …'

'I'm so proud of you for saving that little girl.' She gently poked his chest. 'Your brother would be proud of you, too.'

It was like a wall had fallen, the shield protecting him from the world melted in his expression as he stared at her.

But she had to keep going. She'd had a lot of time to think about this, and it needed to be said. 'I know your father is proud of you and he loves you. Underneath you must love him, too. Yet, you both have this gaping rift between you. And, I think you're both suffering from survivor's guilt. It's why you don't celebrate birthdays, or don't do anything for fun, except work, only focusing on your job. It became your entire career to save people's hearts, but what it's also done is blocked off your own heart from connecting with anyone else.'

He inhaled sharply.

She thought she'd hit a nerve, but she still had to keep going.

'You told me once I was too good to be alone. But it's you who is too precious to be alone, because you have a mountain of love to give if only you opened your heart and let someone in.' She roughly wiped way her tears to take one last look at him. To commit to memory the thick blond hair she liked to comb with her fingers, the strong jawline, high cheekbones, the blue eyes and the charm and intellect that made up the package.

Stewart could have said something, but there was nothing more to say. He was leaving.

Slipping on her ranger's hat, dressed in her khaki uniform, she walked out the back door to try and salvage her job. It's all she had, because her heart was turning into ash, to be forever lost to the wind, after saying goodbye to her soulmate who was leaving her for good.

Forty

It was one final stroll down the hospital corridors for Stewart. One last time to peek at the baby in the nursery.

Alex sat beside the crib, reading aloud from a children's book. 'Hey, Doc.'

'How's she doing?'

'Nugget's as tough as her mother.'

'She looks good. Her vitals are strong.'

'She's freaking perfect.' Alex's smile was wide, his chest rising with pride. 'Thank you, Stewart.'

'I'm glad I was here to help.'

'So, it's true, you're sneaking off?'

'I'm about to catch my plane now.'

'Anything we can do to convince you to stay?'

'I'm on a contract to return to Melbourne.' With a new one being drawn up for the specialist surgical team. He had the job!

'I heard. Some swanky heart hospital. You deserve it after what you did for my daughter. Look at me, a freaking dad.' Alex shared a soft smile at the baby sleeping in the crib. 'You know, it's scary as hell.'

'What is?'

'Being a father. I never wanted it. My dream was simple — to brew my own beer. But now I've got more than I'd ever dreamed of with a partner and a baby. I always thought I wasn't good enough, or smart enough, or rich enough to be with someone like Verily. While Verily reckons she's not pretty enough, not feminine enough, going through her own issues of leaving the world stage of softball. But we both love each other's strengths, weaknesses, and faults, that make us whole. That's what love is, being with the one who accepts you, when you don't want to do the dishes for a few days, and they won't throw out that skanky T-shirt with holes because they know you care about it, so they care about it too,' he said, gripping his faded T-shirt.

Stewart tried not to think of the T-shirts Alice and her family had given him. No pressure here. No guilt here. They were just gifts. T-shirts. Right?

'These past twenty-four hours, I've come to understand what love is. It's ugly, teeth grinding, gut-wrenching. And beautiful. Then when you add a baby into that mix, mate, it's like jumping out of a plane without a parachute. If there's a way to muck it up, I'm there. But I know I've got Verily watching my back, like I've got hers, and that's what gives me the courage to move forward. You dig, Doc?'

Stewart couldn't answer.

'I have you to thank for keeping my family whole, for being that pilot that saved us from disaster. You're a miracle worker for what you did for this little one and for everyone else. Damn, man, you're the best freaking heart surgeon in the world for what you did for my family. You will be missed.' Alex held out his hand over the baby's crib.

'Thanks, Alex.' Stewart shook Alex's hand. 'Take care of your family.'

'I will. And I'll be naming a beer after you too.'

Stewart paused at the doorway. 'Hey, what did you call her? Not Nugget?'

Alex smiled down at the crib, his fingers tenderly cupping the newborn's head. 'We decided this morning to call her Elsie.'

'As in …' Stewart pointed towards the window that led to the main road.

'Elsie, as in this town, Elsie Creek. It's home for Verily, me, and now little Nugget. Everyone in this town will know her name, and I'll make sure she knows your name, Doctor.'

'I didn't do it for the fame.' He wasn't like his father.

Leaving the new father to dote over his newborn daughter, Stewart snuck past the nurses' station, and into his office to collect his bags.

'Dad?'

Thomas rubbed his trousered thighs before rising from the visitor's chair. 'I wanted to see you off. You're leaving sooner than I thought you would. Is it because of the hostage thing?'

'I'm fine. I just wanted to escape the farewell stuff.'

'Did you see Alice?'

'She's out in the park.' Alice didn't come home last night, avoiding him.

But he'd been waiting a long time for this day, even longer to join the ranks as a specialist in his dream job of being part of the best cardiothoracic surgical team in the country.

'Here, let me help you with the luggage.' Thomas picked up Stewart's overnight bag and started dragging his suitcase out the door. 'This it?'

Stewart nodded, picking up his leather work bag off his empty desk, his office looking the same as it did the day he arrived. He had little luggage. But he'd made sure he took his T-shirts with him. He didn't think he'd wear them again, but he'd never get rid of them, keeping them the way his mother kept certain knick-knacks of his past as a child.

Leaving his empty office door open, with the suitcase rumbling down the corridor, the two doctors walked side by side towards the helipad exit.

'Dad, what are your thoughts on survivor's guilt?'

'Um, let's see … Self-blame. Isolation. Flashbacks and a feeling of helplessness. For some it's an obsession to do what's right, to try and rewrite the past. Some struggle, dealing with the guilt of having fun, fighting that constant guilt for living, where the survivor will fixate on …' The suitcase wheels stopped their rumble as Thomas paused, to turn and face Stewart.

Stewart finished the sentence. 'The survivors will fixate on their own faults, asking why they survived, and their son or brother didn't, while denying their own chances of happiness.'

Thomas swallowed hard, raking fingers through his thick hair, the grey blending with the blond. 'H-how?'

'Alice told me. I didn't even recognise it in myself until she said it. I was so mad at her when she said it, thinking she was wrong.' Yet he'd been up all night, packing, thinking, walking around the house, hoping Alice would walk through the door so he could hug her one more time. 'Alice is right, on many things.'

'She's a smart girl, that one. Alice adores you. I suspect she's always had a secret crush on you.' Thomas gave a nod and a wink like he did when sharing one of those lame medical puns or dad jokes.

His father wasn't playing matchmaker, was he? Setting them up from the beginning, telling Alice that she could move in without Stewart's consent.

But then none of this would have happened, his time with Alice, or this conversation that had been long past due with his father. 'I care about her, too. And I care about you, Dad. We both have our faults, but you are my father. Even though I'm flying out, it's not too late to make a start, right?'

'I'd like that. Call me when you get to Melbourne?'

'Sure. I might even book in a weekly zoom call. Alice does it with her parents.' Again, his heart squeezed at the thought of leaving her behind.

'Is there a doctor in the house?' Pushing the back door open was the gravelly voiced airport mechanic, Mickey, tossing an oily rag over the shoulder of his grey coveralls. 'Got me nifty buggy here by the helipad to take you to the plane.'

'Take care, Dad.' They shook hands, and Stewart reached over and hugged his father. The pats on the back were hearty and the hug strong. It felt good, too.

One more look over his shoulder to the corridor he'd patrolled where now only his father stood. He gave his dad a nod and headed into the daylight to begin his journey home.

Forty-one

'Want to do one more sweep of the place, Doc?' Monet asked as she strapped into the pilot's seat of the small red plane.

Stewart sat in the co-pilot's seat, the only passenger on the plane known as Gertrude. 'Sure. As long as I make it to Darwin airport by ten. I've got the midday flight to Melbourne.'

'Direct?'

'Yeah.'

'Cool. That gives us plenty of time to do a bit of sightseeing, get your dollars' worth. So let's get this party started.' Headphones on. Strapped into the mould of the lambswool seat cover, Monet flicked her fluffy dice with the Chinese good luck charm hanging from the mirror. Finalising her cockpit pre-flights checks, she put her tablet into its cradle, the same way Alice put her tablet in the dashboard of her ute. 'Any music requests?'

'I'm not fussy. As long as it's not some audiobook.' A smile rose at the memory of Alice's red face when her audiobook burst through the speakers with him in the car. Or when she hid her face in her hands when he snatched her book to read out a very sexy passage that led to an even more passionate time off the page.

He had to put those memories behind him. He had work to do as part of the best cardiothoracic surgical team in the country. This was his dream, the job he'd been training for his entire life.

Monet started the engine. The propeller spun until it became invisible, and that's when it seemed like the little red plane purred.

Stewart settled into his seat, as the adrenaline rose with the rumble of the plane's engine. With a clear view of the airstrip ahead, he was finally going to see the back of his place of penance. His jail time had been served and now he was a free man.

'Gertrude, let's take the doctor home.'

They taxied down to the edge of the freshly swept runway that Mickey fastidiously cleaned daily. It used to amuse Stewart watching Mickey chase the water buffalo, Cecil, off the airstrip towards the helipad where he'd sat with Alice and Iris watching a sunset together.

Again, it was another memory he forcibly put behind him. He was leaving all of this behind. It was time to turn the page and begin a new chapter of his life.

Mickey waved from his office doorway with the telecommunications tower high above him. Monet saluted at him, then pulled back on the yoke, doing the delicate dance with the pedals, and the roaring plane powered down the white line. Pushing against the mild g-force, he grinned at Monet, embracing its power.

Wheels off, and Gertrude climbed, up and over the outlying scrublands that stretched on forever.

Below him Elsie Creek flowed lazily, with some fishermen sitting in boats barely bigger than the crocodiles sunning themselves on the nearby riverbanks.

The view from the co-pilot's seat was truly remarkable, as Monet glided over the main street of Elsie Creek with its images painted on various rooftops. His artistic mother would be loving this view. So would Alice's father, who loved cartoons on T-shirts.

There was the Mad Hatter, complete with a teacup and saucer stretched over the tea house roof that made up part of the Elsie Creek train station.

On the nearby row of roofs, a snail with a mouthful of mail raced over the post office roof. A glamorous woman dressed from the fifties style era, complete with hair curlers and vintage hair dryer, was painted over the hairdressing shop. Across the road there was a cracked spanner for the hardware store.

Back over to the first responders' region, stood the old ranger station. He leaned closer to the window, following the road that led to the hospital with its red cross on the roof. At the back was his old house, his new lawn a lime-green patch, guarded by the three trailers Alice used for her job. But there was no chunky ranger's ute to show she was home, and one of her trailers was gone.

He wiped his mouth, sitting back in the seat choosing to look elsewhere.

There was the spotty Dalmatian peeing on a fire hydrant painted on top of the fire station. And the police station's roof had the mighty strong arm of the law. He never did get to say goodbye to Marcus.

'I like what you did, Monet.' He pointed to the artworks on the roof.

'I don't know what you're talking about. I failed art in school for doing stick figure drawings.'

'I know of an eyewitness who watched you spray paint the police station roof.'

'Yeah, who?' Monet asked.

'Don't worry, they won't say anything.'

'Marcus knows.'

'I guessed that.' Stewart hesitated, unsure if he should ask, but he wanted to, just one more time. 'You don't think we could fly over the national park?'

'Sure, you're paying for the privilege. But there is some restricted airspace in the park. I'd hate for the new ranger to get on my case.'

'Her name is Alice.' Just saying her name had his heart drowning in a sea of regret—when he had no reason for it.

He'd told her he was leaving, and here he was flying away.

But the guilt made him roll his shoulders, irritating him because he'd done nothing wrong. He was leaving to work in the job he'd always dreamed of. Like Alice was living hers.

'I heard Alice is a hero for rescuing you and trapping them poachers, huh? Now that's a woman I'd love to have a beer with.'

Alice did rescue him, risking everything for him. Who knows where he'd be today without her.

From the air, Monet followed the tarmac road out of town, where it disappeared like a roll of liquorice on the distant horizon. The further inland they flew, the thicker the bushlands got. They flew over the waterfalls he'd swum in with Alice, the valley where Melody lived, that led to the hills curving on the distant horizon like soft green pillows, as the river glistened like shiny ribbons of places he'd explored alongside Alice, never realising how big it was.

Then he frowned at something shiny in a large field. 'What's that? Are we being signalled?'

'Take a peek through these.' Monet handed him a set of binoculars. 'You know how to drive those things?'

'I do. Got taught by the best.' And her name was Alice.

Zooming in on the shiny light, which came from a mirror flashing them. 'Can you fly over that?'

'I can. What is it?'

'Not sure.' Again, he peered through the binoculars that were nowhere near as powerful as Alice's.

Monet leaned forward and pointed. 'Look, it's the ranger.'

Alice was standing on the roof of the ute, her hat on her head, in her khaki uniform, with her long red hair in a braid trailing down her back. The beautiful woman who had infected his world in all the right ways, in such a big way, was now so small and so far away.

But it's what was trailing behind her that made his heart stop in his throat.

Across the black soil plain were a series of large white

rocks spread out in a pattern to spell: *I love you, Doc!*

'I'm taking another swoop, Doc, low and slow. You can open that window and wave.'

'I—I—' He grappled for words, for reasoning, for what was flooding his bloodstream.

Alice loved him.

He'd known she cared about him—but she loved him?

It must have taken her all night to shift those boulders around. Was that why she hadn't come home last night to say goodbye?

Was Alice trying to manipulate the narrative of his story?

'No. Let's go, Monet.' He sat back to face the skies ahead. Alice may have said she loved him, but what she'd done was tear his heart in two.

Forty-two

Two weeks later and it was as if Stewart had never left the city, up to his elbows in the cut and dice world of limbs, aches, and ailments where the revolving operating theatre door never stopped.

At the end of the shift, the hospital's main doors slid open to a cacophony of noise and a busy sidewalk. The traffic shifted, with honking horns, and the roar of a city bus dragging the icy breeze with it.

'Darling?' Priscilla stood by the hospital's front doors, holding two coffees, rugged up in one of her long dress coats.

'Mother? What brings you here?'

'I wanted to see you. It's the only way I can see you now that you're back at work.'

After watching the shifting traffic from his cold apartment, he'd unpacked his bags, sliding a bag of coffee beans into his empty fridge, and he was out the door to front the CEO for a dressing down. Throughout their meeting he ground his teeth as the pompous twit lectured him on not upsetting patients with gold-lined pockets. But he was then given his work tags, a contract to look at, and he was back on the hospital's roster. Two weeks gone in the blink of an eye.

'I'm having a dinner party this Friday,' his mother said, as they strolled down the busy sidewalk. 'Why don't you and Olivia join us?'

'Liv and I are just friends.' There was none of that spark they used to have, all they talked about was work. Nothing about the environment, growing lawn, totem-pole gardens, or staring contests with pig-nosed turtles. And nothing about crazy names for pumpkins or about T-shirts that made him laugh. He tugged at his suit and tie, a requirement for the job.

'How's work?'

He rolled his eyes. 'They've got me doing the grunt work of an intern fresh out of medical school.'

'You knew that was going to happen.'

'Come on, I'm a registrar, a medical officer who has completed specialty training programs to be a cardiothoracic surgeon. I performed open-heart surgery on a newborn, a surgery most of them have never done, and they won't even let me scrub in on a stent placement.'

He was never involved with the complex heart surgeries, assigned to observe basic bypass surgeries where the senior residents fought to work under their few star surgeons. Then there was the politics that went with the job, the hassle in getting a theatre booked, to getting the okay to have a case accepted, and the constant rosters of shifting staff who weren't a team. His job wasn't surgery, it was babysitting the health of stressed-out businessmen with platinum health insurance.

But what his mother didn't hear was the cheap jibes from the other interns and residents about Stewart's time of being an outcast in the outback. 'They think I got the new job because of Benjamin.'

'You did, darling.'

He frowned at his mother, hooking her arm through his. 'I like to think I got the job for my skills.'

'That too. Benjamin told me what you did on that baby girl was incredible. He's never done open-heart surgery on anyone that young. Benjamin said no one on his team has. But you have, darling.' She playfully squeezed his arm, her pride shining in her smile.

'How can I show the team my skills when they won't let me operate?' He'd performed operations with half the equipment and not even one-tenth of the staff. He could do the job, but they just weren't letting him because they were all fighting for the fame of being the top dog.

'Aren't you rostered with the team now?'

'I am, but I've been put on call for any consultation for the ER.' Which made it hard for him to actually perform surgery, not with his pager constantly beckoning him to the ER. 'I forget how rude people are.'

'Coming from you …' Priscilla laughed. 'Darling, take a breath and settle in to reacclimatise to the city life. We can go out for dinner. What do you feel like? Steak?'

'I'm more of a vegetarian these days.' His eye caught on a window display, that made him stop. 'Mum, do you think I don't connect with people?'

'Pardon?'

Back at Elsie Creek bush hospital he'd ruled those halls, where he'd had wheelchair races with visiting children, threw soft toys down the corridor for a baby wallaby to chase. He had parents or partners of patients who'd deliver homemade cakes for afternoon tea he'd share with the staff, until they proclaimed they were on diets, so he'd take those cakes to the police station and share with them. He'd been in a place where their head nurse Jenny took orders for online shopping for the other nurses, where the orderly ran the footy tippings, and the cleaner would waltz with their mop when he thought no one was watching. The whole town was bursting with personality and life that had a water buffalo to share all its good news.

Stewart's nightly walks here were restricted to indoor walkways of the hospital, which was bigger than the main street of Elsie Creek. It was nothing like his nightly stroll under a sea of stars, or those nights at the police station to watch the football with Marcus. He was stuck indoors without outback treasure hunts, ambulance rides, with no time to be part of a sunset vigil for an old friend from the hospice wing.

Here, people were just a number to get in and get out as

fast as they could to make the bed available for the next patient. There was no time to make friends or even remember patients' names. There were certainly no invitations to barbecues, family lunches, and birthdays like he'd received in Elsie Creek—that he never accepted because he chose not to, knowing he was always leaving the place that had been his punishment.

He looked around at the tall buildings blocking the sun, showing only a snippet of a small sky. The scents of concrete blended with car fumes, as the noise rose and fell with the flow of cars and people walking by. In a city of over five million people, he'd never felt lonelier.

'Mother, do I live in a constant state of disconnect, ever since Ethan passed?'

In the large store window's reflection, he watched his mother nervously fiddle with her pearl necklace. 'Well, you chose not to get close to anyone after that, choosing to focus on a future of becoming a surgeon. Which you did. Darling, you did it. You belong to the best cardiothoracic surgical team in the country.'

So why didn't that title excite him the way it used to?

'When did I stop doing the fun stuff that didn't involve medicine?'

His mother shrugged. 'You put away your toys when …'

'Ethan died.' Because he had no one to play with.

'And when your father left, too.'

'And birthdays?'

'You couldn't bear to celebrate without Ethan. We both couldn't.' She tenderly brushed his hair in a motherly manner, then brushed lint off his suit, and adjusted his silk tie.

'Did I ever want to be anything else, before Ethan passed away?'

'Yes.'

'What was that?'

She gave a tender smile at an old memory. 'You wanted to

be a zookeeper.'

'No way.' Had he pushed that memory so far away that he'd completely forgotten it?

'You were forever begging us to take you to the zoo on weekends.'

'I don't remember that.'

'You used to go with your father. Then the three of you would pretend you were camping in the wilderness. You two boys used to upset the housekeeper dragging the clean linen out of the cupboards to make tents in the dining room. You'd have picnics on the balcony, pretending to birdwatch with your brother.' She held up his hand, sandwiching it between her small hands. 'You were so little, my darling. Your whole hand used to wrap around my finger back then.'

It reminded him of the baby in Elsie Creek. Her tiny fingers never reached around his.

And Alice, with her strong nimble fingers turning a page of her book, or tucking her hair behind her ear, or how they intertwined perfectly with his. Or how her green eyes would soften as she smiled at him.

He leaned his forehead against the window's cool pane of glass. It was as cold and empty as his insides that had a hole in need of filling.

Once he used to ignore that empty feeling, but now he'd been made to look at it, especially after having it been filled, he struggled to close that trapdoor shut.

'What's wrong, darling?'

'That is.' He pointed to the window, belonging to a large bookstore. Its busy display had one side showing off the latest hot release in romance novels, and on the other was a display celebrating the children's classic *Alice in Wonderland*.

'Mother, you might hate me, but I need your help.'

Forty-three

*H*is fingertips traced over her face, then glided down her body, lighting up her insides as his eyes darkened with a possessive hunger. His breath flowed in short, sharp, heated bursts along her ear and down her neck, sending a chill racing along her spine …

The back screen door opened.

Alice sat up in her rocking chair, holding her book against the baby pouch that rested in her lap.

'Hello?' Alice swung out of her rocking chair, leaving her book on the coffee table and walked into the kitchen. 'Stewart?!'

Stewart put down his luggage by the door and approached her, but she was too stunned to move as he reached out and stroked her hair. 'Hi.'

She jabbed him in the chest. 'You're really here?'

'I am.'

'Why? Did you forget something? You can take your coffee machine back.' The baby pouch moved. 'Ow.' She cringed, grabbing her ribs. 'Trippy.'

'A new wallaby?'

'A rock wallaroo.' She hung the pouch straps over a chair.

'Is he called Trippy because he got into some magic mushrooms?'

'No. Trips over his feet. Broken leg and tail …'

Stewart peeled back the cover to peek at the joey inside. 'He's much smaller than Melody.'

'Why are you here?' This just wasn't real. Stewart, back

and in the flesh.

'For you.'

'Huh?' She tried to step back, but he held her hand.

'You were right. You told me I lived a life of disconnect, and you were right.'

'But I— After sixteen days of complete radio silence you just show up?' She scowled at him, wagging her finger, hurt and anger flaring in her chest. 'You left, and you never looked back. You shouldn't be here, not when you tried so hard to be free of this place.'

'Hey, I just travelled across the country, you could at least offer me the courtesy of allowing me to say what I have to say.'

'You have the floor.' She crossed her arms over her chest, chin raised, tapping her workboot against the floor. She had planned to change after work, but hey, she had a new book boyfriend to meet, because her real-life boyfriend left and never looked back.

His smile was fleeting as he took a deep breath, nervously running fingers through his hair. 'You told me I lived in a state of disconnect, and I've come to realise that this was because I was afraid of being happy.'

She arched an eyebrow at him.

'Underneath, I wanted to be the guy who wanted to have fun. To be the guy who isn't afraid to say *I'm sorry*, to say *I love you*, to say *hey let's try this* because I found my happiness in you. And it's because of you I can feel.'

She gasped, stepping away from him.

Only for Stewart to take a big step closer. 'I don't want to stop, not now you've turned on this tap of emotions.' He patted over his heart. 'I'm worried that I'll never get that back, to connect again, because the one person I truly connected with is you.'

'You. Left.' She gritted her jaw.

'You know I had to.' He matched her frown.

'What do you want, a medal? You didn't call. You didn't

write. There was no email. Nothing.'

'Because I was fighting my feelings for you, when I should have fought to stay.'

'Your career came first. I get that. You were following your dream, to be the best cardiothoracic surgeon in the country.' Her eyes narrowed with suspicion 'Why are you here, when you have that title as your day job in the big city?'

'Because you're here, Alice.' Again, he took a step closer, his eyes an intense blue she couldn't look away from. 'You make me a better person, just by being with you.'

She angled her head at him. 'Er, no. You're the miracle worker in this town.'

'It's true. Because, through you, I learned that love and family are worth far more than a career. I've met plenty of billionaires who are the loneliest people on the planet, and there's nothing sadder than when they're in the hospital with all this money and there is no one to visit them. Yet, I've seen how some of the poorest families are richer because they are surrounded by love. Those who are truly rich in life are the ones who celebrate together when a baby is born, and those who mourn together when an elderly lady passes. That town out there,' he said, pointing to the front windows, 'is full of people who get that. You get that. And I was an idiot who didn't recognise it. But I do now.'

'What about the dream job?'

'Politics killed it for me. The higher you get, it's all paperwork and politics. I knew it was always that way, but I suppose my time and experience from living out here gave me less patience to deal with it.' His shoulders drooped and his heavy sigh stabbed straight through her hard shell.

'I'm so sorry.' Her hand pushed against her tight throat, getting choked up for him.

'I had to try, right?'

'Can you make that decision after only a few weeks?'

He shrugged. 'I was there long enough to realise I was wasting my time. I didn't fit there anymore, or they didn't fit me anymore. But I completed my original contract with them, and I never signed the second one for the new job.'

'But you wanted that job.'

'After suffering under their first ironclad contract, I was so wary of signing another one with them, I'd sent it away for a second opinion. But I resigned before the lawyer could get back to me with their recommendations. I'm a free man to work anywhere I want to, and I choose that hospital out there.'

'But you hated the place.'

'Like you said, I chose to not connect to that hospital and to this town. I didn't want it getting under my skin, but it did. Because of you. Look, not to sound too weird, but I believe we don't know who we are until we're connected to someone else. As a twin I fully understand what that means. I believe we're better human beings when we find the person we belong with, the one we connect with. And for me, that's you.'

Alice struggled to keep her firm stance, bending that wall she'd been building to forget all about him. 'What do you want from me?'

'I want to rent your spare room. I don't have a house to stay in anymore. The rangers took that contract.'

'Excuse me?'

'I'm taking the job back at the hospital, with some changes. I won't be working like I did, and Dad's agreed to a roster we can share and not avoid each other.'

'Really?'

'I want to build a putting green and watch the grass grow with you. Maybe even a pond for that turtle.' He pointed at the tank where the pig-nosed turtle paused from eating his celery leaves. 'Did Piggy just smile at me?'

She shrugged. 'You were saying?'

'Oh, yeah ...' He cleared his throat, that charming smile growing, it was a mission to not smile back. 'What I want to do first is build a bookcase with you.'

'Huh?'

'You built a rocking chair with your father and said it was like a piece of home. Well, I want to build an entire library of bookcases with you, where we'll fill it with the story of our life to control the narrative our way.' He cupped the side of her face, his thumb brushing her cheek. 'I love you, Alice. And I know you love me, too. Even though you wrote it in rocks, I want to hear you say it.'

She winced, her hand rubbing the back of her tight neck.

'I love you, and I love that I love you, and I know you love me, because you wrote it in stone.' He cupped his hands to her cheeks, trapping her with nothing but raw emotion—there was no doctor's face here. 'I used to think you were this rabbit—'

She frowned, pulling back. 'I'm not a rabbit. Rabbits are feral. They don't last here.'

His fingertips brushed her forehead, as if to wipe away her frown. 'After seeing how fiercely you protect others, and how far you'll go for those you care about—like me—I think you're a queen who rules over her kingdom. You are my queen in khaki.'

Alice sucked in air so fast she lost her ability to speak, unsure whether to take the compliment or cringe.

'Here, I got you this ...' From his luggage Stewart removed a gift-wrapped parcel.

'It feels like a book.' She tugged on the ribbon.

'I was expecting you to have a stack of bookcases taking over the house. The place hasn't changed at all. Did you move into my room?'

'Nope.' Her eyes widened as she turned the hardcover book over in her hands. 'This is a limited-edition *Alice in Wonderland*.' It was also second-hand. 'Why did you give me this?' Was this a joke?

'When we had breakfast at the billabong, with all of those birds, I kept thinking the spoonbill bird was the dodo.' He tapped the book cover. 'You called it Mother Nature's birthing suite. For me, it's Alice's Wonderland. Open it up,' he said.

There was a faint inscription on the first page. '*To my boys and the adventures we'll have, Dad.*'

Stewart tapped on the writing. 'Dad might not have shown up to our soccer games when I was a kid, but he would make the time to read to us every night. But when Ethan passed, and Dad left, I put all my childhood things away in my mother's attic, choosing to forget those memories, to focus on medicine to save people.'

'Is that why you don't read fiction for recreation?'

He nodded. 'I plan to change that in the future. Now, read the bookmark.' He tugged on the heavy paper.

It was a very fancy scripted invitation. 'What's this?'

'An invitation to my mother's next fundraising event.'

As she read the invitation, the words blurred from the tears forming.

Over her shoulder Stewart read aloud: '*You are cordially invited to the exclusive fundraising event for the ground-breaking ceremony for Alice's Animal Sanctuary in Elsie Creek ...* My mother sent one to your parents. I believe they're going. My mother wants to make it an annual event. She's happy to volunteer and take over fundraising—which she's really good at—so you can focus on what you love doing the most.'

'I love you.' She whispered it in a breath, as the joy filled her at what he'd done and that he was here. 'I love you, I love you. I. Love. You.' She playfully poked his chest.

'Does that mean I'm allowed back in the house?'

'Well, there are a few ground rules first.'

'Like what?'

'No lace doilies. If you have a single doily in your luggage, we can't be friends.'

'Anything else ...' He leaned in closer, the smile in his eyes warming her soul.

'I'm sure we can make it up as we go along. Make yourself at home, Doctor.'

'I will.' Pressing his lips to hers, he kissed her so deeply it blocked out the world to fracture her thoughts. Her body remembered him. His touch. Taste. Smile and lips. He was the love of her life, and she was his. They were two halves that made each other whole, connecting in a whole new way, living in a place where they would control the narrative of their own story. Period.

THE END

For now …

I have a gift for YOU!

Learn the secrets of

ELSIE CREEK

Exclusive to Elsie Creek Readers!

Simply go to:

https://melarowe.com/elsie-creeks-secrets/

Did you like the story?

If so, your opinion matters to me!

It's true.

A good reader's review is worth a lot to this author.

So, if you enjoyed this book, please leave a review and

recommend it to your friends.

I'd appreciate it.

With much gratitude,

mel

A. ROWE

ACKNOWLEDGEMENTS

Thank you

I love visiting many of the Northern Territory's National Parks as a neighbour, visitor, explorer, and as an employee of these places. Over the years, I've found myself working directly for the National Park Rangers making Kakadu National Park (Cooinda) my home address. No wonder it ended up in a story, filled with many personal experiences of my adventures of these places that I now share with you in book eight of this amazing series that is very close to home for me—except for the medical side of this story.

This is where I thank the nurses in our local bush clinic for their help with uncomplicating some of the icky side of things in this story. I'd also like to thank all those first responders who live with the daily challenge of working in a remote region. You guys are the real unsung heroes in my book.

As always, I'd like to thank the Handbrake for being my co-pilot on my many adventures. Thank you to the incredible editing Deb team at DP Plus who I torture with my grammar. Thank you to the Fabulous First Readers team for their amazing support; I am truly blessed to have you all join me on my writing journey.

Lastly, to you, dear reader, thank you for taking the time to read this story. It means the world to me, as I look forward to sharing more with you in that *'Escape to Happily Ever After'*.

Until next time,

Mel

A. ROWE

ABOUT THE AUTHOR

Australian bestselling author, Mel A ROWE, creates romantic escapes for today's busy women to enjoy from the comfort of their home.

Delivering stories with a dash of drama, witty humour and quirky family units, Mel is known for reinventing romantic versions of home, taking her common characters on uncommon journeys that lead from boardrooms to billabongs as they try to find their own HAPPILY EVER AFTER.

Living in Australia's Northern Territory, Mel enjoys random outback road trips, fumbling with her camera, annoying her family with her bad singing, and making new friends in the middle of nowhere—except for water buffalos. She's been chased by a few.

Find Mel at

MelAROWE.com

Receive exclusive insights, book gifts, news
of upcoming releases by joining:
https://melarowe.com/newsletter/

Also by MEL A ROWE

ELSIE CREEK SERIES:

The ART of DUST

DIAMOND in the DUST

CAKED in DUST

XMAS DUST

MUSTER in the DUST

ROLLED in DUST

WRITTEN in DUST

DOCTORING DUST

BUFFALO DUST

OASIS OF THE OUTBACK DUOLOGY:

The Station, Volume One

The Station, Volume Two

STANDALONE STORIES:

Avoiding the Pity Party

Unplanned Party

The Football Whisperer

Winter's Walk

Run Beautiful Run

The Sister Trip

For story exclusives & more visit MelAROWE.com